"Julie Beard is one of the few writers who takes the concept of love and passion right to the brink! Keep up the wonderful writing, Julie. I'm a fan for life!"

—*A Romance Review*

* * *

"Look, Mr. Gorky…Vladimir…I think I've done a bad job of communicating here. I believe you're going to murder me."

He put his hand over his heart. "It hurts me to think that Lola's daughter doesn't trust me. I wanted you to think of me as an uncle. Now get in the car."

"Why would I want to get in a car with you?"

"I'm not plotting to kill you, Angel, but I know who is. Now get in the damn car!" He said it with a smile as he pounded a dent into the hood of the limo. I had to give the guy credit for being a master of the unexpected.

Startled into complacency, I got into the car.

To my everlasting regret.

Dear Reader,

What is a Bombshell? Sometimes it's a femme fatale. Sometimes it's unexpected news that changes everything. Sometimes it's a book you just can't put down! And that's what we're bringing to you—four fascinating stories about women you'll cheer for!

Such as Angel Baker, star of *USA TODAY* bestselling author Julie Beard's *Touch of the White Tiger*. This twenty-second-century gal doesn't know who is killing her colleagues, but she's not about to let an aggravating homicide cop stop her from finding out. Too bad tracking the killer is *exactly* what someone wants her to do....

Enter an exclusive world as we kick off a new continuity series featuring society's secret weapons—a group of heiresses recruited to bring down the world's most powerful criminals! THE IT GIRLS have it going on, and you'll love Erica Orloff's *The Golden Girl* as she tracks a corporate spy in her spiked Jimmy Choos!

Ever feel like pushing the boundaries? So does Kimmer Reed, heroine of *Beyond the Rules* by Doranna Durgin. When her brother sics his enemies on her, Kimmer's ready to take them out. But the rules change when she learns her nieces are pawns in the deadly game....

And don't miss the Special Forces women of the Medusa Project as they track down a hijacked cruise ship, in *Medusa Rising* by Cindy Dees! Medusa surgeon Aleesha Gautier doesn't trust the hijacker who claims he's on their side, but joining forces will allow her to keep her enemy closer....

Enjoy! And please send your comments to me, c/o Silhouette Books, 233 Broadway Ste. 1001, New York, NY 10279.

Sincerely,

Natashya Wilson

Natashya Wilson
Associate Senior Editor, Silhouette Bombshell

Please address questions and book requests to:
Silhouette Reader Service
U.S.: 3010 Walden Ave., P.O. Box 1325, Buffalo, NY 14269
Canadian: P.O. Box 609, Fort Erie, Ont. L2A 5X3

Julie Beard

Touch
of the
White
Tiger

Silhouette®
BOMBSHELL™

Published by Silhouette Books

America's Publisher of Contemporary Romance

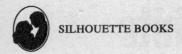

SILHOUETTE BOOKS

ISBN 0-373-51371-2

TOUCH OF THE WHITE TIGER

Copyright © 2005 by Julie Beard

This edition published by arrangement with Harlequin Books S.A.

www.SilhouetteBombshell.com

Printed in U.S.A.

Books by Julie Beard

Silhouette Bombshell

Kiss of the Blue Dragon #5
Touch of the White Tiger #57

JULIE BEARD

is the *USA TODAY* bestselling author of nearly a dozen historical novels. With her first Angel Baker action-adventure novel, *Kiss of the Blue Dragon,* she made a no-holds-barred debut in contemporary fiction worthy of a Bombshell heroine. She loves kickboxing, debating politics and being walked by her Basenji dogs. She lives in the Midwest with her husband and two children, one of whom was adopted from China. Julie is a former television reporter and college journalism instructor who has penned a critically acclaimed "how to" book for romance writers.

To Amy Berkower and Julie Barrett,
for being there when it mattered the most.

Chapter 1

Tit for Tat

Once upon a time, I would tell anyone who asked about what I did for a living that I liked to make men sweat. *Men.* As in plural. And though a double entendre was implied, what I really meant was that I liked to scare big tough guys who like to hurt people.

Scaring bullies is easy to do when you're a Certified Retribution Specialist like me, armed with extensive Chinese wushu fighting skills and a Glock. Did I mention my G136? It's a sleek black semiautomatic handgun that shoots bullets or laser.

In the year 2104, just about any weapon goes. The Wild West of the 1880s ain't got nuthin' on twenty-second century Chicago. With the neo-Russian and Mongolian Mobs running rampant on the streets, in business and in government,

I'd even say we beat the 1920s hands down. That, of course, was the era of the famed Italian mobster Al Capone and friends. The Cosa Nostra has since been reduced to theme park motifs and legal real estate deals, but that doesn't mean the world is any safer.

I recently learned a fancy word that describes my world: dystopia, which is the opposite of utopia. But I digress.

The point is that my unusual profession grew out of a need for order. The Scientific Justice Act of 2032 tried to take the bias out of the criminal justice system by tipping the scales in favor of DNA and other high-tech evidence. De-emphasizing good old-fashioned common sense created unexpected loopholes. As a result, the court system is now a wreck and cops are overwhelmed. So crime victims who feel they've been cheated out of justice often turn to retributionists for help. For a fee, we deliver criminals to their victims for a little payback time.

Some people—especially the police—consider Certified Retribution Specialists vigilantes, but we're professionals serving an important function in society. Granted, we haven't been embraced by the establishment, but we hadn't been outlawed, either. Not yet, anyway.

But the state of my profession wasn't exactly dominating my thoughts. Lately I'd been obsessing over a detective named Riccuccio Marco. Though we'd made love only once, that was all it had taken to show me that lovemaking really can be an art form.

Ah, yes, I know, cops are so boringly upright. Now, there's a play on words. But Marco is different. Not only is he a detective with the Chicago Police Department, he's a former psychologist. And to really complicate matters, I recently found out he was briefly involved with the Russian Mafiya Organizatsia when he was younger. You gotta love a man with a past. Exactly what it was, I didn't want to know. I just wanted to make art again.

But that was proving maddeningly difficult.

I rang the telecom buzzer at his downtown flat and nervously pronged my fingers through my spiked, blond hair, using the brass buzzer as a mirror. Normally, I didn't care what anybody thought about my looks, but this was different. I was here to further pursue my relationship with Detective Marco. That is if he wanted to.

"He-he-he," came a whiskey-rotted voice from a weaving figure to my right. I made the mistake of inhaling just as the toxic cloud reached my nose.

I turned and found a methop junkie, drooling on his ragged shirt, grinning at my chest. He obviously hadn't been to a dentist since the last millennium celebration, and he reeked of Eau de Middle Ages. That's what happened when you cared more about your next hit of methamphetamines and opium than you cared about taking your next breath.

"What are you looking at?" I pressed the buzzer more forcefully.

"You, baby. Are those tits for real?"

I glanced down at my tight, leather V-necked vest. This was as close to cleavage as I ever got, and it wasn't much. If this creep thought my breasts were surgically endowed, he needed more than a long bath. "They're real and they're off-limits, so get lost."

"Let me give those melons a squeeze," he said without sparing my face a glance. When he reached out with both hands, I felt like a fruit stand at a green grocers. "Nice an' ripe, I'll bet. How much do you charge, baby?"

"You don't want to do this," I said calmly. "Trust me."

But he was too doped up or dumb to listen. Hunched over,

arms extended, he zeroed in on his targets with surprising precision, but before he could make contact, I snapped my arm out in a quick backhand punch to his jaw. He went down just as the door opened.

"Hey!" the junkie protested, rubbing his chin. "That hurt like hell."

Marco looked at me in surprise, then frowned at the junkie sprawled on the sidewalk. "What happened?"

"Sticker shock," I replied. "Don't worry. He'll survive. I went out of my way to avoid his windpipe."

"Very thoughtful," Marco said sarcastically. Our eyes locked and sparks flew. He grinned slowly. "He had no clue what he was up against, did he?"

I smiled back. "They never do."

"Come on in. I was just about to take a break."

"From what?" I stepped inside a long, restored loft with shiny blond wood floors and an intriguing maze of pipes looming from the ceiling high above. I breathed in the foreign, pungent odor of turpentine and paint, and quickly surveyed brick wall after wall adorned with large canvasses covered in brilliant hues, some arrayed in geometric impressions and some realistically drawn.

My God, I thought, *is Marco also a painter?*

I whirled around to gaze at him in frank wonder and realized he wore no shirt. How I had missed that was beyond me. Paint-spattered, threadbare jeans slouched at his jutting hip bones. A line of dark, silky hair intersected his naval and spread up his flat belly, fanning upward and outward over the mounds of olive skin and muscle that defined his breast bone. Red paint smeared over an inch of his collarbone. My gaze wandered up to his ruggedly handsome face.

With a square, shadowed jaw, a seductive, lush mouth and brown eyes that could undress you in seconds flat, he made my mouth water. It was amazing. I was right to come here. You can't fight fate.

Wait a minute! Be cool, Angel, I told myself. *Be cool.* Then I shrugged and said, "So. You wanna make love?"

Oh, God, what did I say? Could I turn and run? No, not cool. Could I take it back? Impossible. Nothing left to do but pretend I had planned it. So I crossed my arms, shifted weight, jutting my right hip in a cocky pose. I raised one brow challengingly and waited for what seemed like the most agonizing and longest minute of my life to pass.

Marco simply stared at me as if he, too, couldn't believe I'd been so bold, so blunt. So stupid. Then he moved toward me, his bare feet padding on the floor amid the frayed hems of his jeans, and before I knew it, he'd scooped me up off my feet, both of his deceptively strong arms wrapped around my waist.

I steadied myself, putting my hands on his bare shoulders. His muscles seemed to melt beneath my fingers. I found myself kneading them. Just touching this man made me feel like I was running a fever.

Except for the one time we'd made love, I'd only seen him in suits and long sleeves. I'd thought of him as a studly but aging cop. Now he seemed like a not-so-middle-aged wild thing, more the unpredictable assassin I imagined him to be after his confession about his Mob ties. That's who I saw, anyway, when I caught my breath and looked down into his gorgeous upturned face. Pheromones shot out from him like the grand finale of a Fourth of July celebration. He smelled musky and masculine with a hint of sweat from hard work—my favorite cologne.

"Did you just ask me if I want to make love?" His husky voice vibrated in his chest. His gaze skewered me with a "You'd better not be joking" look.

I spread my hands over his day-old beard and up through his thick, natural dark curls of hair. "Yes."

"Are you sure?"

A touch of gray distinguished his temples, and his long-lashed, bedroom eyes ended with a trace of crow's-feet, the legacy of too many deep smiles in the sun. He was all man, and he was mine. And he was just mature enough to make a relationship dangerous. I craved opening up to him, and dreaded it at the same time. If he really knew me—and he was smart enough to do that in time—would he still want me?

"Yes." A simple reply. The last nail in the coffin.

He roughly grabbed my nape and pulled my lips to his. They were briefly tender, like silk, but soon parted and we melded in a mind-blowing French kiss. I wrapped my legs around his waist, feeling like I'd fallen into the eye of a hurricane. Everything around me was chaos. But something in me knew this was where I was supposed to be, and I grew calm, intent on consuming him.

I hadn't realized he was walking, but we dropped together onto a mattress laying on a low platform in the back of the loft. We scrambled together, still kissing, as we tugged off our clothes. Jeans and leather gave way to the rub of taut muscles and slick skin. I was like a champagne cork ready to pop and nearly did when he stretched out on top of me, his long, strong legs entwining with mine.

I was ready. He was ready. Then I made the mistake of talking. Pulling from his lips, I said, "I guess your answer is yes."

It was a joke. He smiled. But the ironic gleam in his eyes turned cloudy. He didn't move, but I could almost see his emotional retreat, like one of those fancy camera moves in old-time horror flicks, when the dolly holding the camera retreats fast while the lens zooms in.

His interest slackened in the most obvious place. I gripped his shoulders, pulling him closer. *No,* I wanted to say, *don't stop now.* But I wouldn't beg.

He drew up and sank on his knees, straddling me. He put his hands on his bare hips and tugged his lips into a rueful smile. "Now that you mention it, Baker, the answer is no. I don't want to make love."

I was speechless. "I don't...understand."

He rose from his knees to a stand in one graceful swoop, then started pulling on his jeans. "I told myself that when the time came I would say no. But I let my desire get the better of me."

I sat up, crossing my arms over my bare breasts. "Why? Am I so appalling to you?"

"Obviously not," he said wryly as he zipped his pants. He raked both hands through his hair, looking older than he had a few minutes ago. "Get dressed. I'll make some coffee."

Reluctantly, I dressed, my humiliation slowly turning to anger. By the time I found his galley kitchen, which was ultra-high-tech and gleaming with silver, I was ready for a fight.

"You've got a lot of nerve," I declared. He tried to hand me a cup of java. I crossed my arms, so he placed it on a small round table.

"Cream and sugar?" he asked calmly as he returned to pour a second cup.

"You can't make love to a woman like you did with me, Marco, and then just expect her to forget about you! What am I saying?" I laughed bitterly. "You probably do it all the time."

He balanced a small pitcher of cream and a bowl of sugar in one hand, and a second cup of coffee in the other, placing them nonchalantly on the table like a restaurateur making the final touches before opening the doors. Then he turned to me with a look of bored patience.

"You're still angry?"

"I'm pissed as hell."

He pulled me close with a grip on my upper arms, cocooning me in a bearish embrace that was now distinctly brotherly in tone. With a firm grip that was neither rough nor gentle, he lifted my chin and kissed me as if he was teaching me a lesson. I stiffened, but soon my lips succumbed to his sensuous rotation. I resisted as long as I could, but the truth was his kisses were better than drugs.

When he was done, he pulled back and gazed at me assessingly. I dropped my head on his chest, undone again. He scooped up my head with hands on my cheeks and looked at me intensely.

"Do you think I kiss just any woman like that?"

I groaned pathetically. "Yes."

"Then you're a fool."

My swollen lips tugged wryly. "Gee, thanks. You do wonders for my esteem."

"I care for you, Angel. Too much. I haven't allowed myself to do that in a long time."

That implied yet more personal history that I wasn't sure I wanted to know about. "You've been hurt?"

I saw it for an instant in his eyes—pain so deep it gave me a chill. He poured cream and sugar in his coffee, then sat in a little round chair too small for him, crossing his legs casually. "Anyone over the age of thirty has been hurt."

"I'm twenty-eight. Age doesn't have much to do with it."

"The older you get, the tougher you are. The harder it is to hurt. But when someone does manage to do it…"

He trailed off and frowned seriously as he took a sip of the steaming coffee.

"I'm not going to hurt you, Marco."

He looked me up and down as if he was logically considering whether that was true. "You're a beautiful woman, Angel Baker. Fit and energetic, brave and yet grounded. Your heart is…very tender. I know you've been hurt, and I know you would never intentionally harm me. But I can't watch you die. I've done that too many times already."

"Watch me die?" I said with a disbelieving laugh, taking the seat opposite him. I grabbed the cup I'd earlier rejected. "You don't have much faith in my abilities if you think I'm going to die."

"You're a retributionist, kiddo. Do you know what the mortality statistics are for your profession?"

"I'm careful," I said soberly. "And I'm good."

"Have you thought about your responsibility to Lin? What if something happens to you? Where will she be then?"

I shut my eyes and laughed ruefully. "You really go for the jugular, you know that?" I took a fortifying breath, folded my hands and pinned him with my robins-egg blue eyes. "I'm not going to abandon my foster child—not to death, not to the state foster care system. Not to anyone."

"Then you'd better quit while you can. While you're still alive."

"Is this about your police committee that's trying to get the state legislature to outlaw my profession?"

He shook his head. "No. This is personal."

"I'm not going to do it, Marco."

"Do it for Lin."

I shook my head. "I rescued Lin. Remember? I couldn't have done that without my training as a retributionist."

"Then do it for me."

My heart did a funny little somersault. Was he asking me for a commitment? I heard a muted police siren wail down the street in the thick silence that followed. My heart pounded. I wanted to commit, but at what price? I felt like I was trapped in a burning building with no easy exit.

"You're asking me to give up my career to love you? That's not fair, Marco."

He shook his head. "No, it's not. But death isn't fair, either. Do you really know what death is?"

I blinked, stunned by the question. I'd spent my life defying death, even ignoring its existence. I had a feeling he knew much more about it than I, but that didn't mean he could make such an important decision for me.

"I'm willing to take that risk."

"Well, I'm not," he shot back, anger giving his low voice a bass tremor. His fist came down hard on the table. "If you want to make love to me, you have to hang it up, Angel."

"Fuck you!" I yelled and slammed my palms down so hard coffee jumped out of both mugs. "This is my life! Being a retributionist is who I am. It's me. You're rejecting *me*. Why don't you just call it like it is?"

"No," he said, softening his voice. "You are not a retributionist. It's what you do. It's not who you are. And until you realize that, we can't have a relationship." He raised both palms up in acquiescence. "That's not quite true. We already have a relationship. But we can't have sex."

I blinked slowly. "You're kidding?"

"No."

"That's just great." I stood abruptly. "You're a sadist, you know that?"

"Don't slam the door on the way out, Angel," he said matter-of-factly.

I shook my head in disbelief and left. When I reached the sidewalk, I turned back and slammed the door with every bit of flare and might I could muster. Feeling perversely satisfied, I whirled and stepped right into the methop junkie. His grimy, open palms fit snugly around my breasts. He grinned and guffawed in triumph, nearly bowling me over with his rancid breath.

"Like I thought," he said, chuckling, "these melons are just ripe enough to eat."

"How ironic." With lightning speed and force, I jammed my hand down between his legs and gripped hard. While his eyes popped and his throat pumped with unspeakable pain, I added, "The melons might be perfect, but these grapes are *way* too shriveled for me."

I couldn't sleep that night. I tried to relax by watching an old black-and-white flick. I loved the early twentieth century Hollywood classics. Still, I tossed and turned. I told myself a hundred times to forget about Marco, but he was the kind of guy who made you think. Damn him. Was he right about my responsibilities to Lin? I swore I'd be there for her. She was seven years old. Old enough to know whether I held up my end of the adoption bargain or not.

When my mother went to prison—when I was seven, ironically—I'd certainly felt abandoned. While I had no plans to go to prison, I never considered that getting killed on the job would be, in effect, abandonment of my motherly duties. Was I willing to give up a dangerous career for a child? When I'd told the social worker a month ago that I wanted to adopt Lin, I hadn't thought through all the ramifications. Love was more than a feeling when it came to parenthood.

I'd never before considered myself motherhood material. But my outlook changed a month ago when I stumbled onto a plot to sell a dozen Chinese orphans, including Lin, on the black market.

The Mongolian Mob had literally been breeding girls outside Barrington, a northwestern suburb, in a downscaled replica of the Imperial Palace in the Forbidden City. Comfortably imprisoned, Lin grew up thinking she was in China. She had been lovingly cared for by an older sister, but her only kin had been slain when it was time for Lin and the other seven-year-olds to be sold at market.

Pure-blooded Chinese girls were highly prized here and abroad. They were scarce because of China's twentieth-century one-child birth control policy. Back then, parents favored boys, so females were often aborted or sent abroad for adoption. That led to a shortage of Chinese brides, and many of the men had been forced to marry immigrants.

Lin and her friends would have netted the Mongolian Mob millions of dollars if I hadn't rescued them. The other girls were put up for adoption, but I had kept Lin as a foster child. We bonded quickly, even though I practically had to fight for time alone with her. My mother, who now lived in my downstairs flat, and my Chinese martial arts instructor, who lived in my garden carriage house, occupied most of Lin's time. They doted on her and babysat when I was away.

Still, Lin knew I was her savior. I was her new mother. When I realized I couldn't let her go, I set the wheels of adoption in motion. But now that decision was forcing me to consider radical changes in my lifestyle. Could I give up my career for Lin?

The prospect of working behind a desk just to be safe made me go numb inside. But perhaps there was something else I could do with my skills. Maybe I could be a case worker for social services and make sure foster children weren't abused. Having been an abused foster child myself, I would certainly know what signs to look for.

The possibilities churned in my mind. Finally, realizing I wasn't going to be able to sleep, I called Marco. I used my lapel phone because I didn't want to wake up Lin using the omnisystem. I popped the receiver in my ear.

"Riccuccio Marco," I said softly, and his number began to ring. With a tightening in my gut, I waited for him to answer, entwined wrists resting on my frowning forehead.

"Yeah?" Marco answered in a groggy voice after five rings.

"Okay," I said, barely able to get the word past my heart, which pounded in my throat.

"Angel?"

"Yes."

"Okay what?"

"Okay," I repeated impatiently. "I'll do it."

There was a long pause. He said, more alert, warmly, "Okay."

"But only as an experiment."

"How will I know you aren't going to go out behind my back?"

"I'll put away my Glock," I magnanimously offered. "I never leave home without it, at least not when I'm on a job. I rarely use it and have never killed anyone, but it's like insurance. You know that if you don't have it, you'll need it. No Glock, no retribution jobs."

"Can you resist the urge to retrieve it in a pinch?"

"I'll put it in my bank safety deposit box. You can be my witness. In fact, I insist. I want to make sure I get full credit for this charade. I'll take a vacation for one week, but I want something concrete in return."

"What?"

"If I go seven days without taking on a retribution job, you have to have sex with me."

"Ah, such a price to pay," he said, teasing.

"I mean it. I have to have some motivation here."

He let out a sexy chuckle. "Okay. It's a deal. You really want to do this?"

"Sure," I said lightly. "It'll be a cinch."

Boy, was I ever wrong.

Chapter 2

Mirandized

Six days, twenty-two hours and twenty-three minutes into my agreement with Marco, my lapel phone rang. Waking from a deep sleep, I slammed my hand on the bedside table, feeling for the noise. At the same time I managed to blink open one eye and saw 3:12 a.m. reflected on the ceiling.

"Who on earth…?" I muttered as I grabbed the tiny round phone. Plugging the receiver in my ear, I groused, "What?"

"Angel?" came a gruff and vaguely familiar voice.

"Who is this?"

"Roy."

I went instantly alert. Roy Leibman was one of Chicago's best retributionists. I couldn't imagine why he was calling me at this hour. I propped myself up on one elbow.

"What is it, Roy?"

"I need help," he whispered.

The hair on my neck sprang up. Roy had never asked for help from me before. He was fifty-five and I was twenty-eight. He'd been my mentor. He shouldn't need help. That's not how our relationship worked. "Where are you, Roy?"

"At the Cloisters. Can you come?"

I glanced up at the red numbers reflected on the ceiling. It was now 3:13 a.m. I was an hour and thirty-five minutes away from seven days of abstinence from my work. If I answered Roy's call for help, I'd have to start all over again. Since I was self-employed, I could take off as much time as I needed. And I'd enjoyed hanging out with Lin. We'd done everything from making sand castles on the beach to moonwalking in the Virtual Dome. But I couldn't afford to be unemployed forever. More importantly, how could I not help a colleague in need? Besides, what Marco didn't know wouldn't hurt him—or me—would it?

"I'm on my way, Roy."

"How fast can you get here?"

"I'll take a chopper cab. Ten minutes, tops."

Chopper cabs were expensive as all get out, and I splurged on them maybe once a year. But Roy needed me and I was determined to be there for him. Fortunately, there was a cab stand on the roof of the Music Box theater, which was just a few blocks north on Southport.

I dressed fast, wishing I had more than a knife and a whip to attach to my utility belt, woke Lola and talked her into moving from her bed downstairs to mine in case Lin woke up. Then I ran the ten-block distance like athletes used to when humans still dominated the Olympics. When I climbed into the cab, whose blades whooshed overhead, the driver's sidelong glance looked like one he reserved for a con artist who was going to shake him down after takeoff.

"Don't even go there," I said, pulling out my CRS identification card. Then I held out my cash chip. "And, yes, I can afford it. Chicago and State. Pronto."

"Yes, ma'am," he said with a faint East Coast accent. "Buckle up, please."

Like I had a choice. He pushed a button and two belts crossed over my chest and battened me down. While we zoomed up and over the sprawling north side of Chicago, I tried not to imagine the worst and found myself reading the cabdriver's certificate.

Herbert Banning IV. He was a Harvard grad. So many of them flew chopper cabs these days. Ivy League degrees were quaint relics of a past when a well-educated human could still outthink a computer. While a Harvard pigskin looked impressive hanging on the wall, it was no guarantee of a job, as was, for example, a certificate from a Vastnet Nanotechnology program.

I was hoping to help Roy and get back to my place before the clock struck day seven. And Herb was fast, God love him. He'd put his philosophy degree to good use. We flew well above the old-time skyscrapers, like the *Chicago Tribune* building and the Sears Tower, but below the executive level of the newer 200-story buildings, like the AutoMates Starbelisk and the Morgan's Organs Surgery Center. Fortunately, only taxis and emergency vehicles were allowed in the downtown skyways, so we didn't face too much traffic. Before I knew it, Herb settled his small, yellow chopper on a taxi pad in the heart of the Loop. I zoomed down the building's outer elevator and ran hard to Chicago Avenue and State Street.

The buildings were so tall in this quadrant that city officials kept the streetlights on around the clock. Like Victorian gaslights, they did little to quell the canyonlike darkness of the streets. And since this once fashionable part of town had fallen on hard times—with free rangers sleeping in well-appointed cardboard boxes, methop junkies shooting up as if they were in the privacy of their own bathrooms, and emaciated hookers lurking in the shadows—it had a vaguely Dickensian aura.

When I reached the entrance to the alley that led to the Cloisters, I called out, "Roy?" as I stepped through the trash-strewn passageway. Rotting food and urine assailed my nose, which I covered with the back of one hand as I tiptoed through a brackish liquid I didn't want to identify. It had rained earlier, and a trickle—blessedly fresh and silvery—still flowed down a drainpipe, spilling over the broken asphalt.

I focused on the cleansing overflow as I made my way toward the end of the alley. I'd almost reached the open courtyard, where I suspected Roy awaited my help, when I was greeted by the one thing in this world that could make me want to turn and run.

"A rat," I whispered. Not just any varmint, but a rad rat. Rad as in radiation, not trendy. Rats are never in style.

About twenty years ago some idiot Director of Public Health decided the city's rat problem had reached apocalyptic proportions and solved it by feeding the nasty critters radiation pellets. A few—the toughest and smartest—survived, mutated, and spawned offspring so large they could have registered with the American Kennel Association.

One of their descendants stood ten feet away from me right now, the size of a pit bull, daring me to pass. That's what I hated about rats. They had attitude, in addition to beady eyes, creepy tails and vicious teeth.

"Get out of my way!" Out of habit, I reached for the Glock that wasn't there. I seldom used it and had never killed anyone, but it was a menacing weapon to wave around. Instead, I pulled out my whip and cracked it in the air. The rat flinched, but waddled closer.

"What do you think this is?" I shouted. "Showdown at the OK Corral? Go on! Get out of here!"

Just then another rad rat stepped out of the shadows. I'd read somewhere that they mated for life. How touching.

"Okay, which one of you freaks of nature wants to be widowed first?"

I snapped my whip at the one who'd been acting like John Wayne. "Bull's-eye!" I shouted triumphantly as it squealed and ran.

The second rat, apparently outraged by the assault, ran toward me so fast I couldn't use my whip again, so I met it halfway and punted it, literally. The squealing—I swear, screaming—creature flew through the air and landed hard against the brick wall, then limped away.

"Ha!" At least I was warmed up. I only hoped these disgusting creatures weren't an omen.

I ran the rest of the way down the alley to the entrance to the Cloisters, so named because it was a square courtyard surrounded by arches, as in a medieval monastery. It used to be a loading dock where trucks would unload their wares. But it was abandoned about fifteen years ago, and soon after was the site of a terrible shoot-out between police and drug runners that claimed the lives of nine officers.

Since then the Cloisters had been virtually crime free. Word on the street was that the slain cops haunted the place. Retributionists, who weren't as a rule superstitious, sometimes took advantage of the empty real estate because it was centrally located. It was a convenient place to meet with a client who wanted a contract to remain secret.

I found the square courtyard well-lit and littered with the remains of a giant forklift, whose metal parts were scattered like the bones of a small dinosaur.

"Roy?" I called out. "Roy, where are you?"

"Here!" came his croaking reply. "It's safe. They're gone."

Spying his bloody, prone body amid the metal rubble, I raced to his side, scraping my knees as I dropped to the dirty concrete. I touched his damp and cold forehead. He was very weak and, I suspected, badly in need of blood. He eyed me with a glint of affection. "Hey, Blue Dragon."

He often called me that because of the easy-stick dragon tattoo I sometimes wore on my forehead during retribution gigs. It had become my symbol. In Chinese mythology, blue dragons are powerful creatures that live in water. Since one of my great joys as a child was swimming in Lake Michigan, and since I'd learned my best combat techniques from a former Shaolin kung fu monk, the imagery seemed to fit and gave me confidence.

"What are you doing in this shitty neighborhood?"

"You called me, remember?" I squeezed his hand hard, willing my life into him. Blood had splattered his white shirt like a panel from a Rorschach test. His abdomen looked like meat ready for a sausage grinder.

"Shit!" I muttered, momentarily squeezing my eyes tight.

I jammed my earpiece in place and called for an ambulance and police, then snapped it back on my lapel and took Roy's pulse. It was too slow. If the ambulance didn't hurry, he wouldn't make it.

"Angel..."

"Yes, Roy?" I stroked his cheek. "What is it?"

He looked at me with eyes I had once watched so carefully for approval. With a gray mustache and silver hair, Roy was elegant and smart. He was also wily. He'd been the first man to tell me it was okay to be a little bad for a good cause.

"Go help the boy," he croaked.

"What boy?"

He raised his right hand and pointed, then dropped it and passed out.

I checked his pulse again to make sure he was still alive. Then I carefully headed in the direction in which he'd pointed. My stomach surged with vertigo when I spotted a second body, which was so utterly still I knew immediately that "the boy" was dead.

As I knelt, both fascinated and horrified beside the lifeless form, I thought of Marco's question to me: do you really know what death is? Trying to take it in as much as I could, I carefully tugged on the shoulder of the young man's Hawaiian shirt. The weight of his shoulders pulled his still-supple torso toward me, and I winced at the scarlet carnage. I reached down and pulled his head my way so I could look at his face, in case I recognized him.

Who it was nearly stopped my heart. "Oh, my God!"

It was Victor Alvarez, the seventeen-year-old son of the Chicago mayor. I'd met Victor briefly when I'd done a top secret retribution job for his father. This was a disaster of monstrous proportions. What the hell had happened here? Had Roy and Victor been in a shoot-out?

"Angel," came Roy's weak cry.

I ran the thirty feet back to his side and my eyes widened when I saw how white he was. He looked at me with terror shimmering in his eyes.

"Angel, I'm dying." He started to convulse, gasping desperately for air.

I knelt and took him in my arms, but he shook so violently his hand socked me in the temple and I nearly blacked out. When I regained my composure, he was still, his eyes wide open.

"No!" I shouted and began mouth-to-mouth resuscitation. I fought to keep the cold of death out of my lungs while I stubbornly forced the warmth of life into his, one breath at a time.

By the time emergency technicians arrived, I was sweating and frantic, pumping at Roy's chest, willing him to live. Strong hands gripped my upper arms and lifted me away.

"Hold it, ma'am," said a brawny EMT, pulling me around. His round, ebony face was serious and soothing. "We have it under control now. You can stop. We'll take over from here."

I took in a hitching breath and nodded, as an EMT took over working on Roy. I looked around and realized the once-empty courtyard was now teaming with detectives, special forces and beat cops. When I looked back at Roy, the technician was pulling a white sheet over him.

"That's it?" I shouted. "Why did you stop? Can't you take him to the hospital?"

The big guy who had pulled me aside said, "We did a brain scan. There's no activity."

I nodded, finally admitting what I'd known from the beginning. Roy was gone. As devastating as this fact was, I could not cry for him. Not here. I had to know first who killed him. As always, I trusted my own ability to find out more than the cops.

"Angel Baker?" a voice intoned over my shoulder.

"That's me," I muttered, still staring at the white sheet.

"My name is Lieutenant William Townsend, director of Q.E.D."

I tore my gaze from Roy's body and focused on a man who towered above me a good six inches. Gray-haired and quietly arrogant, he regarded me assessingly.

"How did you know who I am?" I asked, refusing to be cowed.

"Detective Marco briefed me when I arrived," he answered in an upper-crust British accent. He was apparently a UK immigrant who'd tenaciously clung to his distinguished way of speaking.

"Marco?" The word was like a bad dream suddenly remembered in the light of day. I glanced over and saw Marco talking to a bevy of crime scene techs and investigators.

"What time is it?" I hissed.

Arching one brow in surprise, Lieutenant Townsend replied, "Four-fifty."

The proverbial clock had struck midnight. In Marco's eyes, I was now officially a pumpkin. I'd failed our agreement. I rubbed my eyes with both hands and sighed.

"I need to see your license," Townsend said in a clipped manner.

Without enthusiasm, I handed over my certification card and studied him as he held it by the edges with his uncallused, manicured fingers, as if I had cooties. I'd always been curious about Q.E.D., which was short for the Latin term *quad erat demonstrandum*, "that which is to be demonstrated." I'd never met a Q.E.D. officer before but I'd heard the group jokingly referred to as the Quad Squad.

An elite group, it consisted of about ten cops who had elected to undergo psychosurgery to limit their capacity to feel emotions. After surgery, the officers took the latest biomeds to spur connections in the logical, left side of the brain, which would then take over functions that had been surgically freed up in the right, or emotional, side of the brain. The idea being that a more logical cop could better solve crimes and would be less inclined to abuse criminals in a fit of anger.

"Are you carrying a weapon, Ms. Baker?" Townsend inquired, handing me back my ID.

"A knife and a whip. No gun."

He fixed me with cold, gray eyes that fronted a brain working apparently with computer-like precision. In fact, he stared down his aquiline nose at me for so long with so little emotion that I began to wonder if he considered me a suspect.

"I didn't do it, Lieutenant. But perhaps I can help you find out who did."

"That won't be necessary." He gave me a perfunctory smile, perhaps one remembered from presurgery days. He motioned above my head and soon another detective joined us. My skin began to tingle ominously in this new presence and I turned to see who it was.

Marco. His jaded eyes that so recently glittered at me with desire now shone with reproof.

"Detective Marco," Townsend said, "I'm arresting Angel Baker in connection with this double homicide. Would you be so kind as to read her her Miranda rights?"

Townsend walked away without waiting for a reply. Marco put his hands on his hips and sighed heavily. Our gazes met again. "You just couldn't wait, could you?" he said accusingly. "What? Another hour was it?"

"Marco, I—"

"You have the right to remain silent," he said in a monotone voice, cutting me off. "You have the right to an attorney...."

Chapter 3

Nothing but the Truth

To say I was stunned by the turn of events would be a gross understatement. I was nearly in shock. I rode calmly in the police aerocar, as if out for a Sunday drive. *This is all a mistake,* I kept thinking. *They have to let me go.* When you step in serious doo-doo, you usually don't realize what a mess you're in until the action settles and your olfactory senses kick into high gear.

I got a powerful whiff of it when I walked into Police Substation #1. Fondly known as the Crypt, P.S. #1 was a highly secure concrete fortress built underground so that mobs couldn't blow it up whenever one of their leaders went there for a pit stop in crime's never-ending rat race. It was hard to get into and out of without a police escort. Not that I planned on trying to escape. I was innocent, after all. I simply had to prove it, right? It was amazing how someone as hard-bitten as I am could be so naive.

Still handcuffed, I rode down a concrete corridor lined with twenty glass prison cells on either side. My chauffeur was a beat cop who transported me in the back of an aero-cart-type vehicle you see at O'Hare Airport that carry disabled passengers and beep obnoxiously at able-bodied passengers in the way.

Slowly accepting the fact that I was a criminal suspect and not a tourist, I hunkered down in the back seat and watched the parade of prisoners with growing dismay and increasing alarm over my predicament. My eyes popped when I saw a tall, shirtless body builder in one of the clear cells. His skin was covered with so many body piercings that he looked like a human pin cushion. He glanced at me sullenly as I passed.

The next cell contained a Skinny—a prostitute who wore no clothes. Ever. Except for the facsimile of clothing permanently tattooed on her body—in this case red short-shorts and a white short-sleeve top. Since it was too painful to tattoo nipples, they remained intact, pink and perpetually protruding from her white "blouse." Skinnies didn't like to waste time undressing. Time was money, after all.

And just when I thought I'd seen it all, we drove past a person I'd hoped I'd never see again as long as I lived.

"Cyclops!" I exclaimed without thinking.

The pudgy, red-haired cop in the front looked back and sneered. "He a friend of yours?"

"Not exactly." More like enemies. Cy ran his own underground prison in Emerald City, the homeless community that dwelled in the abandoned underground subway system.

Unlike the previous jailbirds I'd just seen, Cy wore a green city-issued jumpsuit with a hood, which he'd pulled over his hairless head. He'd been badly burned in an underground gas fire when he was young. Blinded in one eye, enraged and twisted by the incident, both physically and mentally, he'd been nicknamed Cyclops after the one-eyed monster in Greek mythology.

"How did you guys catch him?" I asked. Cops as a rule stayed clear of Emerald City.

"From what I hear, it wasn't hard," the officer replied. "He's blind."

"Blind?" I sat up for a closer look as we drove out of sight, so to speak. Hunched over and scowling, he looked not unlike Shakespeare's Richard III, whom he was fond of quoting. "I thought he had one good eye."

"Yeah," the cop said, "some chicks wandered down in Emerald City and poked his eye out. Ain't that a bite?"

"Yeah," I replied without enthusiasm. The chicks just so happened to be me and my mother. Lola had stabbed Cy in the face with a stick during our fight. It was the coup de grâce that enabled us to escape from his prison. It must have left him totally sightless. Somehow I felt bad about it. Roy always told me I was a sucker for the underdogs of the world.

With a tug of guilt and the loss of Roy squeezing my heart, my numbness began to fade and I felt shaky by the time we arrived at the interrogation wing of the station. My chauffeur deposited me, still handcuffed, into a windowless rectangle and locked the door. If this tactic was meant to make me brood over the evening's events, it worked.

I would miss Roy terribly. And Victor had been cheated out of his future. I felt for his father's loss all the more because Mayor Alvarez was a friend of Henry Bassett, my foster father. Both men would grieve, and it killed me that I had to be associated with Victor's death in any way.

And, as always, I felt abandoned. It was my natural reaction to everything. Marco could have come to my defense at the crime scene, but he hadn't. I wasn't even sure if he thought I was innocent. Now, that *really* hurt.

I'd refused to let Lieutenant Townsend, not to mention Marco, see me cry, but now a tear escaped down my placid face. I cried silently, a trick I'd learned during a two-year stint in an abusive foster home before I'd been mercifully rescued by the Bassetts. It was a trick I hoped Lin would never have to learn. God, I had to get out of here and get back to her.

The door opened with a brisk whoosh and a nerdy little man bearing an underarm full of electronic files, a coffee-stained tie and a suit he must have purchased at the local print shop. I could recognize the unnatural creases of a reconstituted paper suit a mile away. Was this a law student intern? I wondered as I surreptitiously wiped my face.

"Miss Baker?" he inquired, flashing a row of neglected teeth with his overly exuberant smile.

"Yes?"

"I'm your lawyer."

"I don't need a lawyer."

He nodded patronizingly as he dropped his load of files on the table. "I've heard that before, Miss Baker. And I suppose you're going to tell me that you're—"

"Innocent. Damned straight."

He looked up, startled, I presume, by my lack of remorse for the crime he clearly thought I'd committed. "Innocent," he repeated, clearly speculating on the credibility of my reply, adding doubtfully, "Okay."

"What's your name?"

"Terrence Murray."

"Don't be an asshole, Mr. Murray. I've already got one, and I don't need another."

His eyes rounded and he pursed his wet lips. "Look here, Miss Baker, you're lucky to have me. This is a busy place, as you may have noticed. Most people have to wait days for a chance to meet with a public defender."

"Lucky me."

He shook his head and opened the top file, muttering, "You're awfully confident for someone who has caught the interest of Q.E.D."

"What do you mean?"

He looked up from his papers. "Q.E.D. is the police department's latest effort to reestablish law and order and polish its tarnished image. If the members of this elite force were willing to go under the knife just to increase their odds of nailing criminals, they won't back down easily in a case involving a CRS. You're the competition."

"But I'm innocent."

"It doesn't matter."

"Why are you here?"

"To represent you during your interrogation with Lieutenant Townsend."

I shook my head. "I don't want to talk to that inhuman son of a bitch. I'm going to face the Diva."

Murray's nondescript, pale features formed into a nebulous look of confusion. "Are you crazy? You're better off with Townsend than with the Diva. If she finds fault with your story, you'll be facing the maximum charges with no chance of a plea bargain. You'll be stuck in the system for years."

"I'll take my chances."

"Let me put it to you another way, Miss Baker. I know of serial killers who are walking the streets because there was no DNA evidence to keep them locked up for more than two years, in spite of solid convictions. If they'd faced the Diva when they were first brought up on charges, she would have detected their guilt. With no chance of bail, they would have spent longer in jail just waiting for a trial than the time they ended up serving for murder."

I just looked at him for a long moment. "That's pathetic."

"That's the system. That's why you can't face the Diva."

"I know you think you know what's best for me, but I have a little girl waiting for me at home. If I don't go back to her soon, she'll think…" Why was I telling him this? He wouldn't understand. "I have to go home. When I tell the Diva I'm innocent, they'll let me go."

The lawyer's agitation turned to disdain. "Very well, Miss Baker, but he's not going to like this one bit."

"Who?"

He looked down at me with a superior smirk. "Detective Marco. Why he'd bother with someone as ungrateful as you, I have no clue."

"So he sent you to me?"

"How else do you think you were lucky enough to see an attorney so quickly? Didn't you see the gallery of rogues rotting away in glass booths waiting for a chance at representation? And people like you have the audacity to be ungrateful."

The thought of Marco throwing me this bone was too much to bear. "Did Detective Marco, by any chance, tell you that he and I are involved?"

"Not in so many words. But I assumed so. Why else would he bother to call in a marker for this?" He looked at me smugly. "Do you think your relationship with Detective Marco will matter? It will buy you no mercy, Miss Baker."

"Doesn't it strike you as a conflict of interest that one of the arresting detectives has been my lover?"

"Yes. But it won't matter to the judge if he's low on convictions this month. But, of course, that's why we have an appeals system."

"And that lame response is why we have retribution specialists," I snapped, standing up. "This system is so fucked up it's beyond repair."

"That's why you need a lawyer."

I shook my head. "No. I want to see the Diva. The truth has to count for something in this shithole."

He shrugged. "Have it your way."

As he headed for the door, I suddenly remembered something Roy had said. "Before Roy Leibman died," I called out, "he said 'they' had left. Someone was at the crime scene before I got there."

"Tell it to the Diva," he said flippantly, adding with some modicum of sincerity, "Good luck, Miss Baker. You're going to need it. But, as they say, it ain't over until the fat lady sings."

After he shut the door, I muttered, "Let's hope she's got laryngitis tonight."

The Diva is a nickname for the Detection and Interrogation Visual Application System. Big words for a simple and beautifully administered lie detector test.

The suspect sits strapped in a dentist-style chair and talks to a hologram. Behind the hologram projection there's a camera that records the dilations and retractions of the suspect's corneas. Based on eye movements, D.I.V.A.S. analysts, watching the interrogation and programming the Divas's questions from behind a two-way mirror, claim they can distinguish between fact and fiction.

The Diva looked like an oversized opera singer. The program's designer thought it would be clever if "the Diva" looked liked Brunhilde. So she wore a winged Visigoth helmet and fully loaded breast plates. She was a "fat" lady, as the public defender had put it. I use the word advisedly because it's against the law to call anyone fat. According to the *Self Esteem Act* of 2010, I should call her full-bodied, but I didn't plan on discussing her weight. I was in enough trouble as it was.

I felt confident that a session with the Diva would exonerate me. I began to have second thoughts, however, when I entered the interrogation chamber and caught a glimpse of Lieutenant Townsend behind the two-way mirror. He saw me and turned out the light in the observation booth, leaving me to stare at my own reflection.

"It's just you and me, kid," I whispered to myself, as I had so many times before. Lord knows I'd gotten myself out of worse scrapes with nothing more than moxie and determination. And now I had the added advantage of my recently discovered psychic abilities. But I hadn't yet learned to use them on cue. At least, not in a tense situation like this.

The lights slowly dimmed, except for a white beam that encircled my chair. As I climbed into the hot seat, I silently reassured myself I'd made the right decision. Suspects who volunteer for a session with the Diva are generally given credit for believing in their own innocence, and that sits well with judges. However, if a D.I.V.A.S. session goes badly, the suspect is immediately charged for the crime in question, and no amount of fancy footwork by an attorney can get the charges dismissed after the fact. The case has to work its way through the courts.

Suddenly the Diva appeared. Her long blond hair hung in braids. Red lipstick brightened a smile so welcoming that I found myself resisting the urge to smile back. I suspected the program had been designed to relax and disarm. That was doubtless another reason the programmer had used the image of a woman. I would have to stay on my guard.

"Hello, Angel," she said in a rich, melodic voice.

"Hello." I tightened my grip on the arms of the cushioned metal chair.

"I want you to get comfortable," she said, and my chair tilted back a few inches via a remote-controlled hydraulic system. "Straps will hold you in place, but they shouldn't be too tight. Are you comfy?"

"I guess so."

"Good. The constraints are simply there to keep you in the correct position. Now, Angel, what were you doing at the Cloisters?"

I squinted to see through the hologram and briefly spotted the camera lens recording my eye movements. The Diva seemed to notice. She moved her head and focused her large, heavily lined eyes more intently on me. The distraction worked. I forgot about the lens and did my best to make my case.

"I was there to help my colleague, Roy Leibman."

The Diva smiled sympathetically. "Did you know him well?"

I tried to nod, forgetting that my head was strapped in place. "Yes. He was my mentor." A surge of emotion clogged my throat and I let out a deep, pained breath. "He…he taught me everything I know."

"Then why did you kill him?" Rather than being accusatory, she seemed genuinely curious.

Trying to mimic her calm, logical attitude, I said, "I didn't kill him. When I arrived, I found Roy already wounded. Victor Alvarez was already dead."

"You know Victor?"

"Yes."

The Diva frowned, and I sensed her sympathy slipping away. This was a very sophisticated program. The interrogators who were running the show behind the mirror had the power to supply the Diva not only questions, but emotional reactions as well. I waited, but she remained silent. Why? What was the big deal about me knowing Victor? Then it hit me.

"Oh, come on. Are you implying that my association with

Victor makes me more suspicious than anyone else in this building? You think this was somehow premeditated on my part? I'm just being honest. I could have said I knew who the victim was because everyone at the crime scene was talking about him, which they were, or because he's frequently seen on television, but I told you the truth. I have nothing to hide."

"You call it a crime scene," she replied. "So you admit a crime was committed."

"Yes. Obviously. But not by me. Roy called me and said he needed help. I think he'd already been shot when he called, but I didn't realize that until I got there."

"He called you?"

"Yes." When she raised a brow in doubt, I added stridently, "Check the phone records. Go ahead. I have nothing to hide."

"If you didn't kill them, Angel, then who did?"

I paused just long enough to feel a trickle of perspiration itching its way down my right temple. I wished like hell I could scratch it. "I don't know. Perhaps it was a random execution by drug dealers. Wrong-place-at-the-wrong-time kind of thing."

"So your gun just happened to be at the wrong place at the wrong time as well?"

"My gun?" I repeated blankly. When she nodded, I said, "That's impossible. My gun is locked up in a bank. I'm…semiretired."

The image of the Diva faded to black and in her place I discovered a 3-D projection of a crime scene photo. A hand gingerly held a dangling semiautomatic weapon emblazoned with a lapis lazuli dragon imbedded in a pearl handle. There was no question that it was my gun.

"Where was this photo taken?" I demanded. "It could be anywhere."

"True enough," the Diva's voice replied from the ether. "How's this?"

Another photo appeared, a wider shot of the same pose. It was Marco holding the gun for the camera. Behind him you could see Victor Alvarez's body.

I closed my eyes, wishing they could stay that way. Forever. *What could I say to refute this photo?* my mind frantically wondered. Deeper inside, I thought, *Why didn't Marco just cut my heart out with a knife?* It would have been less painful than this. Clearly, he wanted me out of his life. Putting me behind bars was certainly one way to do that. Had he planted my gun at the crime scene?

"I don't know how my gun got there," I forced myself to say, though I felt like a dead woman walking, or rather sitting. "Contact my bank. Someone broke into my deposit box and stole it."

The Diva threw her head back and laughed, her double chins shaking as her voice ran the musical scale from top to bottom. She finally settled on me with twinkling eyes. "Come now, Angel, you don't expect me to believe that."

"You seem like an intelligent woman, Diva," I replied, daring a bit of reverse psychology with my computerized interrogator. "Surely you've figured out by now that sometimes people are set up for crimes they didn't commit. Do you really think I would be stupid enough to risk an interrogation with you if I'd used my gun at that crime scene?"

"Someone used that gun."

"But not me."

The Diva looked back over her shoulder and appeared to be talking to someone, though no one else was projected in the hologram. She turned back to me with a look of grave doubt.

"Angel, Lieutenant Townsend informs me that his men have already run a computer check of your lapel phone records. There was no call from Roy Leibman."

"That's a lie!" I shouted.

Her expressive eyes couldn't quite conceal a gleam of triumph. "Take a look for yourself."

The Diva faded to black and an image of my phone records flashed in front of me. I squinted to make out the numbers that had come in over the last twenty-four hours. Not only was Roy's call absent, there was no evidence of any incoming calls after 10:30 p.m. The only registered conversation was the one I had made when I called for emergency help at the Cloisters.

"This isn't right!" I called out. I tried to look at the two-way mirror, but the padded clamp around my forehead stopped me cold. I moved to yank it off, but the straps around my wrists merely tightened. "There's a mistake in those records."

The Diva reappeared, fading in on a bubble like Glenda the Good Witch in *The Wizard of Oz,* though her change in demeanor reminded me more of Glenda's evil sister from the east.

"What do you have to say for yourself, Angel?"

"I talked to Roy," I said as calmly as I could. I had to remember that I wasn't trying to convince the Diva. She didn't exist. I was trying to prove to the camera lens hidden behind her image that I was telling the truth. "Roy asked me to come."

"Is that so?" the Diva replied, all frowns and pinched lips. "Did Roy Leibman ever ask for your help before?"

I paused. "No. And I'm sure that in Lieutenant Townsend's little logical manual on law enforcement that means it's unlikely Roy would have called on me now. Am I right?"

"I'll ask the questions, missy," the Diva hissed. "Isn't it true that you came to the Cloisters because you were jealous that Victor Alvarez had chosen Roy Leibman as a Certified Retribution Specialist instead of you?"

"What? No!"

"You wanted to be among the most prominent in your profession. That's why you rescued those twelve Chinese orphans last month. Not because anyone was paying you to do that job, but because you wanted the publicity."

"I wanted to help the girls," I shot back.

"You were jealous and angry that when Victor needed a retribution job done, he didn't turn to you like his father had."

I frowned slowly. "Wait a minute. How did you know about—"

"You didn't want Roy to horn in on your domain as CRS for the mayor's family."

"That's absurd."

"So when you found out that Roy was meeting Victor at the Cloisters, you came to express your anger. You were the only one with a gun. Before the night was through, you used it. You killed Roy Leibman and Victor Alvarez."

I shut my eyes. I shouldn't have. It would probably be construed as a sign of guilt. But suddenly my eyelids were too heavy to bear. I could take no more. It had become abundantly clear the Diva wasn't going to cut me any more slack than Lieutenant Townsend had. No surprise there, since he was doubtless programming her with the questions.

The lights came on suddenly. I opened my eyes and found the Diva had disappeared. My chair righted itself and the restraints retreated with a slight hum. Townsend came out of a door near the three-way mirror.

"Speak of the devil," I muttered to myself as I swung my feet to the floor and rubbed my wrists. When he came close enough for me to shiver at the sight of his gray, reptilian eyes, I said sarcastically, "So, did I pass the test?"

"Yes."

I blinked twice and tried unsuccessfully to read his urbane, starched features. The Diva showed more emotion than this automaton. "I don't understand."

"Based on your eye movements, the D.I.V.A.S. program

has come to the conclusion that you did not lie during your interrogation."

I squelched the urge to say *I told you so!*

"However, there is a great difference between not lying and telling the truth. Normally, passing the D.I.V.A.S. test would be enough to free yourself from suspicion. But your phone records offer a compelling contradiction to your testimony. Combined with a compelling motive for the murders, that offers us enough evidence of probable cause to hold you over for trial."

"But I passed the test."

"Article 34.A of the new 2104 Interrogation Bill passed by the city council two weeks ago allows the lead investigator to override test results in the case of probable cause."

I stared at him, speechless.

I was aware that the legislature had passed a law designed to add so-called teeth to the bill that had established Q.E.D. two years ago. But I hadn't realized the "teeth" would be biting my rear end.

"I'm innocent, Townsend," I said. "If you're going to abuse due process in the name of public safety, you ought to at least wait until you have a real criminal at your mercy."

His gray eyes glittered keenly. "Don't tell me you didn't consider the new law when you elected to face the Diva. Didn't the public defender assigned to your case tell you that?"

I hadn't given him a chance, but I wasn't about to admit that to Townsend. "No, he didn't."

"That's a pity." Townsend's lips turned up in a shadow of a smile. "Angel Baker, you are now officially charged with double homicide."

No question about it. The fat lady had sung, loud and clear.

Chapter 4

Guilty Until Proven Innocent

The sun was coming up when I finally emerged from the Crypt under armed guard. We stood a moment at the discreet underground entrance, taking in the fresh air. A pink mist hovered over the lake to the east, and across the street coils of silver steam rose from the Chicago River, an entrenched waterway that snaked through the city, splitting it in two.

Momentarily forgetting my troubles, I breathed in the glorious scent of city grime and baking pastries. A deli at the corner was about to open. Freshly brewed coffee wafted from the storefront's vents. It was a little after 5:30 a.m. Rush hour was a noisy bubble about to burst. Meanwhile, the streets remained surprisingly tranquil. A light breeze picked up, and a little tornado of discarded papers and candy wrappers whirled around us, then rolled away, so much urban tumbleweed.·

God, I love this city, I thought, feeling a surge of affection that brought moisture to my eyes. Funny how the threat of imprisonment could make you appreciate even the downside of urban life.

"There she is! Angel! Angel Baker!"

Tensing, I looked to my left and saw a couple of television live trucks parked on the other side of the street. Several well-dressed reporters hurried toward me with photographers dressed in flak jackets and combat boots trailing after them, cameras mounted on their helmets, their wireless controls imbedded in their touch belts. The photographers looked as if they were ready for a war zone, which was a good description of some downtown streets they had to cruise on various news assignments. The reporters could hang back and do a live report on the set with the anchors, but the photogs had to dodge sniper fire and gang wars to get pictures for air.

"Let's get out of here," I said to the cop gripping my right arm. He watched the approaching media without batting an eye.

Suddenly feeling abused, I realized this journey down the block from the station to the criminal processing center had been arranged specifically so that the media could get me on camera. It was one of many ways the police and the media worked hand-in-hand. We could have taken the underground passageway between the center and P.S. #1, but then the reporters wouldn't have gotten their all-important "pictures."

This was what my foster-brother Hank Bassett, a television producer, called "walking the suspect." The police made sure suspects were paraded for the cameras. In return, the grateful press was more inclined to give cops favorable news coverage. There was nothing overtly unethical about the arrangement, but now that I was a suspect, it all smacked of collusion.

The walking shot would then be used over and over again

on the news as file footage whenever there were new developments in my case. I would be forever immortalized in newsroom archives. Even if I won the Nobel Peace Prize twenty years from now, they'd pull out this footage of me in handcuffs for a retrospective of my life. Oh joy.

"Okay, let's go," the cop finally said when four camera crews were practically breathing down my neck.

"Angel, did you do it?" shouted one female reporter, shoving a microphone the size of a pen in my face.

I jerked my head away and kept walking. The camera operators walked backward in front of me, their head gear recording my every grimace and scowl.

"Angel, do you have anything to say to the Chinese girls you rescued?" said a good-looking male reporter.

"Why did you kill the mayor's son, Baker?"

I turned sharply to see who had shouted this last outrageous question and came face-to-face with Rodney Delaney, a gruff, gray-haired reporter who had been in detox at least five times for five different addictions, according to Hank. Delaney's face had more lines than a sushi chef's cutting board, and his nose had more skeins of broken veins than the legs of an aging drag queen.

"What did you say, Delaney?" I demanded to know.

"Who paid you to kill the mayor's son?" he shot back out of the side of his mouth, clearly trying to egg me into a good sound bite.

I jabbed his chest with a forefinger. "Look here, you presumptuous, drunken, ambulance-chasing—"

"Back off, Delaney!" A man in his midtwenties, with red hair and light freckles, pushed his way through the crowd. It took me a minute to realize it was my foster brother. Hank shoved Delaney back, then pulled me into a fierce hug. Though handsome, Hank was stocky and soft like a teddy bear.

"Wh-what are you doing here?"

He looked down at me with a world of worry creasing his forehead, then said to the cop, "Officer, I'm Hank Bassett, a relative and a producer at WFFY-TV. If you're going to walk my sister, then you're going to have to walk me, too."

The officer nodded and we moved ahead. Hank held out an arm, forcing the reporters to keep their distance.

"Back off!" he shouted. "Come on, give us a break. You got your voice-overs, now go on back to your vans."

Finally, we gained some distance from the news crews. Hank explained that was because they needed some wide shots to intersperse with the close-ups they'd already recorded, not because the reporters were having mercy on us. Accepting the bizarre fact that we were now both newsworthy, Hank placed his arm around my shoulder and held me close. I leaned into him, fighting tears. He was my kid brother and he'd rescued me. He'd fended off his own colleagues to protect me.

"Thanks, pal," I said with emotion. "I owe you."

"Everything's going to be okay, Angel," he reassured me. "I called Mom and Dad when I heard the story on the police scanners. They're waiting for you in the processing center. They're working on getting you a lawyer. Maybe Jack Berkowitz, he's one of the best."

"Okay." I wasn't going to turn down legal help a second time, although I didn't like having to trouble Henry and Sydney for it. They were the Evanston couple who'd rescued me from two years of hell in an abusive foster home after Lola had gone to prison for bookmaking. The Bassetts were well-to-do, educated and had completely accepted me into their family. At times like this, I didn't feel worthy of their unconditional love.

I hated having to face Henry after embarrassing him like

this, and I worried that he'd taken the news of Victor's death very hard. My fears were confirmed when I entered the family conference room on the third floor of the criminal processing center.

Henry sat at the table, looking older than his sixty-five years. His silver hair was not quite in place and shadows lined his cheeks down to his Vandyke. Sydney sat by his side, looking lovely as usual, with her frosted hair pulled back in a bun and the best makeup money could buy, which made her look as if she wore none, except for the coral pink on her quick-to-smile lips.

She was the first to see me, and the look of worry and relief that washed over her about broke my heart.

"Angel!"

"Sydney," I said. We hugged tightly. I inhaled her Armand Gervais perfume and the comfort it brought me made my eyes puddle up. "Thank you for coming."

She patted my back, then gripped my forearms and regarded me fiercely with her pastel blue eyes. "We're here for you, Angel. One hundred percent."

I nodded but was unable to find the words to express my gratitude. I glanced over at Henry. He hadn't budged. He still sat, his tall, lanky frame sprouting from the small chair.

"Henry?" I said, but he didn't respond.

My heart started pounding. I could take just about anything—a bullet, murder charges, even a guilty verdict—but I couldn't bear Henry's disapproval. I walked slowly forward and sat across the table from him, searching his face for forgiveness, just as I had when I was a child reporting for punishment.

My foster sister, Gigi, would always start the trouble, but when Henry demanded to know who was at fault, I was invariably the one who would break the stalemate with a false confession. Henry would look at me doubtfully and ask me if I was really to blame. Yes, I'd insist, but please don't send me away. Never, Henry would reply. Then he'd create some chore as penance and send me on my way with a wink. Gigi would be happy and that meant Sydney was happy. Little Hank would call me a sucker, but he was on my side. Yes, I could take anything but Henry's rejection.

"Henry," I said, willing my voice not to shake, "please look at me."

When he finally did, I winced at the sadness I saw.

"I'm sorry, Henry. I'm sorry I had to drag you into this."

"Victor…" His voice faded and he shook his head.

"Yes, Victor was killed. It's a horrible tragedy. Have you talked to his father?"

Henry nodded, then looked at me in a way that turned my blood cold—as if I were a stranger. "Did you do it, Angel?"

All breath vanished from my lungs. How could he even think such a thing? "Did I do it?" I repeated incredulously.

He leaned forward. "I know what you do for a living. It's a risky business. Did you have a contract out on Victor?"

"Christ, Henry!" I shouted at him, which was a first. I pounded the table three times with my fist until I was sure it was bruised. "Christ! I can't believe you just said that. You make it sound like I'm an assassin. I didn't shoot Victor! I've never killed anyone. Henry, please! Sydney, tell him!"

"Calm down, Angel," Sydney crooned.

He nodded and leaned back, his face regaining some color. "Of course you didn't."

I turned my head away from him so he wouldn't see me struggle with tears. The one thing I'd had to see me through my trying life was Henry's faith in me. Now even that was gone.

"You and I know you're innocent," Henry said, the numbness fading from his voice. "But the police think you are guilty."

"I've been set up for a fall," I said in a low voice, sniffing and turning back to my foster parents. It was time to get down to business. "You know I have lots of enemies. Roy Leibman called me and asked for help, but someone has erased all traces of his call from my phone records. If I can find out who did it and why, I'll be able to prove my innocence. But I need to get out of here so I can investigate."

"Of course," Sydney said. "We've already made arrangements to post bail and have retained the Levy and Berkowitz law firm."

My jaws tightened like rubber bands stretched to the breaking point. "How much?"

Sydney blinked several times, then said quietly, "Ten million for bail and ten million for the retainer fee."

I choked out an incoherent reply. "You don't have that kind of spare change, Sydney."

"We're going to mortgage the house," Henry said.

I blanched. "I won't let you do that. It's absurd. I should be released on my own recognizance. And what kind of lawyer would ask for that much money?"

"A very good lawyer," Henry replied sternly. "A lawyer who is risking his reputation taking the side of a retributionist in such a high-profile case."

Humbled, I nodded. Henry continued.

"I talked to the mayor and gave him my word you wouldn't jump bail. So he put in a call to the judge handling the case. The judge threw out Lieutenant Townsend's decision to override the D.I.V.A.S. test results. If I wasn't a close friend of Mayor Alvarez, you wouldn't have gotten bail even if we had a billion dollars. He's in pain, but he knows I'm in pain, too. And he wants you to have a fair trial, even though he thinks you're guilty. Just be grateful it worked out this way."

My shoulders slumped, and I pressed a hand to my nauseous stomach. Henry had really gone out on a limb for me. But at what price? Henry was a former television news director and college journalism dean who had always told us that his only retirement fund was the house, a beautiful lakefront mansion. If he lost that because of me...

"Don't worry," Sydney insisted, reading my thoughts, and smiled. "We know you're good for it."

"But you've got to clear your name, Angel," Henry said. "Don't let us down."

Don't let us down. At least I was home. I hadn't let Lin down. Not yet, anyway. I had to prove my innocence. Sure, I wanted to clear my name and avoid prison. But even more I wanted to make sure I was here for Lin.

God Almighty, help me, I thought as I trudged my way up my apartment steps late in the afternoon. That I'd even gotten in the door without injury was amazing enough. The tranquillity of my wide, somewhat decrepit north side street had been replaced by a block-party atmosphere.

Television camera crews had staked out my two-flat. Neighbors from nearby redbrick apartment buildings had wandered out to see what was going on. I was shocked to see a young couple who looked like they belonged to the sons and daughters of the American Revolution holding signs that read, Down with the Retribution Movement.

I didn't realize I was part of a movement, I thought with a touch of irony as I shoved my way through a pack of reporters who swarmed around me like killer bees. One of them—Rob Keiser from Channel 3—was doing a live shot and I decided I'd better turn on the digivision system to see what he was saying.

When I reached the top of my building's inside stairwell and swung open the door to my living quarters, I shivered with relief. Thank God I was home. The bad news about being fast-tracked through the criminal justice system was that you could find yourself accused, charged and bonded out for an alleged crime before you knew what hit you. That was also the good news. At least I wasn't going to rot in jail waiting for the rusty wheels of justice to churn.

I saw a note on the living room coffee table from Lola. She and Mike had taken Lin to the Lincoln Park Zoo. My knees nearly buckled when I imagined having to tell them that I was now a murder suspect. But I couldn't think about that now. I flipped on the digivision and a flat projection of the Channel 3 reporter appeared in the middle of the room.

"I spoke earlier with Mayor Alvarez," Keiser said, looking officious and concerned as he spoke directly to the camera, "and he admits using Angel Baker's services for a prior retribution job. Here's what he had to say."

The mayor appeared in what was obviously a prerecorded interview. "I hired Angel Baker a couple of years ago," he said. He was a fit and vital man in his late fifties, but now he looked gaunt and grim. "I employed Angel Baker after my niece, Carmella, was raped. Her rapist was convicted, but only served two years because he was clever enough to leave no DNA evidence behind. I was frustrated by the lack of justice. This is a problem many victims must deal with."

I gasped, unable to believe the mayor had exposed his niece's violation before the entire world. When he'd hired me, he had been so adamant that he wanted the rape and retribution to remain secret out of respect for Carmella's privacy.

"With all due respect, Mr. Mayor," the reporter said, "that's why the retribution profession came into existence. Victims want justice. Are you saying you will throw your support behind the Certified Retribution Specialists, even though their tactics are coming under increasing criticism from traditional law-enforcement groups?"

Mayor Alvarez hesitated only a moment before replying, "No, I can no longer support the CRS profession. Not after the death of my son. We cannot tolerate any group, no matter how well-meaning, if it turns into a rogue force of assassins."

"Do you agree with prosecutors who say that Angel Baker was motivated by professional jealousy? She was allegedly envious that your son had passed her over when he hired Roy Leibman."

"I will not speculate on the matter, nor will I comment on the case until it's settled."

"One last question, Mr. Mayor. If Angel Baker were here right now, what would you say to her?"

Hatred filled the mayor's brown, hooded eyes. "I have nothing to say to her. I hope I never have to see her again."

I flipped off the digivision with a remote control and sank down into a couch, burying my face in my hands. I wasn't sure how much more I could take. But a little voice of logic inside my head wouldn't allow me to wallow long in pity.

"Something's not right here," I said, trying to jump-start my resolve with logic.

The door flew open and Lin bounded in, her flip-flops slapping the blond wood floor. "Angel? Are you back?"

"Lin!" I called out and threw open my arms. She ran into them, and I hugged her as hard as I dared. I didn't want to scare her with the depth of my need for this particular hug.

Lin was a petite seven-year-old, nimble and graceful, with bangs and shoulder-length hair as dark as night. Her lovely almond-shaped eyes always lit up when she saw me, which I considered the eighth wonder of the world.

When Lin had first come to live here, she'd been understandably reserved, but she'd thawed a little with each passing day. And though it would probably take years for her to fully accept me as a mother, we'd bonded in new, unspoken ways during the past week.

"I'm glad you're back," she said, beaming up at me with a resilient smile, minus one front baby tooth. "Was your trip productive?"

I laughed to hear such a sophisticated word from her little mouth, but I quickly sobered and felt cold inside. How and when would I tell Lin that I was a murder suspect? After my disastrous interview with the Diva, I'd called Lola from P.S. #1 and told her my retribution job was over and that I'd decided to spend the night with Marco. I wasn't prepared to admit to my ex-con mother that I, too, was now in trouble with the law. Lola had decided to tell Lin that I'd unexpectedly gone on an overnight trip.

Lola, of all people, didn't want Lin to think I was sleeping with a man. When I was a kid, I'd lost count of her lovers, but I couldn't fault her for trying to be better at grandmothering than she'd been at motherhood.

I pressed Lin's head gently between my hands and positioned her for a loud, smacking kiss on the forehead. "Yes, my darling girl, I had a productive night."

Lola tromped up the stairs, fanning herself. Her frazzled red hair had obviously revolted in the late blast of summer heat. Her cheeks were flushed and, beneath her voluminous red polysynthe gown, her double-D breasts heaved in her bid for air.

"Hello, Lola," I said.

"Honey, you got problems down there. Some idiot reporter just asked me if you'd ever threatened to kill anyone when you were growing up. I said, 'Other than me? No.'" She laughed and I groaned.

Lola was the only person I'd ever known who could catch

her breath and expend it without pause at the same time. Suddenly remembering my alleged sleepover at Marco's, she raised her brows with prudish disdain. "Did you enjoy your *trip?*"

"It's a long story," I said, combing Lin's silken black hair with my splayed fingers.

"I have all the time in the world," Lola replied as she headed for the couch. "Lin, honey, fetch Grandma*ma* a glass of iced tea."

"Grandma*ma?*" I repeated.

She flopped down on the couch and leaned her head back so she could mouth at me: mind your own business. Nothing Lola did was my business, yet everything I did was hers. But now wasn't the time to get in a mother-daughter spat.

"What's wrong with Grandma*ma?*" Lola asked petulantly.

I held up both hands in surrender. "Nothing. Nothing at all."

"What is the matter, Baker?" Mike came up beside me.

I hadn't heard him coming up the stairs. His calm, accented words washed over me like warm, soothing water. "Oh, Mike, am I glad to see you."

I put my arms around him, craving his strength. He held himself upright and firm, yet I felt his affection in the light embrace he gave me in return. "What happened, Baker?"

While Lola and Lin played cards in the living room, I joined Mike in his renovated coach house in the back of my garden. I ended up drinking an entire pot of green tea while I told him all that had happened. Fortunately, I had a twelve-foot wooden privacy fence around my oblong garden, so I didn't have to worry about snooping reporters.

Sitting on the futon on Mike's floor, gazing at his small stone fish pond through the open French doors of his one-room haven, I began to unwind and restore a sense of inner peace.

Mike listened to my incredible tale and took it all in stride. That was easy to do because he was a former Chinese Shao-

lin monk who had survived three years of indentured servitude in the poppy fields of Joliet, Illinois, before finding a
place to call his own in my backyard. Opium production was
legal as long as the harvest was sold only to legitimate phar-
maceutical firms. But the poppy farms kept a low profile,
preferring to hire foreign immigrants. Mike was such a one.
He'd naively signed away his freedom when he signed up to
work for the Red Fields opium plant. I'd rescued him and he'd
been devoted to me ever since, saving my butt on numerous
occasions. Nothing could shock or defeat Mike.

"Who do you think did this, Baker?"

"I've been thinking about that, but can't say for sure. Lots
of petty criminals I've hauled in for retribution might want to
harm me or my friends. But none of them has the power to
alter phone records or get into my safety deposit box."

"What about one of the mobs?"

"That's more likely."

There was so much governmental and corporate corruption
and the various criminal syndicates had so successfully infiltrated the establishment that sophisticated crimes were hard
to trace.

"It could be anybody," I said. "But the person who comes
to mind is Corleone Capone."

That was the ridiculously archetypal alias of the head of
the Mongolian Mob. He'd chosen Capone because he was ob-
sessed with the notorious Prohibition-era gangs that became
rich through bootlegging. As for Corleone, he'd supposedly
chosen the name in homage to Don Corleone, the main character in the novel and movie *The Godfather.*

His alias notwithstanding, Corleone Capone dressed like
an eighteenth-century Mongolian warlord and spent most of
his time trying to outdo the neo-Russian syndicate.

I'd majorly pissed him off last month when I'd negotiated

the release of the Chinese orphans from his archrival, Vladimir Gorky. Gorky had kidnapped the girls from Capone for the sole purpose of foiling the competition. Gorky knew that Capone had spent seven years preparing the girls for sale. For Capone, losing the girls permanently to loving, adoptive homes was humiliating and financially devastating. I had been waiting for him to get back at me in some way. Maybe this was it.

"Yes," I agreed. "It was probably Corleone Capone. But why didn't he just kill me? Why did he involve me in a bizarre and pointless double murder?"

"Maybe he wants to make you suffer."

"Well, he succeeded."

"Do not worry, Baker. We will prove your innocence, Baker," Mike said with his usual lack of expression. He didn't need histrionics to prove his points. Not when he could down three men at once with *fei mai qiao,* "the leg flying like a feather," or *gang jin juan,* "the diamond fist," or any number of the other amazing kung fu moves he used so effortlessly. "You need rest now."

I nodded and stretched out. Mike pulled a sheet up to my chin and tucked it around my shoulders with great care. I felt safe and loved. Why could I feel that way with a friend but not with a lover?

"Marco betrayed me," I said with cool detachment that belied the pain I wasn't prepared to deal with.

Mike exhaled and assumed a lotus pose, sitting next to the futon. "Perhaps he had a reason."

"He could have given me a character reference to Q.E.D., but he didn't even admit to the lead investigator that we knew each other. And I believe he planted my gun at the scene. He was the only one who knew I'd put it in the bank."

"Did you ask him about it?"

I shook my head. "I didn't have a chance. I'm not sure I want one."

Mike mulled this over silently, and I felt a prick of irritation that he didn't immediately condemn Marco. A breeze softly buffeted the wind chimes hanging outside. They tinkled soothingly.

"You should get your crystal ball," Mike said at last. "Find out why Detective Marco betrayed you."

I could do it. Marco himself had forced me to accept the fact that I'd inherited Lola's psychic abilities. I'd used them to help us find Lin's missing friends. I suppose I could use my talents to help myself as well. But the very thought of learning any more about Marco made me feel queasy.

"The less I know about Marco the better," I said, closing my eyes for much needed sleep. For now, ignorance would be my only bliss.

Chapter 5

Date With Destiny

Detective Riccuccio Marco had an inbred devotion to truth, justice and the American way. Granted, all three lived in the shadows of his own crimes and guilt, but he'd learn to compartmentalize his life, and so far the positives still had his dark side on a tight leash.

Two years ago he'd entered a new program to streamline the training of solo detectives to replace those killed by the R.M.O., the Mongolian Mob, and other crime syndicates. His colleagues in the psy-ops department of the Chicago PD assumed he'd been motivated by the desire to learn more about the drug-related shoot-out that killed his rookie-cop kid brother, and in part that was true.

Handsome, articulate, sensitive to emotions and bred into a lifetime of nuance, Marco had easily excelled at crime-fighting propaganda campaigns, psychological profiles on seriously twisted suspects and media appearances. None of his superiors would guess that he'd majored in psychology so he could understand his own horrific crimes. R.M.O. attorneys had illicitly wiped his record clean.

Prior to his long years of study at the University of Chicago, he'd been a *sgarrista*—a foot soldier—for the Russian Mafiya Organizatsia. And before that, he'd been an innocent kid. Everybody started out in life innocent. Few were lucky enough to die that way.

Angel was still innocent, though she pretended otherwise. But she wouldn't be for long if she got stuck in the prison system. She needed help. So Marco made two calls. One was to one of the best lawyers in town, a former prosecuting attorney who was so clean his shit didn't even stink. The other call was to a shyster who acted as an equivalent of a *capo bastone*, or underboss, to R.M.O. leader Vladimir Gorky. That call cost Marco—how much he didn't even want to know.

Both attorneys—upstanding and crooked—essentially said the same thing: Angel Baker was screwed.

Gossip in the substation's coffee bar confirmed as much. While the department sold whiskey-flavored coffee, Marco concluded that he needed a shot of the real thing. Not even the chameleon-flavored alcohol marketed as Vivante would do. So he tossed back a quadruple espresso and headed for the nearest exit, glancing at his watch. Six in the morning wasn't too early, or late, to drink he concluded. Not considering the circumstances. Then it would be time to call in some more chips.

Marco almost made it out the door. His mistake was taking a shortcut through the eastern corridor, which took him past the psy-ops interview suites.

"Hey, Marco, is that you?" came a bulldog voice. Captain

Mitchell Deloire stuck his head out of one of the suites. "Fancy meeting you here. I need you to come in and interview a suspect before you go."

"I'm leaving, Del," he said, waving off the older man.

With a round, seemingly neckless head planted on broad shoulders, Deloire looked like a bulldog. But instead of growling, he whined.

"Come on, Marco, give me a break. I got nobody here from psy-ops and this nut-ball they call the Cyclops says he's ready to talk. I just need somebody to do a quick psych profile. Then you can wash your hands. He thinks he's King Richard III. You can brush up on your Shakespeare."

Marco stopped and looked back with longing. He'd always had a weakness for delusional personality disorder. "I'd like to help you out, Del, I really would. But I hung up my shrink hat. Now I'm—"

"Yeah, yeah, a hotshot detective. Maybe he'll tell you something to help with the Cloisters case. That suspect you brought in with Townsend —Angel Baker—she's the one who brought down this wacko thespian. Maybe King Richard can tell you something about her that will nail your investigation."

News travels fast, was Marco's first thought. Of course, when the mayor's son is killed, the details would travel like wildfire throughout the department. His second thought was that Angel had never told him she'd tussled personally with the Cyclops. To know she had risked her life so thoroughly and hadn't even told him made the low-burning flame of frustration she fed in his gut flare up.

Angel was a damned stubborn woman. She'd never had any intention of giving up her work for him. That he'd allowed himself to think that she would made him feel like a sap. He didn't doubt that she wanted him. What he doubted was her ability to reveal her hand. He wasn't even sure if she could play straight.

From a psychological viewpoint, she was damnably intriguing and gutsy as hell. He was curious to hear what the Cyclops would have to say about his defeat at Angel's hands.

"Okay, Del," Marco said, massaging his frown away, "but this better be quick."

"I heard she was here tonight," Cy said as soon as he entered the darkened room.

Marco always turned down the lights when he interviewed a mole who had spent his life underground in Emerald City. It didn't matter that Cy was blind. He would sense the lack of heat from the ceiling and know it was dark and feel safer.

"Who was here?" Marco asked casually.

"Angel Baker." The stooped and disfigured young man said the name with such loathing that Marco's arm hair bristled to a stand.

"If she were here, would that be all right with you, Scott?" he said, glancing down to make sure he said Cyclops's birth name correctly.

"Call me Richard," Cy said. He took a limping step forward.

According to the files Marco had quickly perused, Cy's legs had been badly burned in the underground fire that had killed or disfigured most of his family about ten years ago. Cy was born and raised as a mole, one of the many descendants of Chicago's homeless who had moved into the labyrinthine subway system in 2020 when the CTA abandoned the train tracks in favor of aboveground superconductor lines. Undesirable though the real estate might be, it had been dubbed Emerald City and had largely been left alone by Chicago politicians and law enforcement agencies.

The moles, who congregated in loose clanlike affiliations, often pirated gas from underground pipelines to light their dreary subway tunnels and stations. Cy's clan had accidentally set off a gas explosion, and many of his family members were killed. Those who survived had been ravaged with burns and were treated like lepers by other clans.

Cy's twisted scars, which covered most of his body, had left him lame and sightless in one eye. His disabilities and the loss of his loved ones had sent him over the edge. Delusional and frustrated by his misfortune, Cy had built an underground prison and hired out his services as a jailer to the various mobs, apparently enjoying his ability to control the fates of others. He called his prison the Globe and was fond of quoting Shakespeare.

"I'll call you Richard if you'd like," Marco said in his neutral therapist's voice. "But according to your file, your name is Scott Owen. And I understand some call you Cyclops. The headlines refer to you as Cy. Who are you really?"

"'I am a villain. Yet I lie: I am not. Fool, of thyself speak well: fool, do not flatter. My conscience hath a thousand several tongues, and every tongue brings in a several tale, and every tale condemns me for a villain.'"

"You're quoting Shakespeare," Marco said.

"Am I? I merely speak the words that come to mind."

"Then what is on your mind? Captain Deloire tells me you wanted to talk to someone."

He lurched forward and felt for the chair on the opposite side of the table. He slunk down into it and stared at Marco as if he could see. "She blinded me, you know. I had one good eye, and she thrust a stick into it to free that worthless old vagabond mother of hers."

"I'm sorry for your loss."

Cy laughed low like a feral hyena. "Don't be. I'll make her pay. That's what I wanted to tell you. Let her know that I will find her if I have to walk through the city streets with a white cane. And when I do find her, I'll make her pay. Tell her, Detective, that I am a hell-hound that crept from the kennel of my mother's womb, and I will hunt Angel Baker down and kill her."

After spilling his guts over the wrongs done to him by Angel, the Cyclops docilely answered Marco's basic questions for an initial profile. As two guards took the prisoner away, Lieutenant Townsend entered the suite.

"Did you learn anything of use about Angel Baker?" Townsend said in his clipped British accent. "Deloire says the mole has information about her."

Marco closed the file and handed it to the Q.E.D. director. "It's all in here. The only thing I learned about Angel Baker is that she has one more enemy to worry about."

"If she attacked this so-called Cyclops," Townsend pressed, "perhaps we can add assault and battery to her case."

Marco skewered him with a look of disgust. "The Cyclops is accused of starving people to death in his prison, Townsend. Aren't you forgetting why he's here?"

"I hope you aren't forgetting why Angel Baker was here."

"Let's keep the two cases separate. Angel Baker confronted the Cyclops in order to free her mother from his underground prison. Is that a crime?"

"Perhaps we can make it one. Whose side are you on, Marco?"

"I'm on the side of justice, Townsend. Aren't you?"

There was a long pause. Townsend's gray eyes studied Marco with silent calculation, but no emotion.

And it was the lack of that simple but crucial spark of humanity that grated at Marco's gut.

Marco had been heartened when legislators first decided to fund Q.E.D. He'd long thought it was time for legitimate law officers to regain control of the city. In spite of his shadowed past, Marco inherently believed in the law and the need for civility in civilization. But at what price? Did investigators really have to dehumanize themselves in order to catch the bad guys? Weren't integrity and strength of character enough to face down evil?

"Your disdain for me, Detective, is obvious," Townsend said. "But can you at least appreciate my dedication to law and order? Do you know how much I have sacrificed in the name of justice?"

Your humanity, Marco thought. "Yeah, you went under the knife so you could think like a computer. But I hope you're going to keep me on the case. You just may need someone who has old-fashioned hunches to help you sort through all of your strategic and logical conclusions. I'm a psychologist. I'm into emotions."

Marco walked away, but stopped when Townsend called his name.

"How is it you were the first on the scene of the crime, Detective? I didn't get a chance to ask."

Marco shrugged. "Fate, I guess. Right time at the right place. I happened to be in the neighborhood." He grinned charmingly. "Don't you worry. We're going to nail her, Townsend. You and me. We'll get that wicked Angel Baker if it's the last thing we do."

Townsend turned briskly and walked away. He may have lost his emotions, but he still recognized sarcasm when he heard it.

There was always a point when Marco realized that summer was over. It would take him by surprise, then make him wistful and, finally, restless for change. Sometimes it was the sunlight, that went from brilliant in June to a mellow August gold. Sometimes it was a noticeable crispness in the air. This morning, as he zoomed in his PD aerocar over the bridge to Little Venice, it was the mist that hugged the shoreline, looming in gray and foreboding tufts. The hawk—Chicago's famously bitter and powerful wind—was getting ready to attack.

Marco made good time over the bridge and parked in the floating commuter lot that sat a quarter of a mile offshore. From there he'd have to take a turbo-gondola to his mother's apartment.

To keep her safe, Marco had moved Natasha Marco Black here to the old neighborhood nearly twenty years ago when he'd broken with the R.M.O. Though she'd raised Marco here until he was five, she'd moved back to her old Russian neighborhood after his father, Luigi Marco, had died. On the north side, she settled down with a nice postal worker named George Black, who passed away five years later. Natasha and George had one son, Danny, Marco's beloved kid brother.

As the gondola sliced through Lake Michigan's choppy, dark water, inching down the Grand Canal, Marco inhaled the cool lake air. He admired the small palazzi as he passed, and the crooked line of multicolored town houses that towered over either side of the waterway.

Little Venice had been built about seventy-five years ago when Chicago became totally landlocked. When the Italian Mafia had been put out of business by a string of federal lawsuits and competition from other ethnic syndicates, the former Mob bosses turned to legitimate real estate.

The idea was to build a replica of Venice in the American Midwest. But when the original Venice in Italy sank into the sea beyond repair, many of the sixteenth-century buildings, piazzas and basilicas had been shipped to Chicago. What resulted was a charming, historically significant piece of lake property that was partly residential and partly a tourist attraction. The tourist angle insured that it was safe.

Marco visited his mother whenever he could, which was not as often as he should, and he steeled himself against her usual admonishments.

"Marco, Marco, why didn't you come see me sooner?" she cooed when he entered her small, second-story apartment.

It was filled with a garish mix of iconography from old Russia, Italy and Vatican City. She'd downloaded photos of the newly consecrated Pope John Paul VI, otherwise known as El Papa Mabuto Ganni, the first Swahili to hold the post. She'd positioned the photo next to a portrait of Rasputin, who'd finally achieved sainthood a decade ago.

"Marco," Natasha said, stroking his cheeks with smooth, warm palms. "You don't look good, my darling boy. What is the matter? You can tell your mama."

He gently gripped her frail shoulders and kissed her forehead. She possessed the best—and most trying—qualities of motherhood shared by her inherited Russian culture and her adopted Italian. She was overprotective, doting and superstitious. Her long dark, silver-streaked hair fell out of a bun, occasionally tumbling in front of dark, lined eyes that ominously studied his face as if his worry lines could portend the future.

"What has happened, Marco?"

He smiled. "Nothing that I need worry you about. I had some time to kill. It's too early to make business calls. Do you have a shot of whiskey?"

Her quarter-moon mouth widened in triumph. "Is the pope Swahili?"

He took two shots of whiskey in the kitchen. The American-made liquor was her second husband's only cultural holdover.

Marco managed to keep the conversation on a light note while he and his mother ate breakfast. When it was time to say farewell, Natasha grabbed his arm just before he could get out the door.

"Did you get him yet, Marco? Is that why you look so worried today?"

Marco set his mouth in a grim, tired line. "No."

"Tell me you did, son." Then she added in a whisper, her nails digging into his arm, "Tell me you've killed Vladimir Gorky. That bastard killed my Danny."

"Yes, Ma," he said patiently, "I know. I was the one who told you about Gorky setting Danny up on that drug raid."

"Then get him! What are you waiting for?" When she started to cry, as she inevitably did at every goodbye, he crushed her petite body in a warm, silencing embrace.

"Don't worry, Ma." He kissed the top of her head. "Justice is always done in the end."

When he stepped out onto the street below, he exhaled loudly, then took in a musing breath when he spotted a familiar figure strolling his way.

"Glad that's over with, eh, Ricco?" called Sasha, his 25-year-old cousin, who stopped when he was close enough to clap Marco warmly on the back. His gruff smile notwithstanding, Sasha looked like an R.M.O. operative, with bluntly cut black hair, pale skin and dark circles under his eyes. His knee-length black shirt hanging over black jeans added to his mobster mystique.

"Sash, what are you doing here?"

"Looking for you. Did the old lady beg you to kill Gorky again?"

Marco nodded and heaved a sigh as he shoved his hands in his pockets. "Yeah."

Sasha shook his head. "You have my sympathies. Aunt Natasha is one determined lady. Too bad she had to find out what really happened to Danny."

"Yeah." Marco nodded toward the canal. He had only recently found out himself for sure—Danny had been gunned down in an R.M.O.-related drug deal because he wouldn't let Gorky buy him off. Danny had tried to make an arrest, but his crooked partner had provided no backup. Danny had been honest. Innocent. Now he was dead. "I'm going back."

Sasha's impassive face relinquished a concerned frown. "Uh, not yet, Ricco. I need to tell you something." He glanced cautiously over both his bony shoulders, then leaned in close. "I followed you out here from the city so I could deliver a message. You have an appointment tonight at Falling Water on the Lake."

Marco's blood turned cold. "You mean—"

"Yeah," Sasha said, this time with sympathy. "Gorky wants to see you. He expects you to be there. And you'd better be."

Chapter 6

Rear Window

At noon, I woke to the sound of Lin shrieking. I flew upright, disoriented, forgetting I'd fallen asleep on Mike's futon in the back of the garden.

"Angel!" came another muted cry from the house.

"Lin? Hold on!"

A second later, Mike ran from the house to the open doors of his shed, every muscle on his fit body strained with danger. "Baker! Come quick. They try to take Lin away."

"Who?" I shot to my feet.

"Government people. Hurry!"

Instantly, I surmised what had happened. Someone working at the Department of Children and Family Services had seen my mug shot on television and decided it was time to withdraw my foster-parenting rights.

I raced after Mike, instinctively negotiating the flower-lined footpath while staring up at the second floor porch, where Lin struggled with a DCFS transporter in an orange jumpsuit. I'd expected this to happen, but not so soon.

Lin escaped his grasp and tried to race down the wooden stairs. She spotted me and cried out, "Angel! Help me!" Distracted, she tripped and tumbled head over heels the rest of the way down the stairs.

"Lin!" I cried out, my heart in my throat.

Mike and I both dashed the distance. Out of the corner of my eye, I saw Lola beating the transporter on the head with a broom on the porch above. Bald and musclebound, he looked like a bar bouncer, but cowered under Lola's blows.

"You keep your hands off her, you scum bucket!" Lola roared like a lioness in winter. "Lin stays here, and that's final!"

Mike reached Lin at the bottom of the stairs first and gently rolled her over, checking for broken bones. She saw me and flung her arms upward, as agile as ever. "Don't let them take me, Angel."

I pulled her in my arms and stroked her head. Heavy footsteps stomped on the stairs. The transporter bounded toward us, either chasing Lin or running from Lola, I wasn't sure which. I scooped up Lin and ran out the back to Mike's shed, where I gently lowered her on the futon.

"Stay here, Lin. I'll be back."

She looked up with terror shimmering in her coal black eyes, but she nodded, and I knew she trusted me completely. I smiled encouragingly and ran back toward the porch, but slowed when I saw an ominous tableau. Mike and Lola stood over the prone, still figure of the transporter sprawled at the bottom of the stairs. My heart stopped a moment.

"Oh, my God, he's not dead, is he?"

Lola cackled and put her hands on her plump hips. "Don't you wish?"

I stopped next to Mike and looked down at the unconscious figure with dread. "What did you do to him?"

Mike rubbed the knuckles on his right hand, then blew on them as if they were lucky dice. "You do not want to know."

"Whatever it was, I should thank you. I think."

"Freeze!" The shouted command came from the upstairs porch. In unison, we looked up to find a Chicago police officer with a fazer aimed our way. "Don't move or I'll shoot."

He carefully walked down the steps, staring at us over his extended arms, two hands clamped on the small but potentially deadly weapon. A second social services transporter followed, dressed in orange like his partner on the ground. When he spotted his colleague, he hurried down the stairs past the cop and knelt by his friend.

"Joe, you okay?"

The bald transporter blinked open his eyes, then pointed toward the shed. "The kid's back there."

The second transporter hurried after Lin. I tried to follow, but the officer shouted at me to stop. When the transporter came out with Lin kicking and screaming in his arms like a whirling dervish, I shouted to the police officer, "He has no right to take her, Officer. She's my foster child. This is kidnapping!"

"He has a warrant to remove her from the premises," the cop shouted in reply. "No temporary foster child can stay in the home of a suspected murderer."

The transporter had almost reached the garden studio door. From there it would be an easy exit through the lower level and out to the street. Then Lin would be gone, perhaps forever.

She seemed to realize the same thing. She reached out with her wraithlike arms over the man's shoulders and wailed, "Angel! Don't let them take me!"

Acting with a mother's instinct that I'd hoped I had but had never truly felt before, I ran after her, not knowing or caring whether 150-thousand volts of electricity from the cop's fazer were about to painfully zigzag through my body.

"Stop!" he shouted. "Last warning!"

I ignored him, and only faintly heard the sound of fighting behind me as I barreled in on the beast who was stealing my girl.

"Let go of her, you creep!"

Startled, the transporter loosened his grip on Lin, and she crawled into my arms like a monkey. I quickly lowered her and gave the transporter a knock-out punch. I wanted to make sure he wouldn't grab Lin again.

When he keeled over, I turned and found her staring at me wide-eyed. I thought she was afraid of me, but her face shuddered with gratitude. She rushed into my arms and I held her tight, feeling as if I had just taken my first breath of air after nearly drowning.

"I'm so sorry, kiddo." I looked up and found Lola aiming the fazer at the cop, whose hands were raised in submission. Mike was finishing off a tight knot on a rope binding the bald transporter's hands behind his back.

"Officer, I'm sorry about this," I said, "but we can't let you take Lin until I speak to her caseworker, Harriet Gross."

Not waiting for an answer, I engaged my lapel phone. Lin wouldn't release her death grip on my waist, so we awkwardly wandered like conjoined twins back toward the fishpond while I had an intense conversation with Harriet. I explained, cajoled, begged, pleaded, and finally threatened, but to no avail. By the time we concluded our conversation, I had to find a way to tell Lin that she did, indeed, have to go.

"Officer, Harriet Gross wants to speak to you," I said numbly. "Can you call her at DCFS headquarters?"

Lola reluctantly lowered the fazer, looking at me as if I'd just stabbed Lin in the back, which I suppose I had. Frowning, Mike began to untie the one transporter, then went to revive the other.

I sat down on the stone bench in front of the pond, pulling Lin into my lap. She clutched at my back, and together we took in hitching breaths, letting out sounds of grief we couldn't stifle. We hadn't known each other long—only a month. But we knew each other well enough to know we were two lost souls who needed each other.

Sometimes at night I would lay down beside her and listen to her short breaths. I'd hear my own heart beat and savor her warmth. If she woke, she'd nestle into my arms with more abandon than she could when she was awake. It was hard to tell which one of us hugged harder. Slowly, silently, she was becoming a part of me. How could I let her go?

I pulled away far enough to press my cheek to hers. Our tears mingled between our flushed cheeks. She smelled like a little girl, and I inhaled that innocence, imbedding it in my memory. I stroked her hair, my desire to protect her burning my insides raw.

"Sweetheart, I'm sorry," I whispered in her ear. She scrabbled closer, pressing her head to my chest. I kissed the silky black hair on top of her head. "Harriet Gross says you have to leave…but only until I can clear my name."

"No!" she squealed, wriggling closer to my heart.

"If I don't let you go now, I'll lose you forever. If I don't cooperate, they'll judge me as an unfit parent. I have to let you go now so I can keep you in the long run. I want you to be my forever daughter, Lin, but first, I have to prove my innocence for a crime I didn't commit. Do you understand? Please, tell me you understand."

Desperate, I took her face in my hands and forced her to

look at me. The light in her shining dark eyes had died. She had shut down on me.

"Please," I whispered, tears pouring down my cheeks. "Please tell me you understand. That you'll wait for me to come get you again. I will. I swear to you." She watched me without judgment or sorrow. "Lin? Do you understand?"

Suddenly, tears welled in her eyes again and coursed down her high, flat cheeks. Her frozen look thawing, her eyes, lit by the faintest of sparks, met mine. She was hurt, angry, but still trusting, just barely. She nodded. That was enough. God, that was a miracle. I let go a shuddering breath and pulled her into my arms, rocking her back and forth.

"Oh, my sweet girl. My sweet, sweet girl. Thank you. I won't let you down. I swear."

Harriet cursed a blue streak on the phone when she found out that the transporters had acted like men in black, bursting in without showing the warrant for Lin. The breach in protocol, topped off by Harriet's esoteric bitch-slapping of the patrolman who'd allowed it, kept me from having my bond revoked. The cop wanted to keep the whole incident as quiet as I did.

Unfortunately, he wouldn't leave without a few ounces of flesh, or rather many pounds of it. He insisted on taking Lola down to headquarters for questioning when he found out she had a rap sheet as long as the Great Wall in China. After all, she was the one who had held him at gunpoint, a no-no under any circumstances.

"Ta-da, dahling," Lola sang as the cop escorted her out the front door, looking like Methuselah the Circus Clown but acting like Queen Elizabeth III, flipping a little clam-wave with one hand over her shoulder. Her flaming red nails and glittering costume jewelry winked in the sunlight as Officer Unfriendly escorted her to his squad aerocar, to the delight of the news crews still staked out in front of my apartment. As they piled into the car, she triumphantly declared, "I shall return!"

I had no doubt of that. Lola knew the criminal justice system like the back of her hand. My birth mother's histrionics had humiliated me as a child. Now she made me proud. I didn't even care that this scene would be repeated ad nauseam on the local newscasts.

Mike and I were just happy that she could escort Lin to police headquarters, where Harriet would be waiting for her. I wouldn't even allow myself to think about what sort of temporary foster home Lin would land in. Harriet promised me it would be a good one. Lin was, after all, a high-profile case since she had been part of the group of Chinese girls I'd rescued from the Mongolian Mob. The media would be following her fate, and that was some reassurance.

In any event, I could waste no more time on tears. I had to prove my innocence. I headed for the front door before the gaggle of reporters shooting footage of Lola's grand exit from the receding cop car back to me. Three enterprising journalists had staked out positions by the door while Mike and I waved goodbye at the curb. One of them was Rodney Delaney.

"Oh, great." I tugged hard on Mike's sleeve. "Let's disappear while we still have half a chance." We made a beeline toward the front stoop. I pushed past Delaney, who had a frenzied, piranha look in his bloodshot eyes. It had been a while since he'd had a scoop. If he didn't produce soon, his reporting contract might not be renewed.

"So, Baker, they got your old lady. The apple doesn't fall far from the tree, does it?"

Something made me glance down. "You've got mustard on your tie, Delaney. You better cut back on the nitro dogs.

They're turning your brain to mush." When he looked down, I turned and nearly crashed into two slender young men dressed in white who had just come down the stairs. I couldn't tell what company they worked for and didn't care.

"Your delivery is complete, ma'am," one of the guys said, holding out an electronic clipboard. "Put your print here."

"I don't understand. How did you get inside?"

"The door was open," he replied. "We thought you left it open for us."

"I don't even know what you—" I stopped abruptly when Delaney pushed his way back into my personal space.

"Here," I said to the delivery guy and I pressed his touch pad with my thumb, then yanked Mike into the foyer and slammed the door shut.

"Whew!" I said. "I can't believe we left the door open. Let's find out what I just signed for."

I bounded up the stairs two at a time and viewed my quiet, empty flat with confusion. "What on earth did those guys deliver?"

"Baker," Mike said a strange voice.

"Yes?"

"I think I know."

I turned around and followed Mike's wary gaze to the corner shadows. How on earth I had walked past this was beyond me.

"Good Lord," I said, dragging the words out in wonderment.

There sat a middle-aged man who had neatly cropped, slicked back auburn hair with a dusting of gray at his temples, a long, amiable face and handsome, hooded eyes. Lean and graceful, he would look good in a suit, but presently sat in tailored pajamas, with a hip-to-toe white plaster cast encasing what was presumably a broken left leg. It was propped up with a foot pedestal, part of his old-fashioned wheelchair, the hand-operated kind used a hundred years ago.

"Who in the hell are you?" I finally managed to spit out.

He gave me a folksy, confident smile, mostly with his eyes, which contained just a flicker of seduction, and handed me a business card. "L. B. Jefferies, here on assignment."

The name rang an ominous bell. I studied the business card. It read:

L. B. Jefferies
Played by James Stewart in
Rear Window
Compliments of AutoMates, Incorporated

"Lights! Grid 4!" I shouted, and the southeast quadrant of soft-fill ceiling lights surged to life. I stepped closer for a better look. "I'll be damned. It is Jimmy Stewart."

"Who?" Mike said. He wasn't a film aficionado. He wouldn't have recognized an actor if he'd won last year's Academy Award, much less a star from the twentieth century.

There hadn't been a U.S. President in the last seventy-five years who wasn't a former movie star. The last politician to take the nation's top spot who didn't hail from Hollywood was President John Turner, a computer geek turned billionaire turned senator. In 2029, he was booted out of office by Cool Funk Indigo, a reality-TV child star turned rapper turned senator. Of course, by then Cool Funk preferred to use the name on his birth certificate and took his place in history as President Bufford Johnson. But the power of the entertainment industry was lost on someone as inwardly directed as Mike.

"This is a compubot," I rasped, unable to hide my impatience. "And one designed to look exactly like the old movie star, Jimmy Stewart. He played the role of 'Jeff' in an Alfred Hitchcock thriller about a magazine photographer who breaks a leg. He's stuck in his apartment and spends so much time snooping on his neighbors through his high-powered camera lens that he discovers one of his neighbors has murdered his wife."

Mike digested this, then exhaled a rare, judgmental sigh. "Angel, did you order him?"

"No!" I snapped, then caught myself. It was a question Mike had every right to ask. I had employed a Humphrey Bogart compubot for years as a lover, I'm embarrassed to admit. I was lucky enough to get a Compubot Classic because I'd done a retribution job for an AutoMates executive. He knew about my obsession with classic movies and was grateful enough to supply me with a top-of-the-line companion gratis. Last month, after falling for Marco, I'd deprogrammed my relationship with Bogie. I guess some wise guy in the supply department of the robotics firm thought I might be getting desperate about now. "Okay, that's it! Jimmy, I'm sorry, but you're outta here. Speaker phone, dial AutoMates, Incorporated."

Sometimes I preferred the house omnisystem over my lapel phone. Especially when I was in the mood to raise my voice. But instead of blasting a customer service representative, I found myself pacing the room, arms crossed, as I battled my way through the company phone directory.

"We're sorry, but all our representatives are busy," a sickeningly sweet female voice intoned. The women in these inclusive corporation answering systems always sounded like reformed vampires who sucked on sugar instead of blood, and the men sounded like defrocked television preachers.

Unfortunately, these days the "If you speak English…" option with international companies was usually nine or ten. If you got impatient and called out "zero" for the operator, which didn't exist, you'd be punished by going back to the beginning of the greeting and then find out the option menu had grown to twenty.

Actually, it was possible to reach a live human being at AutoMates. I'd accidentally done it before. I think it happened when I won a Hollywood trivia contest while I was on hold.

"If you speak Spanish," the orgasmically contented voice intoned, "press 1."

I began to pace. From the corner my eye, I caught Jimmy trying to wheel himself closer to the window.

"Don't even think about it!" I admonished him. "Some reporter will get you on camera and the next thing I know the newscasts will be announcing that I'm sex-starved and emotionally incapable of a real relationship."

I paused a moment when I realized that wasn't far from the truth.

"If you speak Cantonese, press 3," the sugary voice dripped from the omnipresent speaker phone. "If you speak Mandarin, press 4."

"Come on, come on," I muttered. I thought English was 8, but if I was wrong, I'd have to go back to the beginning of the menu.

"If you speak German—"

"Eight!" I shouted, unable to wait any longer.

"Yo!" a hip voice replied, "Watchu want?"

I pounded my forehead with a palm. I'd chosen American slang. Close enough. "Give me customer service," I said, swallowing my frustration.

I spent the next ten minutes being bounced from option to option, then realized the double-murder case I'd been embroiled in would turn cold before I got through to the right person.

"Hang up," I commanded the phone system and sank into the couch. "Jimmy, it looks like you're stuck here for a while. And if you're going to stay, you're going to have to make yourself useful. What can you do?"

"Well, I excel at two things. One is spying. The other is—"

"I don't think I need to hear about the second thing," I interjected. "I don't exactly look like Grace Kelly, do I?"

"Well, sweetie," he said, eyeing me speculatively, "you look pretty darned good to me."

"Save it for Gigi over there." I tipped my chin in the direction of my Personal Listening Device, a head-and-shoulders model stashed in the corner.

PLDs looked like manikins, but had pliable synthetic skin and contained interpersonal reactive programming that made them good listeners. They weren't nearly as sophisticated as AutoMates, but they were an affordable alternative for lonely people on a budget.

Increasingly, PLDs were taking the place of compubot dating services and psychotherapists. People loved having a pseudo human who would listen to them kvetch without interrupting, except for the occasional preprogrammed, "Oh, my!" and "I'm sorry to hear that."

I thought PLDs were a pathetic new addition to our increasingly isolated electronic society. But I'd received this one as a freebie at a CRS convention. With blond hair and pink lipstick, it looked vaguely like my wicked foster sister, Gigi, so I'd kept it to amuse myself. I'd turned it on maybe once.

A PLD was one thing. A resident compubot was another. I glanced at Jimmy, wondering how I could take advantage of his unexpected arrival. I noticed two connected cylinders in his lap. "What's that?"

"Binoculars." He raised them and put them to his eyes by way of show-and-tell.

"Did you get them from a museum? Or are they just pretend?"

"They work," Jimmy replied defensively.

"Then get over to the window and keep an eye out for trouble. But be discreet."

I could just imagine the headlines if a reporter caught sight of an AutoMate at my window: Sex-Starved Murder Suspect Hires Disabled Gigolo.

Jimmy wheeled himself to the edge of the couch and raised his binoculars, scanning the crowd still mingling on the street below. "So exactly what kind of trouble should I be looking for?"

I sauntered to his side and surveyed the scene from over his shoulder. At the same time Marco pulled up to the curb in his aerocruiser. He stepped out of the car and fended off a swarm of reporters as he headed toward my door.

I pointed at Marco and said, "That kind of trouble."

The doorbell rang. Jimmy lowered his binoculars and looked at me with such sober concern I began to think of him as an ally.

"Don't answer it," he warned me.

The bell rang again. "I have to. Detective Marco and I have some unfinished business."

Chapter 7

Lovers and Other Strangers

I ordered the omnisystem to open the foyer door for Marco, then waited for him to climb the stairs. Trying to be cool, I sat in a round easy chair by the fireplace, crossing my legs and assuming a look of ennui. I was so concerned about the impression I'd make on Marco that I didn't notice what Jimmy was doing.

"Angel?" Marco said as his steps sounded outside the upper landing door.

"Come in," I called out.

He took one step inside, but that's as far as he got. Jimmy wheeled his ancient chair forward, held up an old-fashioned square camera with a silver dish light and set it off as close to Marco's face as he could. *Poof!* The lightbulb popped and flashed. Marco shielded his eyes with his arm in confusion.

"Jimmy, stop," I said.

"Go on, Angel," he replied. "Run out the back! I'll hold him off."

I realized he was acting out the scene in *Rear Window* when he fends off the murderous Aaron Burr with the only weapon he had—blinding light in a darkened room. But this was ridiculous.

"That's enough, Jimmy!"

Ignoring me, he backed up his wheelchair and frantically put another bulb in his silver light dish. When Marco tried to walk past him, he set off the flash again.

Marco shielded his eyes, then grabbed the camera, yanking it out of Jimmy's hands with little effort. "Give me that," he muttered.

"Hey, wait a minute!" Jimmy drawled indignantly.

Marco marched to the window, clearly intending to lob the camera to the sidewalk below. But one glimpse at the reporters made him think better of his plan, so he slam-dunked the camera in the waste can by the front door.

"What do you think you're doing?" Jimmy shouted, pounding a fist on his wheelchair's armrest.

"It's already done." Marco thrust both hands into his front jeans pockets and tilted his head as he studied my gallant visitor. "Who the hell....Jimmy Stewart?"

"From *Rear Window*," I said.

Marco turned a scathing look my way. "When you couldn't get me in bed, you turned to—"

"Don't go there," I growled.

"Why not?" he said with a sneer, making his way across the room.

Jimmy wheeled into his path. "You heard the lady," he said, jamming his extended leg support into Marco's shin. "Now why don't you get out of here?"

"It's okay, Jimmy," I said. "Go back to the window."

He shook his head. "Naw, naw, now, look here, Angel, I have a bad feeling about this one. I have instincts about these things."

"You're a damned compubot," Marco said dismissively. "You can't have instincts."

"At least he has manners," I said.

Marco pursed his lips and raised a brow in acknowledgment of the zing. We'd had this argument before. Marco came to my chair, towering in all his splendid and quiet masculinity.

"Let's go out to the porch." He held out a hand for me to take, which I did.

When I uncurled the leg I'd been sitting on and rose, he pulled too fast. I lost my balance. He caught me with a strong arm, then steadied me with a firm grip to my shoulders.

My skin sizzled under his touch, and when he pulled me closer—I swear he did—my breasts and hips seemed to fuse to his lean chest and hard legs. He gazed down at me with a smoldering look that promised a kiss, and I tilted my chin up.

He squeezed my shoulders so hard I nearly winced. "Angel, I—"

"Hey, hey, hey!" Jimmy said, wheeling his way toward us. "Just what do you think you're doing?"

"Isn't it obvious?" Marco muttered sensually, as if I had asked the question.

"Yes, painfully," Jimmy shot back in blustering irritation.

"Yes, pleasantly," I murmured. I would have given a mortgage payment to taste Marco's lips and feel his tongue on mine again. But Jimmy was doing a remarkably good job of staring us down. I notched my head toward the back porch. "Let's go."

* * *

"I don't know how you do it, Marco," I said, leaning against the porch rail in the shade of the elm tree that towered over my house and garden.

"How I do what?" He leaned against the rail a foot away from me.

I crossed my arms in a desperate bid to keep my feelings out of this. "I was ready to hang you from the nearest tree, and you almost got a kiss out of me."

He leaned a forearm on the railing, moving closer. I stiffened against the buzzing excitement his closeness always created. "Let's just face it, Angel. You and I are hot for each other, no matter what the circumstances."

I gave him a cold smile. "That didn't seem to matter when I visited your flat and asked you to make love to me."

"It didn't seem to matter when you decided to go to the Cloisters just hours before our deal was done."

"A colleague was in distress. I couldn't refuse his call for help. You would have done the same thing if you were in my position." I moved to a lawn chair and propped my heels on the railing. Slouching, I massaged my temples. "At least I think you would. Maybe I'm giving you too much credit."

He straightened and regarded me with all the confidence and certainty of an enlightened soul—or an accomplished sinner. A chill wriggled up my spine and down my arms when it struck me that I didn't really understand Marco at all. And the more I knew about him, the less I understood. Hell, even ruthless assassins could be loving when you got them in bed. Whose side was he on?

When I'd thought Marco was merely a surprisingly intelligent Chicago tough who'd grown up to make something honest of himself, I'd felt safe. But he'd been in the R.M.O., and he'd been scary-hurt, and he wouldn't make love to me, and he'd betrayed me. The checks in the "con" column of the "Pros & Cons" list were mounting.

"Why didn't you tell Lieutenant Townsend that we were lovers?"

He heaved a sigh and crossed his arms. "Because it probably wouldn't have helped, and it most certainly would have hurt."

"How?"

"If he'd known you and I were involved, he would have taken me off the case. As it is, I have access to all the details."

"Which you cannot ethically or legally share with me or my counsel."

"Ah!" He mugged a wry grin. "So you've actually deigned to hire a lawyer."

I frowned and blushed. "Yes."

"I don't plan to help your defense case, Angel. I plan to find the son of a bitch who framed you."

"My gun…" I ran out of air. I couldn't look him in the eye. I didn't want to falsely accuse him, but neither did I want to be right. "Marco, you had it at the crime scene…."

"I found it when we investigated the scene." He paused. "What? You didn't expect me to pretend it wasn't there."

"How did it get there, Marco? Did you plant it just to get me out of your hair?"

"What? Are you nuts?"

"Sorry," I said, realizing I'd gone too far, "so who else would have taken it?"

"That's what I'd like to know."

"And the phone records—"

"Would imply that someone with powerful connections is involved. Someone who can have the phone system altered."

"So at least we agree I've been framed. I suspect Corleone Capone. Or Vladimir Gorky."

"Why would Gorky want to get you in trouble? You helped him find his Maltese falcon."

"At least, that's what we think."

Gorky had agreed to free the kidnapped orphans if I could use my psychic abilities to find clues to help him locate a missing treasure. It was a replica of the black falcon statue featured in the 1940s film noir *The Maltese Falcon,* starring Humphrey Bogart. Ironically, Gorky was a Bogie fan, as well. He'd stashed some sort of priceless object inside the falcon replica for safety, but it had been stolen.

In a vision, I located the falcon at a farmhouse in Chechnya. Pleased with this information, Gorky had released the girls into my care. But he'd warned me that if my vision proved false, he'd make me pay.

"Gorky might be trying to punish me if he couldn't find the falcon using my psychic clues. But why kill the mayor's son just to punish me?"

Marco shrugged. "He wouldn't hesitate to piss off the president of the United States if it suited him."

"I still think Capone is our man. He's much more of a fringe player with less to lose. The only thing is he's more known for slitting throats in darkened alleys than elaborate political schemes."

"I think you've just been inducted into a complicated chess game. It's too early to see who the pawns are protecting. Personally, I want to know why the mayor exposed your contract to avenge his niece's rape."

"That makes two of us. Marco, did you tell Townsend about it before the mayor admitted it on TV?"

He shook his head and knelt in front of me. He took both my hands and caressed my knuckles with his thumbs. "Angel, I have many faults, but breaking confidences isn't one of them. You have to trust me."

How could I trust a man who was this handsome and willing to kneel at my feet? I slowly pulled my fingers from the warmth of his and folded them in a fist. "I don't have to do anything. That's the sad thing about it, Marco."

Marco thought about his conversation with Angel when he pulled into Vladimir Gorky's compound on Lake Michigan later that night. As the pink and blue laser gates dissolved so he could drive his new-used land cruiser into the expansive compound, he thought again about chess. Angel's game with the Chicago syndicates had just begun. Marco's had been in play for some time. He wasn't a pawn. More like a rook. Still, he was a long way from checkmate.

He pulled his silver cruiser into the circular drive and left it running for the young Slavic-looking guard who came unsmilingly to park it. He'd get a warmer welcome, he knew from past experience, when Alexia greeted him at the door.

"Ricco," she said, her cool disposition thawing at the sight of him. "How is your mother?"

"She's fine," he said, kissing her cheek. "And you?"

She folded her hands and tilted her head, her eyes wistful with memories of better days they both had known. "I'm okay, Ricco. Better at the sight of you. How long has it been?"

"Two years."

"Well, it must be important if Mr. Gorky wants to see you after so much time. He's in the Romanoff dining room. You remember the way?" she asked with an ironic smile.

"Of course." Marco gave her a wink and headed toward the long corridor that wended in a northwest direction.

He knew every nook and bend in the mansion. The front of the house looked like a columned Southern plantation, but the interior was a faceted hive of eclectic architectural styles and decor.

Though it had been twenty years since he'd been unconditionally welcomed here, he remembered enough to get around and how to make a fast escape if necessary. In the old days a fast escape would mean a raid by Homeland Security. These days, now that Gorky had more control over the Feds, Marco was more worried about Gorky himself. Their truce was uneasy to say the least. And Gorky was a dangerous, unpredictable man.

Marco needed no reminder of that, but he received one nonetheless when he entered the oblong, high-ceilinged dining hall where Gorky was eating his usual late dinner. He sat at the far end of a gilt table big enough for a state dinner, absorbed in conversation with someone hidden behind a huge vase of flowers.

Unnoticed, Marco paused in the doorway and surveyed the place, looking for his favorite pieces among Gorky's vast and priceless collection of early twentieth-century artifacts mounted on gold flocked wallpaper. Marco's gaze caught and lingered on the pale pink enamel and pearls of the Lilies of the Field egg. Inside, Marco knew, was a picture of Czar Nicholas II and his two oldest daughters, Olga and Tatiana.

He then glanced at the Czarevich Egg. Done in a Louis XV style, it was a deep lapis lazuli blue, decorated with chased gold. Fabergé created 140 different translucent enamel colors to adorn the imperial bibelots, which included fifty-six of these priceless eggs, most of which Gorky had acquired for his personal collection.

He also had gathered some bizarre artifacts from the Romanov Dynasty. For example, the famous Anastasia fingerbone mounted on the wall on a flat piece of slate like a rare dinosaur relic. This was the evidence that finally provided DNA proof that Czar Nicholas's daughter had indeed been murdered along with her family by the Bolsheviks in the early 1900s. Marco happened to know that Gorky also kept the head of a Czar Nicholas clone in a jar of formaldehyde, though he was gracious enough to keep it out of the dining room.

"Here he is now. Marik!" Gorky said, waving him closer. "*Zdravstvujte!* Come eat!"

Gorky didn't like Marco's Italian heritage and had insisted on using a Slavic version of the name Mark. It used to bother Marco, but he'd learned to choose his battles. It was the only way to win the war.

"*Dobryj vecher,*" he greeted Gorky. "*Kak vy pozhivaete?*"

"Eh." Gorky shrugged noncommittally, and they chatted in Russian about the weather as Marco strolled along the dozen red velvet dining chairs lining one side of the table.

But Marco stopped when his line of vision cleared the hotel-foyer sized flower arrangement and he recognized Gorky's dinner companion and heir apparent sitting on the left side of the table's end.

"Yevgeny!" Marco blurted out.

"*Privet,* Marik," the arrogant young Turk replied.

He wore a sleek Nehru-style jacket of millifine steel that shimmered in the chandelier light. He'd slicked his jet-black hair from his high forehead straight back to his nape, showing off smooth, handsome features. Marco could see Gorky in his grandson, and the resemblance added to Marco's disapproval.

"I didn't expect you here, Yevgeny."

"I was just leaving." The young man stood and dabbed a smug smile from his mouth with a silk napkin, then tossed it beside his plate. "Grandfather was just showing me some pictures from the old days. I have to say, Marik, I'm impressed. I didn't think you had it in you."

Suspicious, Marco glanced at Gorky, who raised his bushy gray brows almost apologetically, saying, "So I showed him a few photos. I was feeling sentimental."

"Enjoy your meal, gentlemen," Yevgeny said brightly. "I have business to attend."

Marco watched with a bizarre mixture of admiration and sadness as the boy-turned-man strutted out of the room. Then he turned on Gorky, gripping the edge of the black-and-red-lacquer table. "What did you show him?"

The aging mobster shoved a large piece of steak tartare in his mouth with an overturned fork, and chewed forcefully as he considered Marco's question. With a thick head of straight silver hair, a silver mustache, quick eyes of blue steel and a firm, narrow waist, he looked like a sleek machine of vengeance. Yet with broad shoulders, a booming, warm laugh and hands as big as paws, he also had an earthy "old world" air that distracted most people from his lethal reality.

"Sit down, Marik, and have some steak tartare."

Marco knew he'd have to eat something to appease him, so he sat to Gorky's left in the seat opposite of where Yevgeny had been. Silently, servants appeared from nowhere to remove the dirty dishes and gave Marco a plate of raw ground steak and au gratin potatoes. Salad consisted of a sprig of parsley.

Marco pronged a mouthful of the meat with silverware that he happened to know had been a gift to Czar Nicholas and Alexandra from his aunt, Her Imperial Highness the Grand Duchess Marie Alexandrovna, Duchess of Saxe-Coburg-Gotha. Marco took a small bite and turned a scowl to Gorky.

"All right, all right! You want to know what I showed Yevgeny," the older man said with resignation. He reached into his suit jacket pocket and pulled out a small master projector and set it on the table. A thirteen-inch screen rose from the table a few feet away, and when Gorky touched a projector button, an image of three dead naked men dangling from a tree appeared.

"What?" he said with minor irritation. "That's not it. That

was from Chechnya. My brothers. I finally had to do the bastards in when they fought me on the uranium deal. That's what I get for not updating this equipment."

Marco tried to swallow the bite of bloodred meat, but looking at the bulging eyes and tongues of Gorky's brothers dried his throat. He reached for ice water and guzzled.

Gorky punched up another file and a photo of one of his *sgarristas* appeared, a thin man, deathly pale, smiling bravely in a hospital gown.

"Who's that?"

Gorky exhaled irritably. "Not who I wanted to show you. How do you work these damn things? That was one of my men. He accidentally stepped in front of a new weapon we've recently developed and got himself shot full of an unhealthy dose of radiation. He died nine months later from leukemia."

It grated on Marco's firm but tattered belief in law and order to know that Gorky considered him so ethically compromised that Gorky could admit any heinous crime or illegal arms trade without fear that Marco would arrest him. But that was all part of Marco's strategy in their ongoing chess game. Besides, even the police chief had been unable to make charges stick to the slippery R.M.O. leader. Though corrupt— even evil—Gorky was practically a Chicago institution.

Marco nodded. He and Angel had almost been the victims of such a weapon. "What do you call those weapons? Radio-arts. Radiation artillery."

"That's right. Ah, here we are." He rasped out a rusty chuckle when a vision of red and blue appeared on the screen.

At first it appeared to be some sort of modern art, an eddy of blueberry and cherry swirls. Though Gorky had one of the greatest art collections in the world, he wouldn't bother to show it off now.

Marco looked closer, and his chest tightened with recognition. He felt like barfing up the food he'd finally managed to swallow.

"You remember Rayenko," Gorky said lightly.

Rayenko had been Gorky's right-hand man twenty years ago. Part consigliere and part monster, Rayenko was being groomed to take over the reins of the R.M.O. when he was brutally murdered.

"This is the last known picture of my former *vice president*," Gorky said, smiling at the euphemism. "This isn't very flattering. He was wearing a blue wind jacket. After more than fifty stabs to the chest, his heart looked like your steak tartare, and his genitals… Well, they went AWOL. The pool of blood between his legs is all that's left there. But the hands and feet and head are still attached. The police were curious about that. Not the usual R.M.O. *MO,* as it were."

Marco reached for his goblet of wine and drank as if it were water. There was a reason for this. He had to remain cool.

"You always had to do things your own way, didn't you, Marik?" Gorky asked penetratingly, as if after all these years he still couldn't figure out what made Marco tick. "You had to castrate Rayenko and stab him in the heart. Dismemberment wasn't good enough for you."

"Did you show this picture to Yevgeny?" Marco said through stiff lips.

Gorky smiled almost gleefully and nodded. "Yes, I did."

Marco winced and slowly exhaled a tight breath of air. Until now, this had been a secret only Marco and Gorky had shared. "What did he say?"

"I think he was impressed. He should be. It was one of the few times in your life that you acted decisively. Your only mistake was walking away from the R.M.O. after you had checked the king. You butchered Rayenko and then *retired* from the *organizatsia.* How stupid could you have been."

Marco studied his wine goblet. Why was Gorky rehashing the past?

"But I lured you back into the spiderweb in time, didn't I? It only took fifteen years. I hope you haven't forgotten who you work for," the old man said at last, revealing his motives. "I thought I'd better remind you how far back we go. Just because I haven't called you into conference for two years doesn't mean I don't still own your soul."

"What do you want from me? I told Sasha to tell you that Mayor Alvarez has decided to let you off the hook for now."

"Yes, yes," Gorky said impatiently. "I'm not worried about the mayor's posse. He'll be voted out of office long before he can do any harm to me. And I know you've done your best to infiltrate the police department."

"Then why am I here?"

Gorky leaned back in his chair. He dusted his mustache with his napkin and threw it on his plate, smiling like the cat about to eat the canary.

"Because I want to talk about Angel Baker."

Chapter 8

Coup d'amour

I rose at the crack of dawn and called Melvin Goldman, a freelance private investigator who lived in Skokie with his identical twin brother Marvin. I used Mel on occasion to help me stake out targets.

"Hi, Mel, this is Angel," I said in a groggy monotone. I sat cradling my first cup of coffee of the day as if it were the holy grail. It pretty much was, considering my caffeine dependence. "Are you up?"

"Of course I'm up!" Mel boomed cheerfully.

I cringed. How could Mel have more energy than I? He was a sixty-something, potbellied elf of a man. What little gray hair he possessed wreathed the back of his head from ear to ear like the last strip of grass in an Arizona drought.

"What is it, doll?" he continued. "You in trouble?"

"I take it you don't watch the news."

"I only download the *Tribune* crossword puzzles. I'm almost done with this morning's. Hey, what was the name of that Jimmy Stewart movie with the invisible rabbit?"

"I can't believe you just asked me that."

"It's 24 down on the puzzle. Six letters. The clue is—hard-to-see hare."

"I know the answer but I'm having a brain freeze." I slurped more coffee, waiting for the kick.

"You're the movie buff, doll."

"Hold on." I shuffled from the kitchen into the living room. My complimentary wheelchair-bound compubot was still where I'd left him the night before, still looking out for trouble on the street below. "Hey, Jimmy, don't you ever sleep?"

"No," he drawled, raising the binoculars for a closer look at the stalwart collection of media types who still hadn't given up on their stakeout. "Sleep isn't part of my program."

"What was the name of the movie you did—or should I say your prototype did—with the rabbit?"

"*Harvey*," he replied, still preoccupied with his assigned task. "The film came out in 1950. My co-star, Josephine Hale, won an Oscar for Best Supporting Actress. I didn't do *Rear Window* until four years later."

I recognized a monologue when I heard one and quietly walked back to the kitchen while he chattered away. I shared the movie trivia with Mel, but when he asked me about 42 across, I cut him off. "Mel, I have some urgent business."

"Why didn't you say so, doll?"

I quickly explained my predicament and asked him to dig around and find out which bank employee gave some as-yet-to-be-identified bad guy access to my safety box. I offered to pay double if Marvin could help him speed up the search.

Mel responded with a long pause, followed by an even longer whistle of amazement.

"You in?" I asked.

"I'm in."

"Thanks."

"Thank you!"

"For what? I haven't paid you yet."

"Listening to your troubles just gave me the answer to 42 across," he said. "Eight letters meaning "Pile of Kimchee."

"And that would be….?"

"Deep shit."

I hung up and allowed that little morsel of enlightenment to penetrate my brain, along with the caffeine. I collected my thoughts about my case, then made a series of calls—to Hank, Jr., to my expensive and capable new lawyer who I needed to meet with and who said he'd look into Lola's status with the police. I also called Harriet Gross, who said Lin was in good hands and relatively good spirits. Harriet said she couldn't be more specific until after my case was settled.

Finally, I called several of my colleagues in the retribution business and told them to shake down every possible informant with any ties to the Mongolian Mob. They readily agreed, eager to find Roy's real killer. I needed as much support as I could get investigating this case, and I seriously doubted that Capone would admit his murderous deeds to me. My goal was twofold. I had to prove my innocence and find out who committed the murders just in case more were planned.

My fellow retributionists, normally somewhat competitive and territorial, quickly offered to track down evidence. I gratefully accepted the help and suggested that we organize a citywide CRS meeting for later in the day. My spectacular debacle threatened the very future of our profession, and we needed to staunch the flow of bad publicity.

I made a few phone calls to set the wheels in motion, then called Roy Leibman's widow to see if I could stop by and pay my respects, and she said I could come immediately, so I dressed.

The heat had broken. In fact, I noticed a touch of cool in the air. I wasn't ready for fall, much less winter, but God rarely consulted me on such issues. I dressed in a red spandex tank top and tight black pants. I threw on my red high-top running shoes, as I was quite certain I'd have to outrun the media, literally, to get out my front door.

After dusting my cheeks with powder and smudging my lips with a pinky-red gloss, I faced my full-length mirror and flexed my arm muscles. I was stronger than the average woman, but still looked petite no matter what I did to try to enhance my size. If I didn't get back to my daily wushu workouts with Mike, I'd be in trouble.

I was just about to walk out the door to the stairwell when Lola burst in, carrying an armload of boxes from Needless Markups.

"Yoo-hoo!" she croaked. Emphysema from years of smoking made her sound like she'd had second thoughts on a sex-change operation before the surgery but after testosterone therapy.

"Lola!" I shouted, genuinely happy to see her, which was saying a lot. "Thank God you're home safe and sound."

I couldn't see her behind the boxes until she dumped them into Jimmy's lap. "Here, honey, take these, whoever you are."

The compubot clutched at the clothing boxes so they wouldn't slide off his lap.

"You went shopping?" I asked, incredulous.

"Yeah, and I got a makeover, too. What do you think?"

She did a little pirouette, which looked kitschy, rather than cute, as one might expect when a sixty-year-old ex-con with enormous breasts, no rear end and size seven feet stuffed into size six stiletto heels tried to imitate Audrey Hepburn. Lola wore a glittering, tight-fitting lamé gown that shouldn't be allowed out of a closet before nightfall.

"I don't understand." I literally scratched my head. "Where did you get the money? Where did you get the time?"

"Oh, I talked my way out of the police station yesterday."

"What have you been doing since then?"

"Shopping."

"Shopping!"

"And," she said, her blue shadowed eyelids going wide, "I was on the news!"

"What! Oh, my God. Tell me that didn't happen."

Lola sashayed over to the couch, sitting. "You're not the only one, missy, who gets attention from the media."

"This is not about attention!" I wanted to pull my hair out, but I took a deep breath. "Tell me, Lola, and start from the beginning, why you were on television."

"Turn on the TV and see for yourself. Channel 3042."

I ordered the omnisystem to power up the digivision and gripped the back of my love seat for strength. If my mother had said a word to the media about my psychic abilities, I'd throttle her. When the news program appeared in midair in the middle of the room, a commercial for ReOrgy was playing.

ReOrgy was a member of a new class of pharmaceuticals that guaranteed multiple orgasms for women. I hated seeing ads for these intimate products on television. So I took some satisfaction when some women had filed a class-action lawsuit against ReOrgy, claiming they could no longer control where or when they had an orgasm. That would pose a problem if you were, say, in a church. Talk about the second coming. Or third. Or fourth.

"Damned commercials," I muttered. "What exactly did you say?"

"I didn't say anything about your case, honey. I know better than that. But when some reporter stuck a microphone in my face and asked me about Lin, I couldn't help but tell them exactly what I thought of the foster-care system."

My jaw dropped open. "But what did you *say?*"

"I told them it sucked the big one."

I covered my eyes with both hands, shaking my head. Only a month ago Lola blithely declared that I had turned out great in spite of eleven years in foster care, as losing a mother was an everyday occurrence and even good for your development. I was just about to let her have it when the news popped on the screen.

I quickly forgot about Lola when I recognized Marco's square jaw and olive complexion. The camera cut to a tight shot, and his dark, bedroom eyes, now serious and squinting, came into focus. He was answering a question posed by a reporter.

"Sound. Louder!" I commanded, and his voice, a confident burl, filled the room.

"—run by vigilantes," Marco said. "The Fraternal Order of City Police has long been against the retribution profession, if you can call it that."

"That's not it," Lola complained. "Turn it off."

"Be quiet." I waved at her frantically. "I'm trying to hear."

"Detective Marco, do you think the double homicide at the Cloisters will have any affect on the popularity of Certified Retribution Specialists?"

"I certainly hope so," Marco replied. "There's no better argument for the dissolution of the CRS business than this horrific crime. It's time these self-appointed retributionists went out and got real jobs and left fighting crime to the police. My committee will be meeting with legislators soon to discuss this very matter."

"Thank you, Detective." The reporter reappeared and

looked directly into the camera lens. "We'll continue to update the story as it develops."

"Television," I practically snarled. "Off!" The images dissolved into thin air, leaving us in stunned silence.

"Detective Marco," Lola repeated. "Was that *your* Detective Marco?"

"Not mine," I said bitterly. "Not anymore."

"Why, that bastard just hung you out to dry, honey."

"I know that!" I shouted. "God, Lola, you never know when to keep your mouth shut."

"Don't get mad at me. He's the one who just stabbed you in the back. I'm telling you, honey, you can never trust a cop. I didn't say anything at first because you liked him. But this just proves what I've known all along. You can't trust cops."

I wanted to argue with her, but the pain pounding in my chest was quickly spreading to the rest of my body. Uncharacteristically, I *wanted* to be alone, as Greta Garbo had so beautifully put it. I marched to my bedroom, slammed the door, and flung myself on my bed.

Trust me, Marco had said. *Trust me.* The bastard! The bloody, manipulative bastard!

I pounded the bed with a fist and punched my pillow. I didn't hear Lola open the door. I didn't realize she'd come in until the bed sank lower. I looked up at her through a glaze of fury.

"Don't get mad, honey," she said with all the confidence of a sage. "Get even."

"What?"

"You heard me. Get even with the bastard. If he's not being honest with you, you have to find out what he's up to."

"How?"

Lola raised one of her clownishly penciled orange eyebrows. "Don't tell me you're still denying your own abilities."

I rolled over on my back. "You want me to psychically spy on him?"

"I wouldn't put it that way."

"Right now I'm too angry to see anything in a crystal ball but red."

"I understand. You're upset. So I'll just have to do it for you."

I was hesitant to use the family psychic powers on Marco. It made me feel like a Peeping Tom. But Lola was right. If Marco was playing fast and loose with me, I needed to know about it so I could protect myself.

"You really would do that for me?" I asked. I'd never before asked her, or allowed her, to read my fortune. Only recently had I come to realize that she really was psychic, and not a con-artist fortune-teller as I'd always thought. It was hard for me to eat this much crow in one sitting.

"Sure, honey." She winked and smiled broadly. "That's what moms are for."

It didn't take much for Lola to get a vision going. She'd been doing it for years. Though she had always done her sessions in a darkened parlor in her Rogers Park apartment, the velvet curtains and candlelight were mostly for show. She was capable of having visions in broad daylight. Generally speaking, the less light the easier it was to see the images that formed in the scrying ball. But they came fast and furious, daylight notwithstanding, as Lola hovered over her crystal ball at my kitchen table.

She described visions of Marco in Little Venice and at the Crypt. Lola didn't know she was describing P.S. #1, but I recognized the scenery she described. She said nothing earth-shattering until she screamed and covered her mouth. Used to her histrionics, I didn't make too much of it until I noticed her hands actually trembled. A fissure of cold wiggled down my spine.

"What is it, Lola? What did you see?"

"A…a…body." She swallowed with difficulty and force
herself to put her hands back on the smooth, glass ball. Sh
winced, as if it actually hurt, but continued like the pro sh
was. "Someone has been stabbed in the heart. His kille
is…castrating him. The victim is pleading for mercy, but th
man with the knife is stabbing him over and over again."

I moved to the edge of my seat. "Who is it? Is it Marco?

"I can't quite see the face." She regarded me warily. "A
you sure Marco's a cop?"

"Yes." *And a whole lot more,* I silently added. "Okay, let
move on to something else."

When she looked at me, puzzled, I replied, brusquel
"That murder doesn't have anything to do with me." And
prayed it didn't have anything to do with Marco. Either wa
I couldn't trust something that important to my mother's psy
chic powers. If I didn't have the guts to pursue it myself,
wasn't ready to know. "I've changed my mind about Marc
He's beside the point. I have to prove my innocence. Can yo
see anything about what happened to Roy Leibman before h
was killed?"

She turned back to the ball and muttered a lot of oohs an
ahs and ahas. Finally, I snapped. "What? Tell me."

She pulled her hands away and folded them neatly. "I sa
many things, Angel dear, and most of them made no sense
me, but one thing is clear. There's a woman behind thes
murders. And she's heartless."

Chapter 9

Blast from the Past

A heartless woman. I'll say. Anyone who could gun down a cool guy like Roy and a young man in his prime had no heart. But I wasn't sure *cherchez la femme* was the order of the day. It just didn't ring true to me. Corleone Capone rarely used female assassins. So I grabbed Mike from his meditations and we headed off for a visit with Roy's widow to investigate the old-fashioned way—one interview at a time.

"Oh, Angel," she said when she opened the door and, to my everlasting gratitude, pulled me in her arms for a warm, forgiving hug.

"Connie, I'm so sorry."

"It wasn't your fault. I didn't believe that for a minute."

I held her tight, wishing I could cry with her. But emotions wouldn't help either of us, and mine seemed so far away. She finally pulled back and dabbed her reddened nose. Sniffling, she said, "Come in. And Mike! I didn't see you there."

"I am sorry, Connie," Mike said, leaning forward to kiss her cheek. "Roy was a good man."

"Come in, both of you."

We stepped through the door of her northside bungalow into the heady scent of funeral flowers. Dozens of arrangements adorned every available surface. Connie offered us tea and made a pot of oolong, knowing Mike would drink that.

After the chitchat died down, Connie wanted to know what I had witnessed at the Cloisters. I shared the details with her, conscious of her vulnerability. She was a sweet-natured person whose eyes reflected her gentleness. I tried to choose my words carefully.

"The strange thing is," I said after she seemed to be satisfied with my account, "I am certain that Roy called me for help. The police say there is no record of it, though. Did Roy say anything to you about getting in touch with me before he went out that evening?"

Connie shook her head. "He said nothing out of the ordinary. Though I can well imagine if he needed help he'd turn to you, Angel. He always said you were his best student. And he'd rather call someone he'd trained rather than a competitor. He was a proud man."

"That's why I responded immediately. I knew it would take a lot for Roy to ask anyone for help."

"What about the mayor's son?" Mike inquired. "Did Roy speak of him?"

"Of course," Connie replied. "Roy was surprised and pleased that Victor Alvarez wanted to talk to him about a retribution job."

"Did they have a contract?" I asked, eager for the answer. If there was no contract, prosecutors would have a hard time proving I had plotted the murder out of professional jealousy.

"Not that I know of. I believe that Roy talked to Victor for the first time the night they were both murdered. Victor requested the meeting at the Cloisters."

"Why so late?" Mike wanted to know.

I nodded. "And why would Victor want to meet in a public place?"

Connie shrugged. "I wish I knew. I wish I could turn back the hands of time and tell Roy not to go."

"Do you mind if I snoop around in Roy's office?" I asked. "I'd like to make sure there was no contract."

"Go right ahead."

I wandered around Roy's office alone while Mike waited for me out on the street. He said he had a bad feeling and wanted to make sure we hadn't been followed. I chalked his uneasiness up to feng shui.

The Leibmans obviously hadn't considered yin and yang when decorating their home in a typical nondescript Midwest style. They had self-vacuuming brown shag rugs and serviceable air-form furniture in golden earth tones, which was warm and cozy. But every cubicle surface was cluttered with memoragrams of the Leibmans' grandchildren. Memoragrams were six-inch motion holograms created from digital video, looped for endless replay. It was like having a collection of pixies who never stopped moving and never aged. Mike loathed them.

I had to admit it was distracting to sit on the sofa and find a three-dimensional image of seven-year-old Trevor sliding into home base on the end table next to your elbow. Even more disconcerting was a commode-side hologram of three-year-old Maggie picking up her new puppy and beaming happily at you while you were on the toilet.

I ignored them as best I could while I explored Roy's office at the back of the house. With papers on his desk still waiting to be filed and phone messages still waiting for reply, I could momentarily pretend he was still alive. Especially when I got a whiff of his spicy cologne. I inhaled deeply, trying to memorize these final impressions that warmed my heart and made me smile.

Getting to work, I perused his filing cabinets and computer files, but found no evidence of a prior relationship with Victor Alvarez. Nothing else drew undue curiosity. I was about to leave when I rested my hand on the sweater draped over the back of his chair.

Mr. Leibman?

Yes?

This is Victor Alvarez.

I heard their voices as clearly as if they stood in the room with me. Shocked, I yanked my hand away and spun, convinced I'd see them. But I was still alone.

"What in the—" I muttered. I spun back and stared at the sweater, taking a deep breath to slow my galloping heart. "Psychometry."

The word popped from the recesses of my sizzling brain. It was a word I'd learned on a recent trip to the Investigative and Psychic Alternatives Consortium downtown. IPAC was a secret quasi-governmental agency that worked to develop practical uses for extrasensory perception and other mental phenomena in law enforcement and the military.

I'd been in denial about my own abilities. I'd always thought my mother's fortune-telling parlor routine was an act, and I wanted no part of it. But when Marco talked me into being tested at IPAC, and my scores were off the charts, I was forced to accept that I was a natural psychic, and that I'd inherited my ability from my mother. They were two bitter pills to swallow.

I was still learning how to use my talents. So far I'd relied on scrying with a crystal ball. I'd never before dabbled in psychometry. Psychometrists could conjure images, sounds and scenes from the past by touching objects connected to those events. That, apparently, was what I had just done when I touched Roy's sweater. Excitedly I touched the soft material again.

Yes, Victor, what can I do for you?

Do you know who I am?

Yes, of course.

Then you know I want to keep this quiet.

I'm discreet with all my clients, and potential clients.

Can you meet tonight?

Name the time and place.

Two a.m. The Cloisters.

Wouldn't you rather come to my house? We can sneak you in the back door. It will be much more comfortable than the Cloisters at that hour.

Uh…no. I have my reasons.

Very well. See you then.

I pulled my hand away and stood a long moment in stunned silence. Slowly I smiled, then let out a quiet whoop of amazement. This stuff really worked. I had to tell Mike.

When I rejoined Connie in the living room, she was chatting with her Personal Listening Device at a Queen Anne desk. I recognized the head-and-shoulder model because it was similar to mine.

"I'm thinking about having Roy's nephew Robert give the eulogy," Connie said quietly to the PLD. "What do you think, Teresa?"

The PLD smiled and nodded. "That's a wonderful idea, Connie."

"And I'm thinking of wearing the black dress with the gray lace."

"You'll look lovely," Teresa replied.

I hated to interrupt. "Connie? I have to go."

She looked up, startled, and smiled. "Of course, I was just…talking with Teresa. That's what Roy named her. She's been a great comfort to me."

"I'm glad."

"Have you enjoyed your PLD?"

I shrugged. "I don't use it much. But my foster child enjoys dressing her up in pearls and funny hats."

Connie chuckled and gave me a reassuring hug. We said our goodbyes, and I left promising to keep her up-to-date on my investigation. As I skipped down the front steps that led to the sidewalk, I promised myself that I'd take a vow of silence before I'd ever resort to having a personal conversation with a PLD.

"I heard it so clearly," I excitedly told Mike as we walked down the sidewalk.

He glanced at me with his inscrutable eyes, then gave me one of his rare smiles. "I am pleased, Baker. Pleased that you used your talent."

"It's not my only one, you know," I said with mock indignation. "I'm not half bad at wushu."

"Now you are—how do you say?—pushing it." He grinned, gently elbowing me in my ribs.

"Literally." I gave him a playful shove back. "My point is this—now I know that Roy and Victor had no contract. They hadn't even met until the night of their murders. This gives me some ammo. I'm going to call Berkowitz and tell him to get Roy's phone records subpoenaed, which I'm sure he's already done. If Roy and Victor only had one prior phone call, that'll be the proof I need. After all, how can I be jealous of a business deal that I didn't know about and that didn't exist?"

I looked for a reaction and realized he wasn't there. Turning, I found Mike standing utterly still, legs slightly bent and set wide. I knew from experience his finely honed senses registered everything in the environment. Suddenly, I too became hyperaware.

"Where are we?" I hadn't realized we'd taken two turns that put us in an alley. We were still in a friendly neighborhood, but shadows fell on broken chunks of concrete scattered like ill-omened runes.

"Someone is here," Mike whispered, squatting into a wide horse stance.

A low, feral growl sounded behind us. I whirled, crouching. Out of the shadows of a two-car alley garage stepped what looked like a wild dog, slinking with rolling shoulders into attack mode. Bared fangs glinted when it inched into sunlight. I squinted for a better look.

"I felt something was waiting for us," Mike whispered.

"Wait, that's not a dog. It's a gray wolf."

"Her name is Keshon." The stranger's voice sounded an inch from my ear.

"Aaaiiieee!" The roaring attack cry sounded from my diaphragm before I had time to think. I whirled with an aerial roundhouse kick to the head. I spun and lunged, striking his chest hard and fast with my fists three times, then knocked his legs out from under him. Down he went, rolling over with a moan.

I turned just in time to see the wolf galloping toward me. Mike gallantly stepped in its path.

"Keshon, hold!" the man on the ground shouted with great effort. The wolf put on the brakes and skidded to a stop. "At ease!"

The wolf docilely sat. The man sank back on the ground, trying to catch the wind I'd knocked out of him. Then he propped himself on his elbows and looked at me in frank amazement.

Panting, confused, I looked down and recognized the spiked blond hair, the row of earrings adorning his pierced blond brows, the sexy, insolent grin which he managed in spite of his pain.

"Brad?" I asked incredulously.

"I let you do that," he said hoarsely.

"Right," came my snide reply, but I was grinning and reached down to give him a hand. "You really shouldn't have surprised me like that."

He climbed to his feet, which were covered in silver boots that looked like they'd been hammered by a medieval blacksmith. The chains at his heels jangled as he dusted off his white biker clothing. Brad looked tough, but he couldn't abide dirt.

"Jesus, woman, who taught you to fight like that?"

"This guy." I waved Mike over. "This is Mike, a former kung-fu monk from Shaolin."

Mike stepped forward and took Brad's diamond-encrusted hand in his. "I am pleased to meet you."

"Naturally," Brad said, whipping Mike's hand in a complicated gang shake. I was amazed that Mike knew the moves and felt a little left out.

"Are you okay?" I asked when Brad turned back to me.

He touched the corner of his lip with a pinky and examined a dab of blood. "I'm not sure, Angel. I think I need a hug."

He pulled me close, cupping my derriere and pressing my abdomen against his hips where, against all odds, his desire for me stood ready and waiting. Then he grinned and laughed at my appalled reaction.

"You're an animal, Brad." I pushed him away. "I see you haven't changed since I last saw you."

I'd met Brad five years ago at a convention in New Orleans,

where local retributionists were big into creating mystiques and alter-identities. The convention was like a weeklong costume ball. Even though I wore a skimpy black leather outfit and temporary blue dragon tattoos on my forehead and chest, colleagues looked me up and down as if I were an undercover certified public accountant who had come to audit their taxes.

That's one reason I fell under Brad's charms. He looked past my "ordinary" motif and swept me off my feet. Literally. I'm embarrassed to say we had a one-night stand. Actually, we had four in a row. And that was the last we'd seen of each other.

The decision was entirely mutual. We'd had fun in bed, and he still obviously turned me on. But having sex with Brad was like taking an aerobics class. It was sweaty and made me feel better, but I found myself sneaking glances at the clock. I guess you could say he's the guy who taught me that sex without emotion is just...sex.

Still, I got a kick out of the way Brad stood out in a crowd. It wasn't just because he was cocky, young and good-looking. He'd dubbed himself Brad the Impaler. Considering his propensity for untimely erections, the name probably fit in more ways than one. But he'd taken that nom de guerre in an allusion to Vlad the Impaler, the brutal Romanian Count Dracula whose savagery gave rise to the Dracula vampire legends. Brad had even filed his eyeteeth to fanglike points.

They gleamed in the sun as he grinned at me. I put my hands on my hips and scowled in return, determined not to let him cop another free feel. Since feminist indignation could never penetrate Brad's testosterone-saturated brain, I'd have to keep my distance. I really didn't want to beat the hell out of him a second time.

"So, Brad, what brings you to this alley? It's a little far from New Orleans."

He gave me a lopsided grin that creased the scar running from his temple to his upper lip. "I came lookin' for you, honey."

"Cut the crap, Brad."

He shrugged and cut back a notch on the high-octane charm. "I stopped by your house, and your old lady said you'd come here. I want to help you get out of this mess. Don't worry, I'm not thinkin' of *you*. I'm concerned about *moi*. This little murder rap of yours is gonna send some heavy duty shit into fans all over the country, and its gonna land on any poor sap who has the balls to hang out a CRS shingle."

"You're a big, tough guy, Brad, you can handle the fallout," I said. He was right, and I was worried about the same thing, but if I gave Brad an inch, he'd take a mile. I had to hang tough until I could ferret out his real motives.

His blond pin-cushion eyebrows, both adorned with four small hooped earrings, curled into an earnest frown. "Okay, so maybe I am thinkin' about someone other than myself. We're in a brotherhood, Angel. You know that. I have to watch out for my colleagues. Just like you."

He had me there. Still, something in the back of my mind warned me to be wary. I crossed my arms until it hit me. "You mean to say that you dropped your own clients in New Orleans to come and help out in Chicago?"

"I was at O'Hare waiting for a connecting flight to California when I saw your beautiful kisser on the airport's digi-screens. I decided to delay my trip, just for you. After all, it's my vacation. I can do whatever I want with it."

I placed my hands on my heart and said, dryly, "I feel so special."

"Seriously, Angel, you need help. Consider me a consultant."

I thought about the meeting we'd arranged with all the retributionists in Chicago. It might be good to have an outsider's point of view. "Okay, but on one condition."

"You name it."

"Keep your hands to yourself."

He looked genuinely disappointed. "Have you stopped to consider that you might seriously need to get laid?"

"Don't even go there," I snarled.

He raised his hands up in surrender. "Cool. We're cool. Lead the way, Kemo sabe."

Chapter 10

Mama Mia

On the way home from the Leibman's, I called and updated my lawyer on what I'd discovered at Roy's house. I should say I updated his assistant. I couldn't imagine that Berkowitz had a higher profile case at the moment, but he must have be- cause getting through to him was like getting an audience with the pope. I guess ten mil doesn't buy much these days.

Still, I felt I was in good hands. You don't pay defense law- yers to be warm and fuzzy. You pay them to ruthlessly rip the heart out of the prosecutor's case, to cannibalize the DA in front of the jury, and to stand triumphantly over the bodies of fallen witnesses when the prosecution has crumbled beneath his feet. And that's if you're innocent. I could only imagine what tactic my attorney would use if I were obviously guilty. But, as I had learned through my interview with the Diva, truth is no defense

Mike offered to lead Brad through the labyrinthine bullet train rail system to the Retributionists Hall so Brad could help organize the meeting scheduled for the next day. I was looking forward to a nice cup of coffee before I set out on my next task, but that wasn't to be.

"Psst! Angel, come here!" Jimmy said as soon as I let myself in the front door.

I flipped on the foyer light and saw Jimmy's extended broken leg sticking out of the shadows of the ground-level studio. "What is it? Why are you down here?"

He wheeled a few inches forward until his long, handsome face emerged from the shadows like a scene from a film noir. "Do you know who's upstairs?" he hissed conspiratorially.

The Cyclops? Santa Claus? I couldn't even begin to guess, so I merely shook my head.

"Sydney Bassett," he said, with an intensity that made a frisson of danger zip up my spine. "Very dangerous."

"Sydney?" I whispered back. "Dangerous? Wait a minute, you're getting carried away. She is my foster mother."

"Are you sure?" he whispered, looking up as if she might be able to hear us through the ceiling.

"Yes! Of course."

"She could be a compubot who has set you up with this whole murder rap," he whispered dramatically. "You say she hired your lawyer? Maybe that's just to make it look like she's on your side."

"That's ridiculous. I know you must think the world is full of your kind, Jimmy, but you're quite rare." *Thank God,* I silently added. "Sydney is not a compubot. Now just relax and keep an eye out for the front window down here. Okay?"

He looked at me as if I were making a grave mistake, then reluctantly nodded. "Okay. But if anything happens up there, you scream. I'll take the service elevator."

I gave him a thumbs-up. "Ten-four," I said with all the sin cerity of a cartoon superheroine on her way to blithely sav the day.

Sydney wasn't a danger, but her presence here made m acutely uncomfortable. I'd never before invited my foster par ents to my house. My abode never seemed good enough t show off to the Bassetts. It wasn't as if Sydney and Henr were money conscious snobs. They'd always treated me as a equal, even though I was from an entirely different soci strata.

It was more the fact that I didn't have any of Sydney's in terior decorating skills. My flat was comfortable, but undi tinguished. Plus, I'd always sensed that in some way, sma or large, I was a social experiment of Henry's. I didn't wa the Bassetts to see me in my own milieu and find out that had failed the test.

More disturbing still, Lola was upstairs. My foster moth and birth mother had never met. When I threw open the do to my upstairs flat, I found them sitting tensely at opposi ends of the couch.

Sydney looked like the quintessential college dean wife. Her hair was richly frosted and tucked in a loose bu An expensive but subtle strand of pearls wreathed her thi neck. And she gracefully wore a sporty peach-and-whi skirt ensemble so tasteful that it didn't even register Lola's consciousness.

In contrast, Lola wore a fitted polysynthe gown with o ange, red, and yellow swirls that looked like custard flamb Her hair was a brassy red-orange, as was the lipstick painte a quarter of an inch above her lip line, not to mention her n polish, and her eyebrows, which looked like twin St. Lou arches in a blazing orange sunset.

I took one look at the two women—so disparate, each representing irreconcilable parts of my life—and blanched. They both jumped up when they saw me and said nearly in unison, with relief, "Angel!"

I cleared my throat and forced a casual smile. "Sydney, what a surprise. I see you've met my...Lola." My mother, I almost said, but caught myself just in time.

I still hated giving Lola the satisfaction of being called "Mom," considering how little mothering she'd done when I was young. And I didn't want to hurt Sydney's feelings, considering I'd never called her "Mom," either, even though I think she'd wanted me to.

The Bassetts had tried to adopt me, but Lola wouldn't allow it. Memories of that disappointment flashed painfully in my mind. I was tough, but I wasn't sure I was tough enough to stand in the eye of that emotional hurricane right now.

I went to Sydney to give her my usual hello hug. Feeling Lola's angry glare burning into my profile, I then gave her an awkward little embrace.

"Well," I said, nervously clapping my hands together, "you two look like you've enjoyed your little chat." The comment was so patently absurd that I blushed and cleared my throat. "Can I get you something to drink, Sydney?"

"I already served her tea," Lola said in a bad, vaguely British accent as she waved her hand in front of the white, cube-like teacups in front of her and Sydney.

No, Lola, just be yourself, I tried to psychically warn her. She had the most unrealistic view of how "the other half" lived. In her own way, she was a reverse snob. All wealthy people, she assumed, were stupid and heartless. She'd always told me you had to put on airs to get along with the well-to-do.

"Oh, yes, I see the teacups now. Silly me," I said, forcing

a laugh that almost turned into a groan when Lola tried
sneak a quick pour of her flask into her cup. I could smell t
alcohol from where I stood.

Lola had been dry ever since she'd moved in with me
month ago. I should have known Sydney's arrival would
enough to knock her off the wagon.

I nonchalantly walked over to Lola's side of the couch a
pried the flask from her curled hand. I didn't want to emb
rass her, but I knew from experience she'd soon be swingi
from the proverbial chandelier if I didn't intervene. "I'll
back in a minute."

I went out to the kitchen, dumped the flask upside do
in the sink, then clung to my ceramic countertop while I h
perventilated. I'd been through too much in the past few da
to pretend I was up for a tea party. I had to get Lola out
here. Sydney had obviously come for an important reason, a
we needed a chance to talk alone.

I spun around and marched into the living room. "Lola
need you to run to the sto—" I stopped cold when I inhal
a telling whiff of tobacco. I focused on my birth mother w
disbelief, then outrage. A trail of smoke curled up from a c
arette poised in her hand like a movie star's. She took a lo
hard drag, then exhaled in Sydney's direction.

"Okay, that's it!" I roared. "You know cigarettes are il
gal. How dare you subject Sydney to that?"

"Don't worry, Angel," Sydney said in her gentle way.

"No, I'm sorry. Lola wouldn't be doing this if y
weren't here."

"How dare you talk about me as if I'm not in the room
Lola said. "You and your hoity-toity foster mother thi
you're both mighty special, don't you?"

"You need to go now." I strode to Lola's side, forcefu
helped her up from the couch, grabbed her purse and escor

her to the door. "We'll talk about this later," I whispered harshly once we'd reached the top of the stairs.

"I was entertaining her until you got home," Lola returned in a stage whisper loud enough to be heard in the balconies. "I tried to help, and this is the thanks I get!"

"If you want to help, take a long trip to the store. Pick up some groceries. While you're there, get yourself a nicotine injection and stop by an AA meeting on your way home."

"That's not fair!"

"Life's not fair, Lola. You taught me that."

That silenced her. She mugged a conspiratorial, almost proud smile. "Yeah, I did, didn't I? Aw, honey, I'm sorry. I embarrassed you. Will you forgive me?"

"Not today." I shut the door, and she immediately knocked. I yanked it open. "What?"

"Tomorrow?"

"We'll see," I said through clenched teeth. This time I shut and locked the door. When I returned to the living room, Sydney was cleaning up the teacups. Together we brought the dishes into the kitchen and sat at the table. I poured myself the last of the tea and sank down in exhaustion.

"I'm so sorry, Sydney."

"Don't be, dear. I'm glad finally to have met your birth mother. She's quite extraordinary."

I laughed and nodded. "I'll say. But I bet you didn't come here to meet Lola."

"No." She reached out and covered my hand with hers. "I have some important news."

I perked up. "What?"

"Your fath— I should say Henry and I managed to get temporary custody of Lin."

My mouth dropped, then spread into a smile. "Oh! That's fantastic." I leaned over the table and threw my arms around her and we rocked together in joy. "Thank you. Thank Henry! What would I do without you?"

I finally released her. "I can't tell you what a relief that is. I know you'll give Lin a fabulous home."

A sudden blast of melancholy rushed through me and I wasn't sure why. But, as was frequently the case, Sydney knew me better than I knew myself.

"It's only temporary, Angel. I'm not going to replace you as Lin's mother. She'll be back with you as soon as Berkowitz clears up this debacle."

I gave her a thin smile, morosely thinking that even Berkowitz wasn't that good, but I didn't want Sydney to think she'd wasted millions of dollars on my defense.

"Lin wants to come back here as soon as she can," Sydney added.

My blue gaze pinned on her hopefully. "Did she say that?"

"Yes. And I can see it in her face whenever we talk about you."

"I hope…I hope she won't forget me."

"I don't think that's possible. You're her savior, sweetie. She knows that."

"Some savior. Lola had her faults, but at least she was never charged with murder. She spent four years behind bars. I'm facing life without parole. Lin might never see me again."

"No, Angel—"

"Let's be realistic, Sydney. I was a foster mother—what?— a month? Already I've abandoned Lin."

Sydney looked nonplussed. "Abandoned her! This wasn't your fault."

"I doubt it matters to Lin whether I'm guilty or not. She needs a mother. I just took that away from her. Isn't it bad enough that she's already lost one family?"

"Stop! I won't have you doing this to yourself. Lin and

eleven other girls would be for sale on the black market right now if it weren't for you."

I couldn't argue there. I treasured the admiration in Sydney's soft green eyes, and her quiet determination to see the world in a positive light. It was that, even more than the Bassetts' wealth, that set them apart from me. It was her hopefulness, and my cynicism, that made me feel I really didn't deserve to be adopted into their family.

"Okay, so I'm not that bad. When I can I see her?"

"Not until you are cleared of all charges."

"What?"

"I know, it's going to be torture to keep away from Lin when you know she's so close. But they wouldn't give us custody until we promised them you'd keep your distance. You're not even allowed to talk to her on the phone. Not until you've been found innocent."

"Sydney, that could be months. Years, even."

"I refuse to believe that. It will happen soon. It simply must. Meanwhile, she's safe with us, honey. It's the best that we can do right now."

I nodded. "Thank you. For everything."

"We love you, Angel."

Thank God for small miracles.

I went downtown to meet face-to-face for the first time with Jack Berkowitz. He was exactly the kind of attorney you wanted to have for a murder defense. He was good-looking, distinguished, bright and he reeked of success. The odor was even more aromatic than his thousand-dollar cologne. You could tell he was the kind of man who could reach under a table and crush his opponent's noogies without a pause in the drone of his legalize. Best of all, he had a winning track record and wasn't about to ruin it with a guilty verdict in my case.

Gary agreed that the prosecution's case stunk to high heaven and that whoever set me up had friends in high places. I was glad we saw eye to eye. I was also pleased that unlike some high-powered lawyers, Gary wasn't a control freak. He'd had enough success to trust in synchronicity and encouraged me to continue my own investigation, though I was not to give any media interviews without first consulting him. Fine by me.

I left his office late in the afternoon feeling more hopeful than I had in days. But the ride home cast me in a blue funk. That was due, in part, to the fact that while waiting on the train platform, I caught a glimpse of someone who reminded me of the Cyclops.

He looked at me from the middle of the crowded platform, a hooded sweatshirt hiding most of his face and head. I couldn't see his eyes, so I assumed they were intact. I knew it wasn't Cy because he was locked up. Still, it gave me the willies. What if he ever got out of jail? Would he try to get back at me for destroying his only good eye?

I also found myself succumbing to the foul mood I'd been fighting ever since Sydney visited my flat. The state of Illinois saw fit to treat me like a leper when it came to my foster child. For the first time, I could relate to how Cy felt, being judged and separated from others for an act of fate. In Cy's case, he had been badly burned. I had been at the wrong place at the wrong time.

By the time I arrived home, I was ready to go into a vegetative state. Nothing like a double-murder charge to force you to deal with all your emotional baggage all at once. Right now I just needed a break.

I stripped down to my undies and a cranberry satin teddy and curled up on my double bed while the sun set. I watched dust motes dance in the fading skylight until dusk teetered at the edge of darkness. My house creaked and moaned as it settled for the night.

That's when I heard Marco's voice in the garden. The last time I'd heard him, he was savagely betraying me on television.

I sat up slowly, like a snake uncoiling from the center of its body. My hibernation, induced by emotional pain, came to an abrupt end as I focused on the one thing I could control in my life.

There were many reasons to toss Marco out on his ear, but chief among them was the desire to prove to myself that I didn't need anybody, and I'd sooner reject the one person I wanted most than admit I really was as vulnerable as he was proving me to be.

I don't remember running down the porch stairs or striding across the garden to where Marco chatted with Mike, scarcely dressed in my teddy and undies. Like in an out-of-body experience, I seemed simply to have arrived. Meanwhile, adrenaline had pumped me up. When I grabbed Marco's arm and spun him, he felt unusually pliant. I was either stronger than I realized or he was letting me have my way.

"Get out," I said and shoved his chest with both hands. Marco staggered back, but didn't register so much as an iota of fear or anger. Not even surprise. He regained his balance and regarded me serenely.

"Hello, Angel. How are you?"

"Don't you 'hello Angel me,' you traitor." I let hard-boiled rage roll through me like a tidal wave and shoved him again like the aggressor in a wrestling ring. "Come on, you son of a bitch, fight back. I don't want any of this zenlike psychoanalytical bullshit. You stabbed me in the back today, Detective, and I want you out of here. If you won't go, then you'd better be prepared to fight."

"Angel, please do not do this," Mike said.

"Whose side are you on, Mike? Were you plotting against me with Detective Marco?"

"Of course not. He is helping me find my lost brother. You are not the only one with problems, Baker."

That stung. Because I was thinking only of myself. I'd promised Mike I'd help in the search, but I'd been too busy ever since Lin had arrived. Was that why Marco was being so helpful? To make me look bad?

"How convenient," I said sarcastically, "that the good detective comes to advise you in the middle of my murder investigation."

"Marco has been advising me for weeks," Mike said in a tone utterly neutral, yet I could still read the indictment between the lines.

I looked back and forth between the men and sensed a bond I hadn't noticed before. My God, I had been self-absorbed. I had brought them together and thought I was the common denominator, but instead I'd been left out of the equation. Now I could add jealousy to the mix of emotions already seething in my throat.

"You can work with anyone you want, Mike. But not here. Not now."

"Come on, Angel," Marco said in a soothing voice as he reached out to give my shoulder a cajoling pat. "You're not mad at Mike. It's me you want to throttle."

I knocked his hand aside and held my own in a praying mantis pose, daring either of them to make a move. "Don't touch me. I don't trust either of you. And I don't need you."

"Angel—"

"No, Mike, it's too late. I want you both out of here. My life is hanging in the balance. I can't afford to be betrayed by anyone. Marco, you get out now. Mike, you have until the end of the day."

I spun on my heel, enjoying the rush of indignation. But the pleasure faded as reality sunk in. I'd just evicted the best lover and the best friend I'd ever had. But there was no turning back now. As I stomped toward the balcony stairs, certain I had burned my last bridge, I wondered if I could assume something more drastic than a fetal position when I reached my bedroom. Could I temporarily withdraw from the human race? Perhaps induce a temporary coma?

Yes, a coma would do nicely.

Chapter 11

A Sigh Is Still a Sigh

"Angel!" Marco called. I heard his feet fall on the path behind me and quickened my pace past the beds of ivy and Japanese lanterns that dotted the garden.

"Angel, stop this instant!" Marco's shouted. The deep, demanding voice penetrated the thick fire-door to my brain. A coil of caution twisted to life in the logical left side—which admittedly wasn't in control at the moment. *Listen to what he has to say,* my better judgment urged me, but pride controlled my feet and wasn't about to buckle under the threat of his anger.

I had just about grabbed hold of the wooden stair railing when my body jerked back. My feet momentarily lifted off the slab of concrete as he twisted me around, my arm painfully imprisoned in his grip. I'd never seen Marco this strong—or this pissed.

Throwing my weight into the flow, I regained my balance and landed in fighting position. I lunged forward and punched my right fist hard into his gut, but he tightened his abs at the last moment and curled his back like a cat's, avoiding the worst of my blow.

"Well done, Detective! I see my kung-fu master has shared his secrets with you as well."

"Stop it, Angel!" Marco roared.

"Make me," I countered in one of my less articulate moments.

I swung my left leg up in a roundhouse kick so fast it made a whooshing sound. To my surprise, he ducked. I rebounded with a double punch, fists slamming into his chest, knocking him backward.

"Damn it!" he choked out, arms flailing as he tripped backward over a chair. He stumbled against the big elm that lorded over the garden like an old tree god. I didn't see him reaching for the tiny but deadly ultrasound saber in his jogging pants as he regained his balance.

The size of an old-fashioned lady's pistol, the lethal device had a trigger but served the function of a knife, severing significant internal organs without cutting the skin or leaving a trace of evidence. For that very reason, U-sabers were favorites among assassins. You could leave an enemy completely paralyzed and unable to speak with a shot to the cerebral cortex.

Or, if you preferred to snuff out your enemy, a jolt of silent ultrasound could slice open a carotid artery as easily as a surgeon's scalpel, but without external bleeding. No muss, no fuss. At least for the assassin. If you were caught with one on your person, though, it was an instant no-excuses, ten-year sentence without parole.

Marco extended his arm as he aimed the U-saber, taking wide, steady strides toward me until the weapon's tiny snout pressed against my forehead. His muscular chest heaved for breath in the silence. He smelled of sweat, fury, even a hint of desperation. Finally, he had me where he wanted me—completely at his mercy.

"Why am I not surprised by this?" I asked rhetorically, careful to stand very still. I didn't want his finger accidentally pulling the trigger. "And how could I have been so damned wrong about you? You're an assassin, aren't you? Naturally, you have an assassin's weapon."

His eyes fluttered as rage swelled in them. "Shut the fuck up, Angel."

"Too close to the mark?" I asked, unable to keep my bloody mouth shut. "Go ahead and shoot me, Marco. You'll be doing us both a favor."

He smiled grimly. "That would be too easy."

"For you?"

"For both of us."

For the first time, fear began to pound unsteadily in my chest. I shouldn't be playing with fire when he had just poured the equivalent of gasoline all around us. Just because I'd made love with this man didn't mean he wouldn't kill me. In fact, I'd lay odds that he was planning on it. Pulling this weapon was tantamount to an admission of his true profession. He would have nothing to lose if all his covers were blown.

"Are you going to kill me?" I whispered through my tight throat, afraid to look in his eyes.

"No. I just wanted you to let me talk."

"Then lower the gun. I promise I'll be quiet, for once in my life."

When he did, I heaved a huge sigh of relief and looked around to see Mike's reaction. He was gone. He'd retreated to his shed. Damn him! Why did he always have faith in Marco? I just didn't get it.

"Angel," Marco began, shaking his head as he searched for the right words, "I'm not an assassin. I never have been."

I crossed my arms, my body language more than adequately expressing my doubt.

He tossed the weapon on the ground. "I picked that up earlier today when I made an arrest."

"Do you always pocket the contraband that you apprehend in arrests?"

"Okay, I didn't make the arrest. It was my cousin. I just frisked him, confiscated his weapon and sent him home."

"How comforting. Did you also pat him on the head and give him cookies and milk?"

"He's family, Angel."

"And that makes it okay to be an assassin? Is Vladimir Gorky family, too?"

"No."

His face went intriguingly dead, and I sensed I was close to the heart of what made this elusive man tick. "What exactly is your relationship with Gorky?"

"You don't want to know."

"I most certainly do. I also want to know why you betrayed me in that television interview."

"I was speaking for my committee, Angel. I didn't say anything in public that I haven't already said to you in private. My opposition to your profession has nothing to do with you."

"You could have fooled me."

"Even if I had wanted to mince words, it would raise suspicion in the police department. You need me on your murder case."

"Oh, yeah, you've done wonders for me so far."

His eyes glinted with a suppressed smile. "You're damned stubborn, you know that?"

I suppressed a smile in return. "Thanks."

He reached out and ran his fingers through my hair, spiking it up on top. "There. You can't look too tame. It would ruin your reputation."

I endured the coiffing with a stoic frown, refusing to acknowledge the delicious tickling sensation his touch sent cascading down my arms.

Satisfied, he crossed his arms and regarded me with perplexity. "You know, Miss Baker, that you're being awfully one-sided in this whole matter."

"How so?"

"Don't I get any credit for the good I've done in my profession?" He loomed over me with a dangerous *I want to make love* look. He cupped a cheek, brushing my moist lips with a thumb.

I gently but firmly pulled his hand away. "Which profession would that be? Psychologist? Cop? Assassin?"

He wasn't listening. He focused with unusual intensity on my mouth. Now cupping both cheeks, he dipped his head down, kissing me softly, almost reverently, like a bee paying homage to the flower. Could an assassin kiss this tenderly? I wondered. Or was kissing this tenderly just part of his cover?

His hands skimmed down my shoulders, arcing down my silken teddy until they reached the small of my back. His electric fingertips inched beneath the waistband of my low-rise briefs, hot against my flesh. That sizzling gesture brought all my senses to a peak and my breathing went shallow.

I *so* wanted him to reach lower and cup my derriere, but he was tantalizingly circumspect. I was practically panting. What more invitation did he need? Could he doubt my desire? It was possible. So I gave him a kiss that left no questions unanswered.

He groaned appreciatively, then pulled away, seemingly unable to take any more.

"Ah, you're good, Angel Baker. Very good," he murmured

in my ear as he intimately lifted one of my arms over his shoulders, then the other. "But let me ask you something."

"Yes?" I said breathlessly. I wrapped my arms tight around his neck and nuzzled against his square, whiskered jaw. "Ask me what?"

He reached under my loose teddy and ran his hands slowly up my sides. They molded over my ribs until they cupped my breasts. Lifting, he kneaded the full flesh in his warm palms, thumbs rotating erotically over the beaded nipples, all the while eyeing me intensely. "What profession do you think I'm talking about?"

"I don't know," I said on a moan as I tossed my head back and dug my nails into his shoulders.

"Is there anything I could do to make you stop wanting me?"

I shook my head, heedless of the moral implications. I had to tell him the truth. If he didn't make love to me now, I'd go mad. "No. I want you. I thought I'd made that more than clear."

"You want me no matter what?"

"Yes, damn it." I gripped his head in my hands and glared at him. "What do you want? A signed affidavit?"

Chuckling deeply, he cocooned me in his arms and fused to me with a hot, deep kiss. He kissed with his whole body, including his slowly rocking pelvis and a hard-on that wouldn't quit, straining like a tent pole against his thin, military green jogging pants. It was a heady experience. The musky scent of him alone was enough to make me drunk, like a sniff of potent brandy.

Marco was all over me in his uniquely skilled way—caressing all the right curves, laving all the right indentations, scratching my tender skin with his five-o'clock shadow, then soothing with his tongue. I didn't want to know how many women this man had made love to. I was just grateful he was putting all that practice to good use on me.

Finally, *finally,* he reached down and slipped a hand inside my briefs, inching down until his skillful touch found the swollen, moist firecracker that was ready to explode. He smiled as he began to rub.

"I believe you do want me, Angel Baker," he murmured in my ear. "I don't know why, but I do."

"I'm gla—" I couldn't even finish the sentence. My own personal Fourth of July fireworks exploded in early September this year, and it was well worth the wait.

"Give me a whiskey," Marco said two hours later to the bartender at Rick's Café Americain, the reality bar down the street from Angel's two-flat.

"We have a special on Vivante tonight, sir," the polite, neatly dressed man behind the smoky bar said. Marco couldn't tell if he was a compubot or an actor. Either way, he looked like the bartender in the movie *Casablanca.* "Every Vivante is a double tonight, sir."

Vivante was a clear alcohol engineered to assume the taste of whiskey or any other liquor that Marco cared to imagine. But somehow he doubted it would burn his throat enough to suit him tonight. He aimed to get seriously drunk, with all that that entailed, including the punishing hangover in the morning. So he was more than willing to pay ten times the price for the real thing.

Marco pulled out a paychip and slapped the small square plastic on the counter. "Thanks, but not tonight. I want your best. And leave the bottle."

The bartender turned to his rows of old-fashioned liquor bottles—there was Black Jack, Beefeaters, and Glenlivet. He returned with an amber-colored bottle, uncorked it and poured two fingers of the powerful liquid into the glass. Marco lifted it to his nose and inhaled. The scent nearly scorched his nostrils.

"Perfect." He raised the glass in a salute. "Thanks."

"My pleasure, sir." The bartender reached for the pay-chip, but a strong and graceful hand interceded, gripping his wrist.

"That won't be necessary," came a familiar, unsentimental voice. "Detective Marco's money is no good here."

Marco looked up at the Humphrey Bogart compubot that had just spoken. Angel called him Bogie, but the patrons knew him as Rick Blaine. Every night Rick and Ilsa Laszlo, played by an Ingrid Bergman compubot, played out various scenes in no particular order from the classic 1940s film. The bar and restaurant perfectly replicated the movie's sultry and tense setting in Nazi-occupied French Morocco, which was the backdrop to their doomed but noble love affair.

"Whatever he drinks is on the house," Bogie said to the bartender.

Marco tossed back the whiskey in one shot, then wiped his mouth with the back of his wrist. "I can afford it."

"I know you can. That's not the point," Bogie replied. He added in an unemphatic, rat-a-tat rejoinder, "Look, Detective, I think we understand each other rather well. I don't like you and you don't like me. But I like to think we respect each other. And we certainly respect Angel Baker."

Marco poured another three fingers of whiskey. He'd only spoken with this compubot once before, when Angel was flirting with it to make him jealous. Marco had thought it was absurd and said so at the time. Angel had thought Marco was being rude to the compubot, which was even more absurd.

"You're right," Marco said at last. "I don't like you."

Bogie gave him a tight, short smile and pulled a cigarette from a flat holder in his tuxedo jacket. He offered one to Marco, who shook his head, then lit up. Compubots were exempt from the antismoking laws.

. "But I don't dislike you, either," Marco added. "I have n
feelings for a mechanized computer that has no feelings."

Sam, a robust, black compubot, began to play the piano ar
sing "As Time Goes By."

"I had feelings for Angel Baker," Bogie said morosel
"But she ended our affair. For you."

Marco slanted him a grudging look. Compubots didr
need sleep, and this one had moonlighted after hours .
Angel's lover. Nice of him to rub it in.

"Right now she has Jimmy Stewart in her apartmen
Marco said morosely.

Bogie's tough-guy demeanor melted momentarily as I
registered surprise. "You're joking."

"I'm afraid not," Marco said with an ironic smile. "Bu
don't think we have much to worry about with hi
He's...disabled."

"Rear Window?" Bogie asked.

Marco nodded.

"Poor sap. He's got to get another gig," Bogie replied. F
took a long drag on his unfiltered Turkish cigarette. "Dete
tive, I can tell you still have feelings for Angel, too. You ju
won't admit it because old-time heroes don't talk about the
feelings. Am I right?"

He was right about Marco's feelings for Angel. The wa
she'd given herself to him tonight had reminded him just ho
human he was. That he needed love, and his life was emp
without it. Angel was unlike any woman he'd ever met. Sl
accepted him, though her instincts knew better, asking so l
tle in return. She was willing to risk it all for him. But if I
gave her the one thing she needed most—commitment-
she'd be forced to learn everything about him, including I
past. And the reality of that would be far worse than anythi
she'd imagined so far.

Marco poured another drink.

"If you plan on drinking that entire bottle, Detective, then you'd better get something to eat."

Carl, the plump, white-haired Austro-Hungarian waiter, set up a meal for Marco at a private table. Bogie sat with him and gave terse greetings to any customer rude enough to interrupt their tête-à-tête. "Rick" was famous for refusing to drink with his patrons, so his presence at Marco's table drew stares.

By the time Bogie and Marco had finished off two bottles of wine, they were in complete agreement on one subject—women.

"You can't live with them," Bogie said, "and you can't live without them."

"No!" Marco said, grabbing his arm, "You can't live with them and you can't live with them."

They both laughed.

"I'll drink to that." Bogie swilled the last of his wine. He loosened his bow tie and stared morosely at the candle burning in the table's centerpiece. "Still, some women are hard to forget."

"Hello, Rick," came a soft, emotion-laden voice with a slight Swedish accent.

Marco looked up in his quasi-drunk state and found the Ingrid Bergman compubot staring longingly at her co-star. She wore a trim cap and conservative suit—very much a lady, but vulnerable in a touching way. Her large, innocent eyes were swollen with unshed tears. Her soft, pretty mouth was moist with a ready kiss.

"What do you want?" Bogie replied with surprising venom. He slammed a fist on the table so hard the silverware jumped. "Why don't you go find Victor Laszlo? He's the one you married. Not me. You left me in Paris, remember?"

Marco watched the lovebirds argue, wondering if true love always ended this way.

When she finally walked away, Bogie ran a hand through his hair, bemoaning, "Of all the gin joints in all the towns—"

"Let's cut to the chase," Marco said dismissively. "You know by the end of the movie you're going to sacrifice everything for her—including her love for you. And all you get in the end, is the guy. You walk off into the sunset with that little French detective."

"He's a captain. And we walk off on a foggy tarmac."

"Whatever."

"I have no regrets about how my story ends because I did what was right. If Ilsa didn't get on that plane with Victor Laszlo, she would have regretted it the rest of her life. Sometimes you have to make tough decisions because they're the right ones for everyone involved."

Marco wiped a cloth napkin over his mouth and pushed aside his plate. "You're right. I have to figure out what's best for everyone in my situation. I've just learned that Angel's life is in grave danger."

"If she's in danger, you have to protect her."

"It's not that simple. I'm hip-deep in crocodiles. She might be better off without me. Maybe I should just disappear from her life."

"Don't ever do that," Bogie admonished him. "Do you know what kind of pain that causes to the one left behind?"

"Not as much pain as I'll cause when she finds out who really am. And what I've done."

"We all have pasts we'd like to run from, Detective. But few of us have that privilege. My advice to you is to stick around and protect the dame no matter what. It's in the movie hero code of honor. You're now an unofficial member of the club." He raised a glass. "Here's to doing the right thing."

Chapter 12

Picture This

When I woke the next morning, I wanted to pinch myself, but I didn't dare. There wasn't an inch of skin that Marco hadn't rubbed to the point of tenderness in our marathon of lovemaking. I couldn't remember ever feeling so contented.

He was amazing. The only reason he'd stopped was because I couldn't take anymore. And he'd intimated that he didn't use any of the new ever-ready erectile dysfunction drugs endlessly advertised on television. He had to be telling the truth, because the men who took the once-a-month pills usually had to resort to wearing codpieces, which looked like decorative athletic cups sewn on the outside crotch area of pants. Nothing like a thirty-day stiffie to bring back twelfth-century fashion.

I couldn't bask in the afterglow for long, though. I had to

get ready for the CRS meeting. Meanwhile, Mel Goldma
called with a report on the bank. Administrators found no rec
ords of my safety deposit box contract. They didn't even ac
knowledge that I was a customer.

This confirmed what I already knew, that I was bein
framed by someone with incredibly powerful connections
Someone powerful enough to tamper with a national bank'
database. I didn't expect the branch employees to remembe
me. Hell, most of them were automated tellers anyway. Bu
my name should have at least popped up on somebody'
computer.

I thanked Mel and went down to apologize to Mike for m
tirade. Normally, I found apologies difficult, but I was eage
to beg his forgiveness. Mike deserved better than I'd give
him last night. I went to his shed and heard the soft dronin
of his Chinese chanting. I hesitated in the doorway. He sat i
a lotus position on his straw floor mat. I must have made
sound, because he opened his eyes, though he didn't stop hi
Om mane padme hum. He gave me a quick wink, then low
ered his eyelids, falling back into his meditative trance.

Mike's ready forgiveness left me grinning in amazemen
and relief. After spending three years as an indentured servan
very little rattled him. In gratitude, I said a silent Hail Mary
followed by a quick thanks to Kuan Yin to cover all the bases
and headed back to the house.

I heard Lola rattling around in her downstairs bedroom, s
I knew she was okay. But I wasn't ready for a mother-daughte
heart-to-heart. Frankly, I found them excruciating. I'd grow
to appreciate Lola's strengths in recent weeks and had trie
very hard to overlook her weaknesses. But it didn't seem lik
she was according me the same favor. I always felt as if I wer
letting her down.

That's one good thing about compubots. They didn't seer

to understand anything about guilt or resentment. Their interactions were refreshingly straightforward.

With that thought in mind, I went into the living room and found Jimmy at the window.

"How's it going? All quiet on the northern front?"

"Shhhh!" he hissed. "Get down! Get down!"

He waved downward so emphatically that I dropped into a squat. "What is it?" I demanded sotto voce.

"That's what I'd like to know," he rasped, rubbing a hand nervously over his perspiring upper lip. He was in a real tizzy. Bogie never perspired. Jimmy must have an upgraded anatospheric program. "This…this…this hooded young man. I've seen him before."

"A hooded man?"

"Yes, it's as if he's trying to hide his identity."

"Maybe he's making a fashion statement." I started to rise.

"Get down! Get down!"

I dropped on my knees without thinking, then took a deep breath. "Jimmy, I'm going into the other room now. Don't panic. I'm going to do a reading on my crystal ball, and I don't want to be interrupted. Just try to be cool, okay?"

"Be cool?" he repeated incredulously. "What does that mean?"

"It means relax."

"Aren't you going to even try and find out who this joker is?"

I let out a beleaguered sigh and marched forward on my knees until I reached his wheelchair, saying, "Give me the binoculars."

I raised my head just far enough over the window ledge to see without being seen. I focused the lenses on the guy standing across the street.

"Oh…my…God."

"What?" Jimmy whispered, leaning toward me. "Who is it?"

I swallowed the lump of dread that had instantly congealed in my throat. "A homicidal maniac." I slowly rose to my feet.

"Don't let him see you!"

"Don't worry," I said in a deadened tone. "He can't see me. He's blind."

Jimmy grabbed the binoculars out of my hands and took a closer look. "Well, I'll be damned. He's facing this way, but you're right. His eyes are a mess. If he's not watching your apartment, why is he just standing there?"

"He wants to intimidate me."

"Why?"

"He's probably planning on killing me."

"Won't that be hard if he can't see you?"

"Not if he has help. Obviously, someone brought him here."

"Maybe the person who killed Roy and Victor?"

I shrugged. "Maybe. But lots of bad guys have used Cy's underground prison. Any of them might be helping him. I'm calling the cops."

That didn't do much good. I found out that Cy had been set free from the Crypt on a technicality. I hung up on the desk sergeant in the middle of his "There's nothing we can do about it, ma'am" speech. How come authorities could never do anything about the true psychopaths of this world but they had no problem holding me accountable for a crime I hadn't committed? I shelved that question beside "What's the meaning of life?"

By the time I hung up, Cy was gone. But I knew he'd be back. A lot of my clients were women who hired me to intimidate restraining order violators, or ROVORS as they were quaintly called. I knew how persistent a stalker could be.

I gave Jimmy one of my digital cameras, since his old-fashioned Kodachrome had been trashed by Marco. Jimmy agreed to take a picture of Cy, or anyone else, who decided to loiter down below. I wasn't going to panic about Cy's visit. Not yet. I'd gather proof that he was staking out my place and then call out the dogs. Or a wolf, if Brad the Impaler was willing to loan me Keshon.

Meanwhile, I set up my crystal scrying ball at the kitchen table. I still felt a little silly using it, but I hadn't yet been able to conjure visions at will without focusing on the ball. I was finally ready to learn more about Marco. Until we made love last night, it had never occurred to me that he might have insecurities, too. I wanted to support him and make him feel accepted, but to do that I needed to understand more about his past than he was prepared to share. I guess I wanted a glimpse of the worst-case scenario so I could keep a straight face when he finally decided to clue me in.

I placed my hands on the grapefruit-sized glass. Immediately, it began to glow, which gave me a boost of confidence. My concentration seemed to improve every time I did this.

Let me see Marco, I thought, and he appeared, fuzzy at first, then clearer.

"Yes, I know Angel Baker," Marco said to someone I couldn't see. *"What of it?"*

"I want you to leave her alone," came a deep voice with a Russian accent. The speaker stepped into view, and I immediately recognized his brusque outline and silver hair.

"Vladimir Gorky," I whispered in shock.

"Why should I leave her alone?" Marco inquired.

"Because I have plans for her. And they don't include you."

I was so shocked I whipped my hands off the glass and pressed them to my gaping mouth. Blood pounded in my ears. What on Earth did Gorky want with me? More important, why hadn't Marco told me he still had contact with the most dangerous man in Chicago?

I reluctantly put my hands back on the crystal. I was both disappointed and relieved to see the scenery had changed. I looked closer and saw an apartment that seemed familiar.

"Getty," I said, finally placing the scene. This was Getty Bellows's place. She was a CRS who lived ten blocks south. I couldn't figure out why this image was important—or even if my psi abilities included any kind of filtering process.

Then it all became clear. I saw Getty in her living room. On the floor. Slaughtered.

I hoofed it the ten blocks to Getty's bungalow because it was faster than hailing a cab. I threw on some joggers and hit the pavement at a dead run, dodging pedestrians, potholes and windblown trash cans. We can send a woman to Mars, I muttered, but we can't invent trash cans that remain upright on a windy day.

I leaped over more than a few, adrenaline lifting me high as I stretched my taut legs over each hurdle. My mind raced even faster than my body.

No, no, no! I thought. *This can't be. My vision was wrong. Getty is okay. I'll get there and realize that my so-called psychic abilities had been nothing more than imagination gone wild. She's probably watching cartoons. I love that about her!*

When you don't know whether someone is dead or alive, you immediately started recalling even their most bizarre habits with fondness. Getty was forty-two-years-old, but she watched kids' shows and dressed in plaid school uniforms, complete with white bobby socks and tennis shoes. She kept her orange hair in braids tied with blue ribbons and applied freckles to her nose with an orange eyebrow pencil. She looked like the psycho president of a Pippi Longstockings' fan club.

The weird thing is, she was one of the most levelheaded

people I knew. She loved kids, and her retribution business specialized in crimes against children. If someone had killed Getty, I'd be *really* pissed off.

I stopped abruptly when I reached her corner lot. A trash can rolled back and forth in front of the steps leading up to her small house. Panting as I caught my breath, wiping away a trickle of perspiration that ran down my temple, I studied the can. Had it been wind tossed or knocked down by an escaping murderer?

Dread rushed through me, congealing like glue on the bottom of my feet, and I walked up the steps with great effort. Each step burned. I felt like I was dragging a freight train behind me. I finally reached the screen door and knocked. I waited. And waited. If she didn't answer soon, I was afraid my heart would leap out of my chest. I knocked again.

"Getty?" I called, opening the screen door when no one answered and stepped in the small entryway. "Are you home?"

A man stepped into my path, towering over me. "She's home."

I jumped and stifled a cry of surprise, then did a double take. "Marco?"

"Hello, Angel."

He sounded so sad I reached out and touched his arm. "What are you doing here, Marco? Where's Getty?"

He swallowed and cleared his throat. "Did you…did you know her well?"

I blinked rapidly. "Yes, I did, I mean I do. We're colleagues. And friends, but not *close*. So, what are you doing here? Where is she?"

When I tried to walk past him, he stepped in my way and gently gripped my arms, bolstering me. In spite of his familiar strength and warmth, I felt cold inside. I pulled away and pushed past Marco, walking down the hallway into the living room. I stopped when I nearly stumbled over Getty's body sprawled on the floor.

I took in several rapid gasps of breath, staggering back. "No! No!" I cried out, then slowly walked to her side, staring down in numb disbelief. It was just as I had foreseen it—horrible then, worse now. More details.

Bullet holes had pockmarked her chest, little geysers, now frozen with blackish blood that stained her navy blue and forest green plaid jumper. A brighter red stained her white lace baby doll collar.

"Ah, shit," I moaned, kneeling at her side. "She deserved better than this."

"Don't touch her," Marco said. "The homicide techs are on their way."

Surprise whipped my head in his direction. Why would he call homicide investigators if he'd murdered Getty? I covered my face with both hands. Jesus, had I really thought, even for a second, that Marco had done this?

"I didn't do it, Angel," he said coolly, as if he didn't really care whether I believed him. "I was on my way to your place when I heard a neighbor's call to the dispatcher. I was simply the first to arrive on the scene."

Sure. Of course. I would never have suspected you capable of such a crime, I wanted to say, but the words stuck in my throat, so I wiped all emotion from my face as I lowered my hands and simply nodded. The damage between us was already done.

"I want to know who did this, Marco. What inhuman, worthless slime would cut down someone as well-meaning as Getty?"

"Very likely that young man right over there."

Marco's nonchalance left me unprepared for what I saw next. He pointed to another dead body I had somehow overlooked, this one sitting at Getty's small dinette table. He looked like he'd lowered his head into his soup bowl to take a nap.

"Who on Earth...?" I slowly approached the frozen figure of a skinny kid who had obviously died at that awkward see-saw stage between childhood and adulthood. Angry splotches of acne marred his otherwise baby-smooth face. A patchy, failed attempt at a goatee scarcely covered his chin. I stepped around the other side of the small table to better view the tableau and saw that he clutched Getty's orange pistol. He'd also violently vomited on the table.

"What happened here?" I muttered. "She was killed with her own weapon?"

Marco came to my side and placed a hand gently on my shoulder. "It looks like he was poisoned. He must have shot her before he died."

"Getty would never have poisoned a kid!" Just as Roy Leibman would never have shot Victor Alvarez. I was beginning to connect the dots to a picture I didn't want to see. "Retributionists are being painted as assassins. Why don't the police realize there's a conspiracy here?"

"I'm sure the detectives who are on duty will be more than willing to skirt the answer on that one. Speaking of," he added ominously, turning me around and giving me a quick good-bye hug, "you'd better get out of here before they arrive. You're in enough trouble already."

"That's an understatement," came the crisp, British-accented voice of Lieutenant Townsend as he stepped into the room. Marco released his hold on me but clasped my hand in his. His loyalty in this moment didn't go unnoticed, by me or Townsend.

"Fancy meeting both of you at a murder scene," the Q.E.D. director said, fixing a pointed look at our hands. "Again."

He gave me an uninspired smile that I in no way felt obligated to return. A phalanx of evidence technicians filed in behind him and began to swarm over the bodies, scanning for injuries, fingerprints, DNA evidence and a host of other high-tech analysis factors. Townsend motioned toward the other end of the house, and we followed him through Getty's kitchen into a small family room.

"We can hear better in here," Townsend said, glancing around with disapproval at the cartoon posters covering Getty's wall.

"This is your fault, Townsend," I said with barely contained fury. "You falsely arrested me for murder, which gave the real murderer plenty of time for a repeat act."

"Oh?" He raised a brow and regarded me with amusement I wasn't sure he could really feel.

"If you hadn't wasted your time charging me with those other murders, you might have been able to find the real killer by now."

"She's right," Marco said. "Angel didn't commit this murder or any others. And now two more innocent people are dead."

"This is a conspiracy," Angel said.

"We'll see about that."

"I was here when she arrived, Lieutenant," Marco said. "I know she's innocent."

"You *know* her in many ways, don't you? Why didn't you tell me you were in a relationship with our suspect in the Alvarez case, Detective Marco?"

"I didn't think it would matter. You clearly had your mind made up that she was guilty from the beginning."

"Are you accusing me of professional bias?"

Marco shrugged. "I suppose I am."

"You're officially off that case," Townsend said, clipping his words. "And I want you to leave now before you contaminate this case as well."

Marco clasped my upper arm. "I'm not leaving without her."

"Letting her go now would be in violation of protocol."

"You can take your protocol and shove it up your bionic ass. You know that if she's in any way questioned for this murder, her bond will be revoked."

Townsend raised his brows in surprise. "Actually, Detective, my ass is completely unaltered. It's my brain that has been improved."

"That's a matter of debate," Marco shot back. "A heartless cop is the worst kind."

"I suppose your brother Danny was full of heart. Isn't that how he got himself killed, by using his heart instead of his head?"

Marco's muscles turn to stone and I sensed he was about to pounce, so I tugged on his arm. He glanced down. I shook my head and he forced himself to relax.

"We'll wait outside," Marco said. "Let us know how the tech scan goes. If you find any evidence connecting Angel to this crime, we can talk again. But if there's nothing, we're leaving."

We went outside, where a dozen evidence technicians, beat cops and homicide detectives buzzed around, gathering evidence, talking to headquarters, cordoning off the sidewalks. Marco led me by the arm to a corner of the yard that was relatively private.

"Why did you admit we were lovers?" I asked. "I thought you wanted to work my case?"

"Not anymore." He scratched the back of his neck and regarded me almost sheepishly. "I hate to admit it, but this is now officially over my head."

I looked at him in horror. "What do you mean?"

"Angel, there is no question that you are embroiled in a huge conspiracy. Now, I have to ask you, and I want you to be totally honest with me—why did you come here today?"

"I saw Getty. I had a vision."

He nodded.

"You believe me, don't you?"

"Of course." He rubbed both my arms reassuringly. "I was the one who encouraged you to develop your psychic skills, remember? But what I think doesn't count."

"Marco, if this is a plot, I can't be the target. Or at least I'm not the only target. How would the murderer know I would have a vision and come here just before the police arrived? The first time I was called to the scene. This time I came on my own."

He broke into a slow, clever grin. "Now that's the best deduction I've heard all day. I couldn't stand for you to be the prime target, Angel. But before we kick up our heels in joy, let's wait and see if the investigators find any Angel Baker memorabilia strategically planted inside Getty's house."

"At least they won't find my gun," I said wryly, "smoking or otherwise. It's still locked up in the evidence vault down at P.S. #1."

"You were right," Townsend said a half hour later as he joined us in the garden. He blinked in the bright sunshine and regarded us almost amiably. I was beginning to think this automaton might have a soul after all.

"You didn't find anything?" Marco asked.

"As much as I hate to admit it, there is not a shred of evidence connecting Miss Baker to this scene. I'm going to let you go."

"Thank you," I said, releasing my pent-up breath. I even conjured a smile. "I appreciate that."

"But not before you tell me how you arrived at this murder scene at such an inopportune time? It couldn't have been coincidence."

I exchanged a look with Marco, wishing I could read his mind. Should I tell Townsend the truth? I'd found from experience that was usually the best policy, but in this case...

"I had a psychic vision of Getty's death," I said, trying to sound businesslike. "I'm...psychic, believe it or not."

Townsend scrutinized me for several moments and said, "I don't believe you."

"Some people are logical," I answered, "and some are intuitive. I was tested by IPAC researchers. The police force uses IPAC-trained psychics all the time, although most of them have been implanted with computer chips to enhance their perceptions. Surely, Lieutenant, you can relate to surgical enhancements."

"I have my doubts about the use of psychics in detective work," he replied. "Logical examination of evidence and unbiased interrogation is all an investigator needs to do his job. You are a sentimentalist who ascribes a lucky, or unlucky, turn of events to innate ability. Your leap of logic is laughable."

"Laugh as you may, Lieutenant," I said gruffly, "the killing has to stop. There are two more murders. Another retributionist and another kid."

"The press will have a heyday with that, I daresay," he replied. "Getty Bellows poisoned a young teen. When he realized he was dying, he killed her with her own weapon. This is the second time in as many days that a retributionist has turned into an assassin, and again the victim is an innocent child. I'd suggest, Miss Baker, that you hire a public-relations consultant in addition to that high-profile defense lawyer of yours. You're going to need both."

I put my hands on my hips and shifted weight as I tried to comprehend the extent of his arrogant and misguided assumptions. "Excuse me, Lieutenant. Can your logical mind wrap around the concept that there might be some sort of conspiracy going on here? Or am I completely wasting my time expecting help from your end?"

He sniffed and looked down his nose at me. "What sort of conspiracy?"

"To frame retributionists for murders they didn't commit and then kill them so they can't expose the truth."

He considered this a moment. "And who do you suppose would be behind such a plot?"

I shrugged with exaggerated ignorance. "Oh, I don't know. Maybe one of the mobs running our fair city? Criminals do tend to consider retributionists like me a real pain in the ass, and Corleone Capone has good reason to want my scalp."

Townsend crooked his mouth in a half smile. "You may be on to something. But I still think you're guilty in the Alvarez murder."

Next NOVEL™

An Important Message from the Editors

ar Reader,

you'd enjoy reading novels about rediscovery nd reconnection with what's important in vomen's lives, then let us send you two free Harlequin® Next™ novels. These books celebrate the "next" stage of a woman's life because there's a whole new world after marriage and motherhood.

By the way, you'll also get a surprise gift with your two free books! Please enjoy the free books and gift with our compliments...

Pam Powers

off Seal and
Place Inside...

EDITOR'S
FREE GIFT
SEAL
THANK YOU

THE EDITOR'S "THANK YOU" FREE GIFTS INCLUDE:

▶ Two BRAND-NEW Harlequin® Next™ Novels

▶ An exciting surprise gift

YES! I have placed my Editor's "thank you" Free Gifts seal in the space provided at right. Please send me 2 FREE books, and my FREE Mystery Gift. I understand that I am under no obligation to purchase anything further, as explained on the back and opposite page.

PLACE FREE GIFTS SEAL HERE

356 HDL D736   156 HDL D72J

FIRST NAME	LAST NAME

ADDRESS

APT.#	CITY

STATE/PROV.	ZIP/POSTAL CODE

Thank You!

Offer limited to one per household and not valid to current subscribers of Harlequin NEXT. All orders subject to approval. Credit or debit balances in a customer's account(s) may be offset by any other outstanding balance owed by or to the customer. ® and ™ are trademarks owned and used by the trademark owner and/or its licensee. © 2005 Harlequin Enterprises Ltd.

(HN-SA-11/05)

The Reader Service — Here's How It Works:

Accepting your 2 free books and gift places you under no obligation to buy anything. You may keep the books and gift and return the shipping statement marked "cancel." If you do not cancel, about a month later we'll send you 3 additional books and bill you just $3.99 each in the U.S., or $4.74 each in Canada, plus 25¢ shipping & handling per book and applicable taxes if any.* That's the complete price and — compared to cover prices of $5.50 each in the U.S. and $6.50 each in Canada — it's quite a bargain! You may cancel at any time, but if you choose to continue, every month we'll send you 3 more books, which you may either purchase at the discount price or return to us and cancel your subscription.

*Terms and prices subject to change without notice. Sales tax applicable in N.Y. Canadian residents will be charged applicable provincial taxes and GST.

If offer card is missing write to: The Reader Service, 3010 Walden Ave., P.O. Box 1867, Buffalo, NY 14240-1867

BUSINESS REPLY MAIL
FIRST-CLASS MAIL   PERMIT NO. 717-003   BUFFALO, NY

POSTAGE WILL BE PAID BY ADDRESSEE

THE READER SERVICE
3010 WALDEN AVE
PO BOX 1867
BUFFALO NY 14240-9952

NO POSTAGE
NECESSARY
IF MAILED
IN THE
UNITED STATES

Chapter 13

Date with the Devil

Marco drove me the short distance to my home. On the way we talked a little bit about Getty's murder, then fell silent. I think we both wanted to forget about it, if only briefly. It was all getting to be too much. There was only so much bad news a person could take before tuning out on some level.

Instead, I focused on the interior of Marco's hydrocruiser. Unlike aerocars, which hovered just above the pavement, hydrogen-powered cruisers had wheels. Marco had purchased it used, but it was fancier than his previous SUV, which I had accidentally destroyed. The polyurospandicottonastic seats of this vehicle were plusher, and I settled in to enjoy the comfort.

When Marco pulled up in front of my two-flat, something was different. It took me about ten seconds to realize what.

"How about that?" I mused as my seat belt unfolded. "The press has finally given up."

"For now," Marco amended as he glanced around the quiet neighborhood and killed the engine. "They'll be back as soon as they hear about Getty."

"You're right." I turned slightly in my seat and allowed my eyes to feast momentarily on Marco's physique. I hadn't really taken a good look at his outfit until now.

He wore a retro short-sleeved, sky-blue shirt with pressed mother-of-pearl studs, taupe twill pants that hugged his muscular legs and a bullet gray Aussie outback bush hat. He looked tanned, rugged and casual. I guess he was enjoying a day off.

Smiling, I said, "You look like Harrison Ford in *Indiana Jones*." I reached across the seat and grabbed his hand. Heat warmed my palm and the air thickened like soup on a slow burner. I could make love to him right now. Hell, I could make love to him in the middle of a three-ringed circus.

"I look like *who* in *what*?"

"Harrison Ford." I chuckled at his blank reaction. "Never mind. I forgot that you don't watch movies."

"I do. But only ones that have come out in the past fifty years."

"You don't know what you're missing. The black-and-whites are the best."

"Why?"

"I guess because you have to color them with your own imagination. With movies today, all you have to do is strap yourself into a hydraulic seat that moves with every action. The olfactory and sensory effects leave nothing to the imagination. And now, with hologram-in-the-round, you may as well be *in* the movie instead of watching it."

"I think that's the point, Angel."

I smiled at his gentle sarcasm. "I know, I'm such a fuddy-duddy. I guess I like to make things hard for myself. Somehow life seems more meaningful when you have to put in some effort on your own."

"That explains a lot," he said, teasing.

Simultaneously, we sighed and tilted our heads against the headrests, becoming lost in each other's eyes.

"Marco?"

"Hmm?"

"I really, *really* loved making love with you."

"Likewise," was his husky reply.

"You really know how to make a woman feel…good." I almost said *loved,* but after I had momentarily suspected him of murdering Getty, it seemed hypocritical to mention the *L* word.

"You're pretty damned good yourself."

His words flattered, but the barely contained hunger gleaming in his eyes thrilled. I felt like a vamp. He leaned forward in slow motion, each millimeter a lost battle for self-control.

"I can't resist you," he groaned, then murmured with a hot breath in my ear, "I want you, Angel."

"I want you, too," I whispered, shivering and nestling my ear to his caressing mouth. "But we have miles to go before we sleep."

He rubbed his sandpapery chin lightly along my cheekbone, inhaling my scent, but managed to pull himself back no more than a second before I was going to give in.

"Okay. You're right." With a sigh of resignation, he resumed his position in the driver's seat, gripping the wheel with an almost comical look of determination. "We can't make love now. I'm glad one of us can resist temptation."

"Right," I said without enthusiasm. "I'm going to meet with my colleagues. We'll be hit from all sides with this latest double homicide. Anything you can tell me about your committee efforts to shut us down?"

He pushed his hat back and eyed me speculatively. "I can't reveal anything confidential. But I can tell you my committee members are out for blood now that you've been charged. They think this is the perfect opportunity to demand action from legislators, and they're right."

"What are you going to do about it?"

He smiled wanly. "For your sake, nothing. At least not now. But you know where I stand, Angel. As soon as your name has been cleared, our little truce will be over."

I nodded, not happy that Marco was still camped out in enemy territory, but grateful that he was cutting me some slack when I needed it most.

"I understand. By the way, Cyclops was staking out my place earlier today. He was released from jail on a technicality."

"Cyclops?" The muscles in Marco's square jaw tightened. "He wants to kill you, Angel."

I raised my hands in a *je ne sais quoi* gesture. "Who knows? Maybe he's bluffing." After a dead pause, I said, "It's a joke. Blind man's bluff. Get it?"

"I get it," Marco said, but he didn't laugh.

Neither did I.

When I went upstairs, I found Lola trying on outfits for Jimmy Stewart. Open clothing boxes littered the couch, chairs and coffee table. I entered just as Lola came out of the bathroom in a sleeveless white beaded formal gown. Her arms looked like deflated beige balloons.

Jimmy made a wolf whistle. "Now that's a good-looking dame if I ever saw one."

I wondered if he ever had seen a good-looking dame. At the very least the image of Grace Kelly, who co-starred in

Rear Window, had been imprinted in his memory bank. But my mother was a far cry from Princess Grace.

From Lola's fringed hem to her ample and glittering table-top of a bosom, she looked darned good for a sixty-year-old recovering alcoholic and ex-con. Whoever had done her makeup, though, should be shot. It was so thick it looked like somebody's final project for a PhD in Mortuary Science.

"You like?" Lola said coyly, doing a pirouette on high heels that bound her feet better than any three-inch Lotus slipper could.

"Looking at you is enough to make a man wish he wasn't in a leg cast, Lola honey," Jimmy said. He turned to my Personal Listening Device in the corner. "What do you think, Gigi? Isn't she something?"

The eyes on the PLD opened in an instant, going from the human equivalent of a deep sleep to fascination in seconds flat. It gave me the creeps, which is one of several reasons why I never used the darned thing.

"What do you think of this outfit, Gigi?" Jimmy asked.

"It's beautiful," the robotic device said in an eternally buoyant voice. Her head turned toward the compubot. "You're right, Mr. Stewart, she is something."

I pinched the bridge of my nose as it hit me. My PLD was having a conversation with my compubot. My world really had spun hopelessly out of control.

"All right, let's break up the love fest," I said, revealing my presence in the shadows of the doorway.

"Oh! Angel!" Lola said. Her self-satisfied grin faded. "I didn't know you were back."

"I'm sure you didn't, or you would have had this little fashion show downstairs. Come to think of it, why don't you and Jimmy use the elevator and get this stuff out of here?"

"What do you think of my dress, honey?"

I grudgingly gave her a closer look, and she worried her lower lip, awaiting my approval.

It touched me and made me mad at the same time. We were hopelessly codependent.

"It's…nice." I couldn't bring myself to say anything more positive than that.

"You think it's too much?"

"I didn't say that."

"But you thought it."

"Lola," I said in a slow, threatening voice, "don't start."

"Honey, I just—"

"Wait a minute, I just thought of something. Where did you get the money to buy these things?"

She puckered her fire-engine red lips and pinched her heavily blushed cheeks. "As a matter of fact, I have an admirer. He's picking me up tonight to go dancing."

I tried to keep a straight face. However unlikely a boyfriend might be, it was possible. To me, Lola looked like Delta Dawn of the Dead, but I knew she had a way with men. Her enthusiasm was infectious, and she loved games—especially poker.

Still, she wasn't exactly trophy-wife material. Whoever she'd hooked up with had to be not only rich but a geezer as well. She'd probably been staking out the skilled nursing facility over on Waveland Avenue.

Twenty years ago, when Lola was on trial for bookmaking, prosecutors revealed that she'd managed to talk three elderly gentlemen into naming her executor of their estates. Turned out they were broke, but Lola didn't know that at the time.

Five years ago she informed me out of the blue that I had a new grandfather. She'd managed to get herself adopted by a billionaire only ten years her senior. But a year later when Gramps died, his relatives contested his revised will and Lola was left with nothing but disappointed fantasies. She could have saved herself a lot of trouble if she'd simply bought a losing lottery ticket instead.

"What?" Lola said, crossing her arms and frowning at me.

"What what?"

"Why are you looking at me like that?"

"Like what?" I asked.

"You're frowning at me in disapproval."

"Honestly, Lola, you're way too sensitive. I just don't think you should be buying all these clothes when you have no money."

"Don't be too hard on her," Jimmy said, waving me off with an amiable smile. "She deserves it."

"Yes, she deserves it," the PLD parroted.

"That's right!" Lola smoothed her hands over the glittering beads. "Besides, this has nothing to do with you."

"As long as you're living in my apartment—" I stopped abruptly when I realized I was sounding like her mother. I held my hands out, trying to get my mind into the right frame. "Just be careful. Okay?"

"Sure, honey," Lola said much too quickly. Scooping up a box, she singsonged over her shoulder, "Come along, James. I'm going downstairs to try on the pièce de résistance. Take the elevator and bring the rest of my clothes."

"Sure, doll," he replied.

I waited until I heard her stilettos spiking their way down the wooden steps, then I went to Jimmy's side and said in a low voice, "I want you to keep an eye on her."

"On Lola?"

"That's right. See who she's going out with tonight. Give me a full description. Better yet, take a photograph."

He pursed his lips and pressed them against his steepled fingers, giving my suggestion a great deal of thought. "You're suspicious of your own mother?"

Was I? I suppose I was. I didn't think Lola would intentionally betray me, but it was possible she'd taken money in exchange for another television interview. She might have been contacted by one of the national daytime talk shows. Maybe this date of hers was really an appointment with a producer.

"I don't know, Jimmy. I just want to be careful."

The hint of intrigue in my voice was of more importance to his program than the hots he'd momentarily kindled for Lola. He reached out and shook my hand.

"You have a deal," Jimmy said. "You can count on me."

"Thanks." I started to walk toward the back of the flat, but realized Gigi was watching me with those perfect topaz glass eyes of hers. I scowled in return. "What are you looking at?"

"You," she said in her equally perfect and serene cadence. "You look lovely today, Angel."

I looked questioningly to Jimmy. "I thought PLDs were only supposed to respond to direct questions."

"It's an updated model. I set it to random-sequence-voice-activation mode. The newest programs allow for conversation initiation."

"I'm turning it off, and I want it to stay that way." I marched around the back of the head-and-shoulders unit and flipped the switch. "I have more than enough chaos in my life as it is without adding her—its—two cents into the mix."

"Aye-aye, Captain," Jimmy returned with a tolerant smile. When he flipped two fingers off his slicked-back hairline in a mock salute, I left the room shaking my head.

Men! You can't live with them. Even if they're robots.

Chapter 14

Meeting of the Minds

The CRS meeting was just north of Irving Park Road on Clark Street, near historic Graceland Cemetery. The spacious 119 acres of rolling grass and trees and an idyllic pond contained the remains of Chicago's original power brokers. Names like Marshall Field, George Pullman and Potter Palmer graced mausoleums that looked like miniature Parthenons.

I always enjoyed the sense of history as I passed by the tall, stone walls that enclosed these ancient graves. I liked to think my life would be worthy of a mausoleum. But when I died, my remains would probably be cremated and pressed into a man-made diamond and wind up in some resale shop. At least that's what would happen if I predeceased Lola. If for some reason I did end up with a headstone, I'd be on a budget, so I'd need a pithy epithet. So far I'd settled on, "No Comment."

I arrived at the CRS meeting just as Mickey Larson, the head of our organization, waved his hands overhead at the podium, trying to command order from the buzzing confab. Mickey was a short, squat man whose face looked like it had been broken and glued back together. He was both tough and humble and prone to wincing with impatience, as he did now.

"Okay, okay," he shouted in a gravelly voice, "everybody take a seat!"

About one hundred of our colleagues milled around, commiserating over recent events, catching up, sharing new weapons and combat techniques. By nature, retributionists tended to be loners, so we crammed a lot of socializing into these rare get-togethers.

I stood just inside of the doorway, indulging in a few moments of anonymous sentimentality. Aware that our very profession was at stake, I savored the camaraderie. Those who spotted me gave me a hug or a word of encouragement. I welcomed the support and relished the rich and exotic blend of personalities. Getty Bellows hadn't been the only odd egg to excel in this business.

There was a retributionist who called herself Mae West. She wore a white wig, a black sequin dress and a boa constrictor around her neck. Mae was dating a guy who called himself Kent Clark, a sort of reverse Superman. He wore a red cape in his off-hours and put on a conservative suit and brass knuckles for retribution jobs.

DCR was an incorporated group of four men about my age who modeled themselves after Dead Corpse Rising, a band that was popular about thirty years ago.

At the moment all I wore was the blue dragon tattoo on my forehead. Tory Rockwell was a twenty-two-year-old knockout who looked like a football cheerleader. She used her all-American smile, blond hair and sweet disposition to seduce criminals to locations she'd arranged with her clients.

Of course, there were lots of retributionists who didn't need to adopt iconic personalities in order to command respect. Roy had been your average middle-aged white guy who used his intelligence more than his fists, although he had been a boxer when he was younger. His generation rarely used costumes or alter-identities. My generation had picked up the costume trend from New Orleans, which set the CRS trends for the rest of the country. There was no question that an intimidating prop or outfit could help give you the upper hand. But Roy had never needed that.

Stupidly, I glanced around the hall, looking for him, then shook my head, trying to comprehend that I would never see Roy again. I realized that my mentors and professional friends were more than half the reason I stayed in this business. Without them, I'm not sure I'd continue.

"Okay, that's enough!" Mickey shouted. "Quiet down now. It's time to get started."

This time, the crowd quieted and everybody sat in the rows of chairs Mickey had set up. I lingered in the darkened rear of the studio, giving quick hugs to the few who noticed me. As soon as I took a seat in the back row, a shadow loomed over me. Then two fangs bit into my neck at the carotid artery, not breaking the skin but coming damned close. Expensive cologne flooded my nostrils.

"Brad!" Out of my mouth, his name was a four-letter curse word. Already he'd broken our agreement. I rammed my elbow back in a blind attempt to sock his gonads.

Apparently anticipating this, he caught my elbow, kissed me where he'd pretended to draw blood, chuckled and sauntered over to the empty seats on the other side of the aisle.

With Keshon, his familiar at his side, Brad slouched into a chair, thrust his hands in his skintight jeans, spread his knees wide and tossed his head back to listen to the proceedings with a bored expression. I wasn't sure if his eyes were even open behind his too-cool sunglasses until he caught me staring and waved.

I turned my head forward, pretending not to notice.

"I've been in the retribution business for nearly thirty years," Mickey began, rubbing his hands together in the spotlight. "This is the worst I have ever seen it. You all know about Roy."

At the mention of Roy, someone began to cry. It was something I'd never heard from a CRS before, and it gave me goose bumps. It was easy to be hard and fearless when you weren't confronted with the realities of death. But Roy and Getty had shown us just how high the stakes were in this game we played.

"I've been in touch with Connie Leibman. She gave me information on Roy's funeral arrangements, which I'll pass out at the end of the meeting. Obviously, we're all devastated by Roy's death. Unfortunately, I have more bad news. Some of you may not have heard about Getty Bellows."

"What happened to Getty?" Kent called out.

In a somber voice, Mickey shared the details, then said, "I'm going to ask Angel Baker to come up here and talk to us, since she's obviously involved in both these tragedies. We all know that Angel has been set up. Now it's time to figure out how we're going to find out who is responsible. But before I do, I want to talk a little about what we do, and why we do it."

I looked around and saw that everyone listened with rapt attention. I think we all needed a pep talk.

"To be a retributionist, you have to have a lot of heart. You put your life on the line every day just to make sure that crime victims receive some sort of justice, whether it's just an apology or some kind of payback. To that end, you have to be a little fearless.

"The burnout rate in our job is high. Some lose their courage. Some come to realize they enjoy scaring the hell out of people just a little too much. Still others become discouraged because no matter how many of us there are, we're never going to conquer man's inhumanity to man."

A few heads nodded as we absorbed Mickey's words of wisdom.

"Now, some of you were pumped up recently when Judge Gibson started issuing execution warrants on ROVOR cases. Suddenly, you discovered we could prevent crimes against the innocent, not just react to crimes already committed. The Gibson Warrants increased our effectiveness, but they also raised our public profile. Where once we were considered a small band of vigilantes, distantly admired by the average citizen and barely tolerated by the police, we suddenly became assassins in the eyes of a lot of folks."

That was true. Judge Gibson's new unilateral policy had sent shockwaves through the entire city and thrust retributionists further into the limelight. Disgusted with all the restraining order violators, or ROVORs, who were murdering their talking victims, Gibson started giving out warrants enabling retributionists to kill any ROVOR caught on a repeat order violation. The power to legally kill excited some retributionists who saw it as the only way to protect ROVOR victims. I, personally, was troubled by the idea.

"So what?" Tory called out as she rose from her seat, tossing back her curly blond hair. "I would never use a warrant, but I applaud those who do, if it saves the life of an abuse victim."

There was a grumble of agreement. Mickey held up his hands to quiet the group. "I know some of you feel that way, and I'm not taking a firm stance. I'm just saying that it might be significant that these murders happened after we started crossing the line between seeking justice for crimes alread committed and killing in order to prevent them."

Mae stood up and thrust out her rolling hip, planting he arms akimbo. Her boa twisted around her neck, finding more comfortable position, its forked tongue darting nov and then. "Listen here, big boy, you've got it all wrong That's like blaming a rape victim for wearing a prett dress."

"No, no, Mae," Mickey countered, shaking his head, "yo misunderstood me. Look, we can debate philosophies som other time. Right now we have to figure out what's going o and protect ourselves. Angel, why don't you come up here an tell us what you know."

I walked up the aisle to the podium with as much enthus asm as if I were walking the plank.

"First, let me say I am so sorry to all of you for the pass ing of Roy and Getty." I paused to swallow the dull ache i my throat. "I know many of you cared for them, as I did. wish I could have prevented their deaths, but I still don't eve understand what we're dealing with here. One thing is clea we have to work together if we're going to prevent any mor deaths, because I'm convinced that we, as retributionists, ar being targeted in a well-funded, high-powered conspirac that may go to the very top echelons of the city government

Exclamations of disbelief and anger broke the crowd's si lence. When they returned their attention to me, I continued

"I took the liberty of inviting Brad the Impaler to this mee ing. Many of you know him from New Orleans. Brad, woul you stand up, please?"

He did so like a reluctant movie star caught unawares the New Cannes Cyber Film Festival. He nodded and flashe his fanged smile, then slouched back in his seat. It was all could do not to roll my eyes.

"Brad has graciously offered to help us get to the bottom
f this problem, which unquestionably threatens the entire
rofession. Hopefully, as an outsider, he'll be able to offer us
different perspective."

I went on to share some of the details of both murder
ases that hadn't been mentioned in the press. We debated
arious scenarios and ideas. At one point or another during
ur impromptu brainstorming session, just about everyone
resent offered to help me with my investigation, either by
oing legwork themselves or by loaning out their private in-
estigators.

"So we're all in agreement," I said in conclusion, "that we
an't rely on homicide detectives to get to the bottom of this."

"No shit, Sherlock," one of the DCR guys replied, then
aughed like he was high on something other than life.

I smiled. "So, we have a game plan. We need to—"

A retributionist I didn't recognize called out from the back
f the studio, "Hey, the media has arrived, everybody."

"Great," I muttered to myself, then said to Mickey, "I guess
t was inevitable."

"Our meetings aren't exactly like conventions of the Milk
oast Society," he said with a rumbling laugh. "We tend to at-
ract attention wherever we go en masse. I'll go talk to them."

"Brad's talking to the TV stations now," the messenger in
he back added.

I shared a speculative look with Mickey. "Maybe that's
vhy he offered to help," I said. "Brad can't resist the lime-
ght. You think?"

Before Mickey could answer, another person burst in, vi-
lently shoving aside the messenger. I recognized him imme-
iately and gripped Mickey's arm.

"What's the matter, Angel? You know this guy?"

I nodded in slow motion. "Oh, yeah. That's Cyclops."

Chapter 15

Wait until Dark

"'**N**ow is the winter of our discontent made glorious summer by this sun of York!'" Cy shouted from the back of the hall. "'And all the clouds that lour'd upon our house in the deep bosom of the ocean buried! You do me wrong and I will not endure it!'"

Cy's melodramatic declaration was followed by absolute and complete silence. Dressed as he was in a relatively normal pullover cotton jacket, with his scarred, bald head tucked under the hood, no one else recognized him, even though several of the more experienced retributionists had run into him on visits to Emerald City.

"Angel Baker!" Cy shouted. "You have ruined my life and now I'm going to ruin yours."

With that simple declaration, he left. The door hadn't even

...nged closed behind him when I took off, racing down the ...ain aisle, ignoring the questions and suggestions coming ...om my confused colleagues.

"Don't you run away!" I shouted after him. "Cy! Get back here!"

I shoved the doors open, stunning the reporters crowded ...ound Brad on the sidewalk. I saw Cy disappear around the ...rner of the building and tore after him.

"Keshon, go!" Brad commanded his wolf.

I hesitated only a moment when I reached the edge of the ...ilding and realized that Cy had run into a pitch-black maze ...construction scaffolding. It filled a neighboring site that had ...parently been entirely gutted for remodeling. In the dark, ...y blind opponent would definitely have the advantage.

Keshon loped to my side and looked up at me, as if to say ...ome on, I'll lead the way." When he trotted in the build-...g, I followed.

I kept a hand on the wolf's back, trusting it entirely to lead ...e somewhere. Anywhere. Filled with sawdust, broken plas-... and bird dung, the air was dark, suffocating and hot. Sweat ...on drenched my clothing, partly from the stifling heat, but ...so from nerves. It was nice of Brad to send in his alter iden-...y, but it would be even nicer if he had volunteered to fol-...w us in.

I had to believe the wolf was working on some kind of ...ent, because he took a series of abrupt turns that I would ...herwise have never even known existed. If Cy was still in ...e building, he had chosen not to reveal himself. I heard ...thing but my own steps. We finally stopped when we ...ched the back end of the building.

"That clever little devil," I muttered, squatting and look-...g out of an old air shaft that opened to the light of day. The ...ent of freshly cut grass was a welcome reprieve for my

clogged lungs. "He's gone, Keshon. He must have crawled o
just before we got here. But thanks anyway."

I didn't expect the wolf to respond, and certainly not wit
an ominous growl. I stood slowly, trying not to look frigh
ened, and glanced down to see if the wolf was getting read
to attack me. What I saw scared me even more than I alread
was. Keshon's gray, narrow snout, snarling with her inna
need to viciously tear apart the enemy, pointed to someon
or something, in the darkness. She'd dropped her shoulder
preparing to pounce.

"Who's there?" I called out. No response. "Show yourself

And he did. Unfortunately, I couldn't even see my ow
hand in front of my face. And I certainly didn't see the fis
dense as a brick, that plowed into my right eye.

"Ah!" I cried out as I staggered back, knocking my hea
hard against a bare concrete wall. If it was possible to se
black in pitch blackness, I saw it as consciousness started t
fade. *No!* I commanded myself. If I didn't win this fight I'
be dead. I could tell by the savageness of the blow. It sudden
occurred to me that Cy was just the bait. I'd chased him int
a trap.

As I doubled over and wretched from a combination o
pain and disequilibrium, I heard Keshon snarl, snap an
growl. She'd finally found her enemy. Clothing ripped.
man gave a deep-chested curse of outrage, then a howl of pai
Scaffolding rattled as man and beast flailed. I grabbed a co
metal bar and hung on, determined not to pass out.

After a moment that seemed suspended in time, I finall
recovered, blinking in the darkness to see if Keshon was win
ning or losing. When they fell in an embattled embrace i
front of the air vent, I could finally see what I was up agains

A Shadowman. His stringy, shoulder-length hair fell arour
shoulders so broad and scantily clad that he could have starre

in the old Hercules movies. He had a radio face, though, I noticed when he twisted his head next to the vent, trying to keep Keshon's snapping teeth away from his throat. Someone had smashed his nose nearly as flat as a pancake. Scars mottled his cheeks. He was missing a few teeth.

In an instant I surmised what an interrogation would later reveal. This was one of the Shadowmen who had been on Cy's payroll, helping him run his underground prison. Normally these inarticulate, rat-eating, jack-booted thugs lived with an underground gang, but occasionally a freelance contract brought them aboveground.

In one monumental show of strength, my would-be assassin threw the wolf through the air. I heard it land with a sickening thud and a whimper in the distance. Then he grabbed my ankle, yanking me down onto the concrete floor.

I cursed and twisted out of his grip. It was time to use all the techniques that I'd learned from my wushu mentor. The only problem was that I couldn't judge distance in the dark. My opponent was used to working in shadows, as his gang's name implied.

Mike might have been able to beat him by going into some zen trance, anticipating his moves on some unspoken, unseen level. I couldn't quite get my act together. I kicked into the darkness where I'd last seen him but there was only air.

The thug grabbed my ankle again, lifting me up. I slammed down on my back, banging my head. I heard a scraping noise that sounded ominously like the spikes of a medieval-style cudgel dragging along the concrete floor. If it was hard for this powerful brute to pick up, it would be a thick steel ball that could crush my skull with one blow. I'd seen them in Cy's cave prison.

I rolled hard to the right, but before I could flip up into the air, a boot stomped down on my solar plexus, knocking the wind out of me, pinning me like a live butterfly to a hobby board.

"Die, bitch!"

Finally, my own zenlike senses had kicked into high gear. I knew without seeing that he had raised the cudgel over his head and was about to hammer it down onto my head, making mincemeat of my brain.

Suddenly, Keshon's growl cut through the air. I never thought I'd be happy to hear a wolf about to attack. When she did, the Shadowman rasped in pain. The cudgel thudded to the floor. I squirmed out from under his foot and tackled his legs.

He struggled to keep the wolf from his throat. I should have had the advantage, but this guy was one determined son of a bitch, and his survival instincts were far more honed than his intellect. He'd been inbred to brutal perfection. He threw off the wolf for a second time, then peeled my arms from around his legs and began to fling me around like a doll, up against a steel support beam, a stack of wooden pallets, then into the back wall, which was mercifully made of wood.

He's going to kill me, I thought. It was a quiet, certain notion. Oddly, it didn't bother me as much as the idea of disappointing Mike. He would want me to win this fight. I couldn't give in now. If only Brad would come. I needed help.

As soon as the words formed in my mind, a light swarmed into my bleary sight, suspended in the air, growing stronger as it neared.

"Stop!" a theatrical voice commanded. "Let her go!"

"Brad!" I called out. Thank God.

"Keshon, hold!" he thundered in an impressive voice. The wolf released its hold on the remarkably resilient Shadowman and trotted to its master's side. The Shadowman let go of my arm, and I fell to the floor in a puddle of bloody scrapes and aching bruises.

"Who are you?" asked my attacker.

Confusion and awe softened his guttural voice. I was impressed myself. I'd never seen Brad in action. His cape shone with dozens of little lights that I had assumed were only sequins. He was as bright as a walking used-car sign. Not only did his illuminated cape enable him to see us, the light cast long shadows on his face. With his hair spiked straight up, his pale skin eerily aglow, and his pointy eyeteeth bared, he looked like Dracula. The slack-jawed Shadowman apparently agreed. Sort of.

"Are you Frankenstein?" His slow, choppy cadence made him sound like Bela Lugosi in the eponymous movie's title role.

Brad's lips twisted with disdain. *What an idiot,* he would be thinking. Some people were just too stupid to scare. Then again, Shadowmen barely qualified as people.

"I am Brad the Impaler," he said ominously, "but you may call me Dracula. Now, be a good shit-for-brains and back up to the wall behind you, very slowly."

I could almost see the wheels churning, ever so slowly, behind the Shadowman's overhanging forehead. His confusion transmogrified to manly belligerence.

"Fuck!" he shouted without finesse, leaving us to wonder which of the roughly twenty-seven different meanings of the word he was using.

"That's cool," Brad said, raising a miniature crossbow from the folds of his cape. "I have just the right implement. Where do you want it?"

The Shadowman and I both gaped at the vicious little device. It consisted of a steel bow and metal arrow mounted perpendicularly on a sophisticated and, doubtless, powerful firing mechanism, all of which was strapped onto Brad's forearm. The trigger was mounted below the weapon on a pistollike grip that fit snugly in his hand.

"If I give up," the thug said, "you won't kill me?"

"Aw, man," Brad moaned, shaking his head. "You gonna

give up that easy? And I wanted to rip this baby straight through your heart."

The Shadowman didn't quite know how to respond. Showing more good judgment than I'd given him credit for, he raised his arms in surrender and backed up to the wooden wall, as Brad had instructed.

"Very good," Brad said as if to a dog in an obedience class. "Back up a little more. Keep your hands above your head. That's right. Back up just a tad more and...perfect!"

Brad raised the crossbow with swift precision and fired. The arrow whistled through the air and thwomped into the Shadowman's right palm, nailing his hand to the wall.

"Ahhh!" the big thug shrieked, looking at his crucified limb in horror, then regarding Brad as if he were Judas. "You said—"

"I said I wouldn't kill you, you stupid dick," Brad said. "I didn't say I wouldn't impale you."

He slipped the weapon off his arm and reached down to help me up. "Angel, I'm so sorry I didn't come sooner."

"Jesus, Brad," I said, wincing as he placed my hand around his shoulder and hoisted me up, "you just...nailed the guy to a wall."

"Hey, my sweet, anything for you. No need to thank me."

I didn't say another word. If Brad hadn't taken such a drastic step, this guy would probably have killed us both.

"Looks like I got here just in time. I was trying to keep the press away, and that little shit Cyclops closed off the entrance after you and Keshon went inside. He must have been hiding near the entrance. He had obviously planned this one out."

"He had to have help," I said, wincing in agony when he hoisted me up.

"You okay?"

I nodded and bit back a moan, breathing deeply instead as

Mike had taught me. "Yeah. We have to find out who helped a blind man and a Neanderthal plot this attack. It had to be somebody who knew about the meeting."

"It's a damned good thing you have an outsider here to do a little poking around."

"By the way, you're wrong," I said, leaning heavily on him for support. "I do need to thank you."

He flashed me a sexy smile and grabbed my butt. "Oh. Good. I know just the way for you to do it."

I smiled. Clever boy. He knew I was too weak to knee him where it would really count. And he knew my behind had enough padding to ensure it was the only place he could grab without causing me more pain.

After filing a report with the police, I stopped by a drive-through doc-in-a-box shop to make sure I hadn't broken anything more serious than my pride. Mickey insisted on playing the chauffeur. I had some bruised ribs, too many contusions and lacerations to count, and a long cut on my neck that required laser stitching. Otherwise, my bones miraculously had remained intact.

On the way home, I was groggy and thankful that I felt virtually nothing, thanks to the wonders of modern medicine. I must have passed out in Mickey's car, because when I came to, I was stretched out comfortably on my couch in the living room. I lazily inhaled the delicious scent of moo goo gai pan and egg foo yung. A familiar voice brought a smile to my lips, though I couldn't quite place it.

"I think she's coming to. Hey, sis, are you awake?"

I pried open my eyes through sheer determination and found Hank leaning over me. I combed my fingers through his wavy, red bangs. "Yes, Hanky, I'm fine."

He laughed with obvious relief that I was well enough to

tease him with an old and hated nickname and sat on the edge of the couch. "Mike said to tell you he'll be back later. He went to old China Town to get some herbs that he says will help you heal faster."

I nodded. Mike was not only a friend and mentor, he sometimes took on the role of nursemaid.

Hank then frowned. "When your friend pulled you out of that building, I thought you weren't going to make it. Jesus, Angel, you really scared me."

I breathed shallowly to avoid the pain in my battered chest. "I'm sorry, Hank. Sorry that you were there to see it. I was scared, too."

He blinked back what I suspected was an imagined scene of my demise, then said, "You'll be happy to know we diverted a horde of reporters from your doorstep. Everybody wanted an exclusive with you."

"You're a magician," I said, coughing to clear my throat, then wincing at the sharp chest pain that resulted. Hank offered me a sip of water, holding the glass to my parched mouth. It was cool and delicious. "Thanks. How did you get rid of the media frenzy?"

"I sent them to your lawyer's office. I called and warned him, giving him the lowdown. He said he'd make some kind of statement."

"That was nice of him."

"Hey, sis, it's the least he can do for ten million. Soji and I brought some dinner. Why don't you try to eat?" He fluffed up the pillow tucked under my head.

I managed to sit upright, though every inch of my body protested with mutinous spikes of pain. "I have never hurt so much in my entire life."

Soji entered from the kitchen, carrying a tray a steaming Chinese food. "Hi, Soj. How are you?"

"The question of the hour is how are *you?*" She placed the tray on the coffee table in front of me and gave me one of her knock-out smiles that had, along with her killer instincts, won her a new multiyear reporting contract with WFFY-TV. That's where she'd met Hank.

In a way, they looked like a mismatched pair. She was nearly six feet tall, as thin as a clothing store manikin, and boasting a luscious caramel candy complexion. She really stood out in a crowd. Plus, she had a rich and creamy voice with a slight colonial British accent.

Hank, on the other hand, was just another overgrown descendant of Irish elves—a charming and handsome, slightly freckled and huggable fellow who stood five foot nine.

I was happy to see them both, and even happier that they'd brought food.

"I just realized I'm famished, and I always enjoy Soji's cooking."

"Chinese is one of my specialties," she replied, filling a plate and handing it to me so I wouldn't have to reach.

"Chinese take-out, that is," Hank added.

"I also make very good reservations." She winked at me, and I appreciated the fact that she wasn't cooing over me as if I were an invalid.

We chatted as we ate, filling in the gaps over the day's dramatic events. Soji had been covering the CRS meeting for WFFY and witnessed the chaos that followed my attack. When she realized I was the victim, she handed over the story to a colleague, called Hank, and they helped get me into an ambulance. She then made some calls to find out what was happening with the Shadowman.

The police arrested him, but he refused to point the finger at Cy. There were plenty of retributionists from the meeting who could testify that Cy had threatened Angel, and that was enough to have him put back in jail. But authorities held out little hope of finding him.

"I've never seen such a vicious attack," Soji shook her head. "It's a wonder you're still alive, Angel."

"You didn't exactly see it, Soj," Hank amended.

I let out a rueful chuckle. "I didn't even see it. But I certainly felt it."

"That retributionist from New Orleans was quite the hero," Soji said as she leaned over the coffee table and helped herself to seconds. She could eat a Green Bay Packer under the table and never gain a pound. I swear she had a hollow leg. Soji sat down with a full plate and eyed me curiously, putting on her reporter's cap. "Who is he? How do you know him?"

"His name is Brad the Impaler."

Hank's pale eyebrows curled doubtfully. "With a name like that, he must be a nice guy."

"He's a good-looking guy, anyway," Soji said, then gave me one of those needling woman-to-woman looks. "He seemed very concerned about you, Angel. Are you...dating?"

Laughter burst out just as I swallowed a bite of egg roll and I choked. I slugged down half a glass of water before I could breathe again, then raised an index finger, begging another minute.

"We'll take that as a no," Hank translated for me, laughing.

"Or," Soji said, "it's a 'No, but I'd *like* to be dating him, though I'll never admit it.'"

"Ah, yes," Hank said, "you're using that 'reading between the lines' special parts assembly given to all women at birth. I don't have that kind of equipment."

"Neither does Brad," I said, finally recovering my composure. "I owe him my life, but he'd be the first one to point that out. He's not exactly modest or subtle when it comes to interpersonal relationships. I'm sure he does care about me, but not as much as he cares about himself."

"Still, he's a delectable piece. I think you should grab him."

I shrugged noncommittally. I couldn't deny that I found Brad attractive. I always had. And now I could add gratitude and respect to my feelings for him. But it was easy to fall for a guy who dressed like a vampire and crucified a thug on your behalf. Too easy.

How much more intriguing to fall for the guy who might blend into the crowd or the establishment, but whose thoughts were truly unique, who was worth listening to, especially when he spoke quietly. And who listened in return. The same one who wouldn't grab your tush just because it felt good, and insisted that lovemaking should be exactly that.

"What about Marco?" Hank asked.

I looked up in surprise. "You read my mind, little bro. You may have some intuition after all. I think it's fair to say that Marco and I are hopelessly stalemated at this point."

"I liked him a lot. So you're still interested in him?"

"Oh, yes," I replied with an exaggerated nod.

Then it struck me, if Marco really cared more about me than Brad did, why hadn't he called? Marco had been on both murder scenes just minutes after or before I'd arrived. But when I was badly beaten, he was nowhere to be found, even though the local television stations had broken into programming with the story. No phone call. Nada.

"I'm interested," I clarified, choosing my next words carefully, "maybe that's just because he's playing hard to get."

Hank waved an invisible watch fob back and forth in front of my face and gave me a look that would have made Anton Mesmer proud. "Look into my eyes."

"No way!" I waved him off with a laugh, avoiding eye contact. This was one of our running jokes. Whenever Hank wanted me to spill the beans, he'd pretend to hypnotize me.

"You will tell me the truth, Angel Baker," he said with a bad Viennese accent. "Is it possible you are the one who is playing hard-to-get with Detective Marco?"

"Not a chance."

"Analysis paralysis," Soji said, reprimanding us both and scooping up our empty dishes. She ferried them out to the kitchen, adding for good measure, "Go with the flow. Make love, not war."

"Any other clichés you want to throw my way?" I called after her.

"Buy low, sell high!" she shouted over the sound of running water and clanking plates.

Hank and I grinned, but tensed when the service elevator clanged, squeaked and groaned to a stop at the top of the stairs.

"What in the hell...?" Hank frowned suspiciously at the closed door to the apartment. "Did the circus just arrive?"

"That was my service elevator."

"Good God, that thing actually works?"

"I used it once when I first moved in, but it lurched so much I feared for my life."

"What brave soul is using it now?"

"I'll let you see for yourself." I opened the door just as Jimmy was about to knock and stepped aside so he could wheel his way into the living room. I made introductions, explained Jimmy's presence, assured him that Hank, who was clearly amused, could be trusted, then took a seat. I gratefully accepted the coffee Soji brought me and prepared for a long-winded explanation of another one of Jimmy's conspiracy theories. He was clearly agitated.

"L-look here, Angel," he stammered, waving a stack of prints hot off the printer in my downstairs office. "I took some photographs when Lola left on her date earlier to-night, just as you asked me to. I think you'll find this very interesting."

I reluctantly set down my coffee mug and started flipping through the images. All of them were taken from the window behind me. There was the postman, making his once-a-week delivery of snail mail earlier in the day, a return appearance of those antiretributionist kooks with their handmade signs, and several shots of various windows in the old redbrick apartment building across the street.

"Okay, Jimmy," I said as I quickly flipped past these, "this isn't a scene out of *Rear Window*. Nobody in the building across from ours has murdered his wife. You're going to get arrested as a Peeping Tom, if you're not careful."

He wiped a graceful hand over his mouth. "Well, you never know when someone has done something they shouldn't."

"Yeah, yeah, yeah, welcome to my life." I quickly flipped through the rest until I found a shot of Lola crossing the street, decked out in a red sequined gown with a black boa—and it wasn't a snake. Far from it. She looked like Lucille Ball going to the Academy Awards. Okay, Lucille Ball after losing a se-rious battle with gravity. Still, I had no idea Lola could clean up this well. She'd been holding out on me.

"Wow!" I whispered.

"What is it?" Hank leaned forward, eager to see.

"My birth mother. I had no clue...."

He grabbed the photo and whistled in appreciation, shar-ing the photo with Soji.

"This is your mother?" Soji's chestnut eyes twinkled. She crossed a long, svelte leg over the other and leaned toward Hank for a closer look. "She's lovely."

I grimaced. "Sort of. I'm not sure she'd look so great if it were a close-up. She's been around the block a time or two. She's kind of like the main character in the movie *Stella Dallas,* played by Barbara Stanwycke. Pretty but hardened by life."

"You really love those old movies, don't you?" Soji remarked.

"When I was little, before Hank's parents took me in, Lola used to get drunk on a regular basis. Whenever she did, I'd watch classic movies. We both had our way of escaping, but mine didn't result in hangovers."

"I don't think I've ever seen a classic movie."

I gaped at her. "Get out of here."

"Nothing certainly before 2080, I'd say. I'm invited to lots of premieres because I work in the media."

"Oh, Soji, you don't know what you're missing."

"So tell me, what am I missing?"

"A lot of handsome leading men, classy dames, a wonderful world where everyone has manners and money, where justice always wins in the end."

"Sounds good to me," Soji said with a dry smile.

"If you decide to catch up, start with a Spencer Tracy movie. He reminds me of Hank."

Hank straightened his collar and showed off his profile. "What do you think, Soji? Movie star material?"

"I don't think so, boy wonder," she teased.

"At least somebody in my family is good-looking," he said, wagging his thumb my way. "And now we know where your beauty came from."

Hank tossed the picture of Lola on the table. I focused on the remaining photos. "Here's another one. Ooh, she looks even better here. Good shot, Jimmy."

When he didn't respond, I glanced up. He was back at his post, watching the street with his binoculars.

"Look at this, Hank," I said. "Lola's looking back at the building as she steps toward a waiting limousine. A nice one, too. Looks like a newer hydro. She must be waiting for her date to catch up."

I passed that photo to Hank and studied the next one. "Ah, here we go. The man of the hour has stepped into the picture frame, I'd say twenty paces behind her. From what I can tell by looking at the back of his head, he looks handsome enough."

"Go to the next one," Jimmy urged me.

I did as he instructed, had to turn it right side up, then let out a slow, hissing gasp when I recognized the man in the picture. I would have screamed, but I couldn't quite get another breath.

"What is it?" Soji asked. "What's wrong?"

Hank snatched the offending photo from my hands. "Oh, my God," he groaned. "It's Vladimir Gorky."

Chapter 16

Et tu, Brute?

"Damn!" I pressed my eyes with my fingertips. Fury and betrayal scalded me from the inside out. The painkillers were wearing off, and pain stabbed my head in a screeching rhythm. "Oh, God, I can't believe Lola would do this to me."

"I don't understand," Soji said, taking the photo from Hank. "Why on Earth would your mother be dating the most notorious mobster in Chicago?"

"Unbelievable," Hank muttered, thrusting up from his chair, clenching and unclenching his fists. "I need a drink. Soji?"

"No, thanks."

"Angel?"

I just shook my head. "Damn her! How could Lola be this

esponsible? Strike that. She's always been unreliable. But
aought she'd turned a corner."

"What's going on, Angel?" Soji asked in a soothing voice.
ola and Gorky obviously didn't meet through a dating ser-
e. What gives?"

While Hank went to the sideboard next to the fireplace
d poured himself a shot of Vivante, I tried to explain the
xplicable.

"My mother and I lived for years in Rogers Park after my
her skipped out on us. One night Vladimir Gorky got nailed
a shoot-out in front of our apartment, which also doubled
Lola's fortune-telling parlor. She heard the ruckus and
lled him into our building, saving his life. She even removed
ullet from his leg so he wouldn't have to go to the hospital
d get arrested. Afterward, she became his favorite fortune-
ler and bookmaker. I guess they're back in business."

Soji sat back as if she'd been shoved. "What an amazing
ry. I don't suppose you'd be willing to—"

"No," I said emphatically, "I will not repeat it on camera
you can use it on the news."

"I wouldn't waste it on the news. I was thinking of a doc-
entary."

I skewered her with a threatening glare. "No."

"I'm sorry, of course not. I just can't resist a good story."
e shook her head wonderingly. "Whatever happened to
ir association. Was it romantic?"

"No!" was my instant answer. I couldn't even go there.

Hank sighed. "Give Angel a break. It's personal."

I automatically grabbed his hand and squeezed, just like I
d to when we were kids. Gigi would make my life a mis-
, and he would be there to make me feel better.

"When I met with Gorky last month, trying to arrange the
ease of the Chinese orphans, I asked Lola to contact him

to set up a meeting at Rick's Café. When she did, they mu
have rekindled…something. So in a way, this is my fault. Sti
I can't believe Gorky is really romantically interested in her

"Maybe she offers him something he can't get anywhe
else," Soji posited. "She seems attractive enough, but Gor'
has been photographed with some of Hollywood's younge
and sexiest starlets."

"Lola went to prison for bookmaking," Hank said. "Do y
think they're running some kind of illegal business together

"No. I had to take her in last month after Gorky's goo
destroyed her apartment and killed her cleaning lady. Sl
was broke and had nowhere else to go. That's why I was su
picious when she recently bought new clothes."

We wrestled in silence over possible explanations th
would prove Lola innocent. Finally, I leaned back in my cha
and carefully crossed my arms over my bruised chest. "Y
know, maybe I'm making too much of this. I did a psych
reading for Gorky in exchange for the girls. When we talke
he seemed genuinely impressed and grateful to Lola for h
psychic visions, though she had failed to help him find t'
Maltese Falcon—his version of it, anyway. Maybe he's fo
given Lola and she's just back in the fortune-telling busines:

"Dressed like that?" Hank pointed to the glamour shot
Lola crossing the street in stiletto heels and enough glitter
light a casino marquee in Vegas.

I held up my hands in surrender. "Okay, let's take a stab
a worst-case scenario. Suppose she and Gorky rekindled
friendship—I'll give her the benefit of the doubt here—wh
she contacted him last month. Then he decides to use her
keep tabs on me. He's either paying her to give him inform
tion on me, or he's treating her like a queen-for-a-day in t
hopes that she'll talk too much, which she usually does."

"No offense," Soji said in her rich contralto, "but wl

uld Gorky go to so much trouble to keep tabs on a small
h like you?"

"Because he asked me to locate the Maltese Falcon when
la failed to deliver. I told him that the statue was back in
s homeland, Chechnya. But if my vision was wrong...." I
pped my face in my hands. "God, am I a fake psychic?
uldn't that be ironic? That's what I called Lola for years
fore I realized she was the real deal."

"You're being too hard on yourself," Hank said, tipping
ck the last of his drink. "As usual."

I grabbed his arm. "No, Hank, I'm just trying to be logi-
l here. I know I have visions and hear things that are right
. But it may be a hit-or-miss talent. Gorky warned me that
he couldn't find the falcon in Chechnya based on my infor-
ation, he would do me serious bodily harm. Maybe he's try-
g to woo Lola to get close to me for the coup de grâce."

"But he wouldn't have to do that if all he wanted to do was
l you," Soji argued. "He could have any one of his minions
ck you off in the dark without leaving a clue."

"Which brings us back to the assassinations," I said. "I'd
eady concluded that it would have to be someone as evil and
werful as a syndicate boss, but I'd assumed it was Capone."

"Why?" Hank leaned back and shoved his hands in his
ckets, relishing the role of devil's advocate. "Why couldn't
ust be some demento fixated on retributionists?"

"Maybe it was Cyclops," Soji offered.

I paused to mull this over. "I don't think so. Why go to such
borate lengths to hide your identity in three murders and
en go ape shit in front of a bunch of retributionists and re-
rters? Now, the mastermind might have set Cy up to cause
uble, but Cy couldn't have planned those murders. He was
ked up in P.S. #1 until recently."

"Why a mastermind, Angel?" Hank persisted.

"Because someone got into my bank safety deposit box an took my gun and delivered it to the scene of the crime. Th same person monkeyed with my phone records. Those are tw different legitimate private institutions that are difficult to i filtrate. To do that you'd have to be both well connected ar criminally minded."

"As far as I can see, there is no reason to connect Cy's a tack with the murders," Hank argued. "He's obviously a loor

"Yes, but Cy knew exactly when and where the CRS mee ing was taking place. His attack was elaborately planned. M whereabouts had to have been divulged to this psychotic mol either by one of my colleagues or by my mother, via Gork Either way, it's not good."

This prospect was so bleak that no one could respon Normally, my birth mother's crimes and emotional misd meanors embarrassed me, but I no longer had the luxury that petty emotion. I had to nail down the real murderer so or I'd be screwed.

"Dad has been working closely with your attorney," Hai said, trying to cheer me up, and it worked.

"Really?"

"Dad and Berkowitz have assembled a virtual war room clerks, private investigators, ballistic experts, shrinks, y name it."

"Henry's actually helping me?"

Hank frowned. "Angel, come on. This is your foster fath we're talking about here. My dad. He adores you. It's not e actly a family secret that you were his favorite."

Tears stung my eyes. I blinked several times, shruggin "I know your folks have risked everything for my defense. B it's one thing for Henry to foot the bill. It's another thing f him to invest his time, his reputation. And I...I thought might still blame me for Victor's death."

"He might," Hank said, as frank as usual. "But that doesn't
ean he stopped loving you. You are every bit as much of a
ughter to Henry as Gigi. And don't you forget it."

I nodded, moved beyond words.

After Hank and Soji hugged me goodbye, admonishing me
go directly to bed, I took a long shower. The hot water
rned my scrapes and cuts but sluiced soothingly over my
robbing muscles. I gingerly donned a loose nightgown, then
ent into the kitchen to call Marco.

I just want to see if he has any new information on my case,
old myself, but myself didn't buy it. I was growing increas-
gly agitated over Marco's lack of contact. God, had he de-
led to blow me off at a time like this?

When his voice message answered, I hung up, disappoint-
ent burning like indigestion. There had to be a reason he'd
ne AWOL on me, but I wouldn't try to figure it out now. I
ally was exhausted and needed rest. As usual, things would
ok brighter in the morning. Before I checked out for the
ght, though, I wanted to see how Cy's attack was being por-
yed in the news.

"Lead story," I said when my picture appeared over the an-
or's shoulder just after the opening credits. "No surprise
ere. If it bleeds, it leads."

I'd learned a thing or two about news judgment, or the lack
ereof, growing up in the home of the dean of the Medill
hool of Journalism at Northwestern University. It would
ve taken a plane crash at O'Hare to bump me out of the top
ot. Not that I wanted to be there.

I splayed myself on the couch, watching a replay of what
ad lived through just a few hours earlier. It was downright
rreal. The reporter's news package included shots of me
ing loaded into the ambulance on a stretcher, the Shadow-

man being hauled away in handcuffs, cop cars and flashi
red lights everywhere, retributionists milling around like
convention of outlawed superheroes.

The holographic images flashed in the middle of my li
ing room, so lifelike that my survival instinct kicked into hig
gear. I had to grip the arm of my couch to keep from boltin
My heart pumped like I'd just run a marathon. I was ju
about to turn it off when the scene then shifted to a two-sh
of the reporter and Brad.

With the sound turned down, I couldn't hear what he w
saying, but I could well imagine. With his hands akimbo d
a sequin studded white belt, his white shirt splattered wi
blood, and of course his cape, he made for a dramatic witnes
His blue eyes danced as he entranced the reporter. I could te
by the way his lip curled smugly now and then that he w
bragging about his rescue.

"Sound. Full." At my voice command, the digivision pr
duced audio.

"What makes you so certain?" The reporter's voice can
off camera.

"Angel Baker is one of the most capable and moral peop
I know," Brad said. "She's incredible. You should have se
her fighting off the Shadowman in there. The only reason sl
needed my help was because she couldn't see in the dark."

"You're from New Orleans. Perhaps you're not aware th
Miss Baker is a suspect in a double-murder case involving t
mayor's son. Does that change your opinion of her?"

"I'm aware of it," Brad said, bobbing his head with obviou
almost pitying disdain for the reporter and anyone else stup
enough to believe that I was guilty. "Let me tell you somethin
Angel Baker is innocent. Someone has set her up." Jabbing
forefinger at the camera lens for emphasis, he delivered his la
line to the television audience. "And the truth will come ou

That was the end of Brad's interview.

"TV. Off."

The room went silent. I just stood there, blown away by Brad's generous, virtuoso performance. Clearly, he had matured a great deal since we'd spent that week together in bed.

"Amazing," I muttered. "Why couldn't Marco stand up for me like that?"

I padded into the kitchen for a glass of water. I lowered myself into a kitchen chair, every move precise and slow. I would definitely need another pain pill before I went to sleep. I let out a big sigh after what seemed like the longest day of my life.

I flipped through Jimmy's pictures again, amused over his choice of subjects. He had very capably followed my directions to photograph Lola. I was intrigued by the other choices he'd made on his own. He had been able to discern which passersby were worthy of scrutiny, like the protestors, and which ones should be ignored, like my neighbors. But he hadn't been able to overcome the *Rear Window* subprogram imbedded in his mainframe. He just couldn't resist taking a few shots of the neighbors's windows, like Jimmy Stewart's character had in the Hitchcock film.

Engineers had made so many improvements in compubots it was almost scary. For years, robotics firms had proudly touted products that looked and felt like human beings, but reacted like computers. They were attractive, brilliant, fast and logical to a fault. As a result, the robotics industry had never really taken off in domestic settings. Human beings didn't like hanging around walking, talking machines that were clearly and vastly more knowledgeable than they, but didn't have enough emotional intelligence to figure out they were supposed to hide that fact. Plus, the early models were totally lacking in spontaneity.

AutoMates, Inc. had been the first robotics firm to incor-

porate sophisticated "Gray Zone" reasoning and deductio
abilities that enabled compubots to wing it, as it were, in ci
cumstances that weren't preprogrammed, and to show a re
alistic facsimile of emotions.

Still, I'd noticed that AutoMates Classics, like Bogie an
Jimmy, had a tendency to default to their prime film moti
for no reason and often when you least expected it. I shoul
probably pass that feedback along to the company, since I wa
one of the few people lucky enough to have intimate conta
with the Classic models for any length of time.

That reminded me that I'd better try to contact the firr
soon just to make sure I wasn't going to be billed for Jimmy
little visit. He hadn't exactly been invited, though I woul
admit he had been useful.

I put my glass in the sink and collected the photos, the
found something in one of the apartment building photos th
I'd overlooked at least a dozen times this evening.

"Holy moley," I whispered.

I flipped on a counter light and held the photo under
bright, narrow beam. Unfortunately, a better view only co
firmed what I thought I'd seen—someone standing in one
the windows across the street, taking a photograph of m
apartment.

I hurriedly flipped through the photos, collecting the tw
other apartment building pics. After close examination, I four
a total of two still cameras and one video, all pointing my wa

Someone was spying on me. And they weren't foolin
around.

I decided drastic action was needed. I had to break into th
apartment across the street and surprise the spies. If I coul
find out who was watching my apartment, I would probabl
also find out who had murdered Roy, Victor and Getty.

But three cameras might mean three operatives, and I didn't like those odds. I would need help. Mike was apparently still in old China Town. Who should I call instead?

"Brad," I whispered.

My choice, which was immediate and instinctive, rocked through my consciousness like an earthquake tremor, signaling to my brain that all was not well in paradise. I had this vague but profound gut instinct telling me that while I could trust Marco with my heart, I couldn't quite trust him with my life. It was a perverse distinction, and one that broke my heart.

I wanted so desperately to love Marco, to be loved by him. Even to have a happily-ever-after with him. I would admit to that absurdly sentimental and boringly commonplace aspiration. But clearly that wasn't my destiny.

Like Jimmy's, my mind teemed with conspiracy theories. I just hoped that when and if my new leading theory proved to be reality, Marco wasn't behind the plot. It pained me to admit my suspicions about him, but I could no longer ignore them. Nor could I deal with them right now. I was too busy putting out fires.

Brad was all too happy to come to the rescue for a second time in one night. I wasn't sure his ego could handle the overload, but it was obvious when he strutted into my apartment, smoothing back his mussed, bleach-blond hair, that he didn't share my concern. For a retributionist, saving someone from an act of violence was like a surfer catching the perfect wave. Brad was riding the big kahuna and wasn't about to take a dive in order to play it safe.

Fearing that my apartment might be bugged, I invited him down into the garden and showed him the photos. We discussed strategies and decided that he and two other retributionists would go for broke, break into the apartment, and capture the slime bags who were snooping into my life. With all the violence that had been directed at our colleagues over the last forty-eight hours, the time for discreet recognizance had already passed. It was time to bust some butts.

Brad e-flashed Tad and Tom Crain, twin brothers who comprised two of the four members of the DCR retribution team. They arrived quickly, adorned with so many weapons I began to understand why some people thought retribution-ists were turning into assassins, even if they were used only in self-defense.

Dressed in forest green flak jackets, camouflage paint and headbands, they looked like members of a Marines special ops unit, with one notable exception. In keeping with the Dead Corpse Rising theme, winding sheets, used in precoffin days to wrap the dead, encircled their waists and crisscrossed over their shoulders, giving them the vague look of Roman gladi-ators. All told, Tad and Tom looked like two dudes you didn't want to mess with.

Jimmy and I took our decoy positions in the living room. We set up a card table in plain view of the window to keep our spies busy while the guys snuck around to the back of the building. I wasn't cut out for the role of lady-in-waiting and didn't like it one bit. Everything seemed to be happening in slow motion.

"Are you going to deal those cards or are you going to just shuffle them all night long?"

"What do you want to play?" he replied.

I glanced nervously at the window, then forced myself to look at Jimmy and pretend I was having a good time. "I don't know. Anything."

"What do you like to play?"

"Go fish."

He raised one provocative brow and began to distribute the cards. "Is that an invitation?"

"No, it is not an invitation," I said sharply through a smile meant for the cameras across the street. "I can't believe you're flirting with me at a time like this."

"Brad was flirting with you."

I picked up the five cards he'd tossed my way and began to organize them in pairs. "Brad is allowed. He's human. You're not."

Jimmy studiously organized his hand. "As I understand it, you didn't mind it when Bogie flirted with you."

"Bogie!" I looked at him incredulously, then took a calming breath and smiled again. "Who told you about my association with him?"

"Lola. As I understand it, you had much more than an *association* with his Rick Blaine character."

I shook my head indignantly. "That's none of your business, and if you insist on continuing this conversation, Jimmy, I'm going to have to file a complaint with your programmer."

His eyes twinkled. "Oh, now, don't spin off into a tizzy. Do you have any threes?"

Chapter 17

Body and Soul

A half hour later, I was surprised to see Tom and then Tad exit from the building's front foyer for all the world to see. Where was Brad? For a heart-stopping moment, I half expected to see a couple of thugs exit the building, dragging Brad's body behind them.

Thankfully, he appeared a moment later with Keshon trotting at his side. He ambled with apparent ease into the glow of the streetlight, where the three guys consulted, joked and high-fived one another.

"Why are they being so obvious?" I wondered aloud.

"They apparently have nothing to fear," Jimmy replied.

The men nodded and shook hands, then the brothers departed.

I buzzed Brad in and met him at the top of the stairs. "Am I glad to see you. Come on in and tell me what happened."

Master and wolf strolled into my apartment. Keshon took one look at my PLD and started growling at it.

"Keshon, back!" Brad commanded, and she circled around to the door and stretched out, still eyeing "Gigi" warily.

"That's just a contraption I've been meaning to get rid of," I said and turned it so it faced the wall. "I growl at her sometimes myself. So, what happened?"

Brad crossed his arms, assuming his normal wide and cocky stance. I noticed he'd changed since the meeting. He wore a black leather jacket studded with silver. In stark contrast, his bleached hair stood stiffly.

"Well," he said, dragging out the suspense, "you were right. It was the R.M.O. keeping an eye on you."

"I'm not surprised. I guess it's a relief to know for sure."

"They were gone when we got there. I thought we had done a good job sneaking up on them, but apparently not." He pushed his way past me and went to the bar, pouring himself a neat shot of Vivante. "Whiskey," he murmured, and tossed back the shot.

"How did you figure out it was the R.M.O.?"

"And what about the cameras?" Jimmy inquired.

Brad looked over at the wheelchair, noticing Jimmy for the first time. Brad made a big deal of licking the last of the Vivante from his lips, frowning dubiously, as if debating whether to treat Jimmy like a person or a thing.

"The cameras were gone," Brad finally replied, and I was glad he didn't ask me to explain Jimmy's presence. "Thanks for the drink, Angel. Mind if I stretch out a moment?"

He made himself comfortable on my couch, kicking his boots up on one end and fluffing a throw pillow on the other. "Nice digs, Angel. Mind if I spend a few days here?"

"Yes, I do mind. No offense."

"None taken."

As hot and hip as Brad looked to me at this particular moment, I had a mental flash of him lying on a couch watching the digivision, tossing aside empty beer cans, belching and farting. It was really hard to predict which men would improve with age like a fine wine, and which ones would balloon like bread dough with too much yeast. Brad was still in the questionable category.

"So they saw you coming somehow," I remarked, trying to steer the conversation back to business.

"I guess. We figured they were R.M.O. operatives because of this."

Brad reached into his pocket and pulled out a crumpled piece of paper. I took it and tried to make heads or tales out of it.

"That's obviously Russian, or some related language," Brad said. "Maybe a Chechen dialect."

"What does it say?"

He shrugged. "Doesn't really matter, does it? It's the smoking gun we needed. For whatever reason, somebody in the R.M.O. wants to keep tabs on you, babe. I'd watch your pretty little ass if I were you."

Little. He called my ass little. Maybe I should let him stay after all, just by way of thanks. I helped myself to a shot of Vivante as I recalculated the risks based on this new information.

"Brad, the way I look at it, Gorky's *organizatsia* is either keeping tabs on me, or I'm being set-up as the next murdered retributionist."

"That's cool. I mean it's not cool, but it may be accurate."

"Jimmy?"

The compubot winced soberly, "Well, uh, Angel, ah, I guess I'd have to agree."

Having Jimmy second the frightening notion made my

stomach drop down into my little ass. "For the first time in my life, I wish someone would disagree with me."

"Angel?" Lola called out, then knocked on the door. "Angel, are you awake?"

"Oh, my God!" I whispered. "She's back!"

Jimmy and I both began to move without direction. I stumbled into the card table. He banged into a wall with his extended leg. Brad bolted upright, but was obviously confused about why we all were reacting in such a panic. I explained, sotto voce, "It's my mother. She may be involved with those spies. She had a date with Gorky tonight. I don't know whether I can trust her anymore."

No one spoke for a long moment while we all seemed to register the same thought. If Gorky had picked Lola up, he most certainly had dropped her off.

Brad twisted around to look out the window. I made a dash for the couch. Jimmy started wheeling our way, but crashed into the coffee table.

"Damn," he muttered.

Brad and I reached the window just in time to see Gorky's limousine drive out of sight.

"Crap!" I cursed, although I wasn't sure why. It wasn't as if I wanted to confront Gorky. *Oh, by the way, Vlad, have you been spying on me as well as schtupping my mother? Well, isn't that quaint. And you plan to murder me, too? Fancy that.*

"Angel, is that you? Why don't you open the door, sweetie?"

"Lola?" I inquired, stalling for time. "Is that you?"

"Yeah, honey, it's me. What's the matter? Open up."

"I can't." I went to the door and conversed through the wood. "I'm…busy."

"Busy with what?"

"I'm…giving…a reading."

"At this hour?"

I had no response and turned back to Brad and Jimmy, whispering, "What should I say? I can't see her right now. She'll figure out that we know that she knows that Gorky has been spying on me. Then she'll tell Gorky."

"I'll distract her," Brad offered.

"Angel, what is going on in there?"

"Um…I'm having trouble concentrating. I'm going to send my…client…home. We'll try another time." I opened the door. Lola's hair was more tousled than usual, and I wondered if she and Gorky had… No, I wouldn't go there. Surely a man who could have any starlet he could buy wouldn't bed my outrageous mother simply to camouflage his apparent plans to assassinate me.

"Mom," I said, knowing that would soften her up, and I could tell by the surge of moisture in her rheumy blue eyes that it did, "this is Brad. Brad, this is Lola, my mother. I'm sure she'd be happy to show you to the front door. Wouldn't you?"

"Whatever you want, honey," she said in her froggy smoker's voice. "Come on, Brad, let's go downstairs."

She clabbered down the wooden stairs in her impossibly high heels. Brad stopped in the doorway, pressing me against the frame with his lean, hard body. Though scarred, his face was fresh and unmarred by the cynicism that creeps in with age.

"I'm going to kiss you, Angel Baker," he whispered, smelling hot and horny like the stud he was, "like you've never been kissed before."

For a moment, I thought, what if he's wrong? But he wouldn't be. Brad succeeded by virtue of the risks he took and the outrageous promises he made, which he did confidently because he'd never known failure, lucky devil. Doubtless, he was even convinced he'd outwit death in the end. Looking into his audacious, bright blue eyes while he pressed

s erection provocatively against my pelvis, I willingly sus-
:nded disbelief.

He tilted his head to the side, like a curious bird, then
oved in suddenly, pressing his mouth to mine. Surprisingly
nder, I felt the briefest flicker of his tongue. Just as I warmed
 his style, he pulled back and stroked my jawline with one
1ger, murmuring, "You think you know me, but you don't.
ve learned a lot since we last…met."

I swallowed back a tsunami of lust and managed a faint,
Oh?"

"Yeah. And since you now owe me big-time, we'll have a
1ance to really get reacquainted."

"But I'm…injured," I croaked.

"Bruises and scrapes. I'll give you forty-eight hours to re-
ver." With that, he slowly marched down the stairs to his des-
1y.

With some effort, I shook off his temporary spell and
rned back to Jimmy. "We have to unravel this whole assas-
1ation plot in forty-eight hours, because I am *not* going to
d again with Brad the Impaler."

"Why not?" Jimmy said, eyes full of mirth. "Afraid you
on't like it?"

"No." I sighed. "I'm afraid I will."

When I finally went to bed, I fell asleep as soon as my head
t the pillow. I didn't dream. I didn't stir. I think I even woke
e next morning in the same position, which exasperated the
iffness that settled in my bruised body overnight. But the sun
as shining and the air smelled of autumn, crisp and cool, and
was in the mood to count my blessings. It didn't take long.
was all for looking at the bright side, but only after the dark
le had been fully exposed.

And that led me to another session with my crystal ball.

I'd been in denial of my psychic abilities for so long I had to remind myself to use them. Now that I knew the R.M.O. was spying on me, I needed to know why.

Unfortunately, the crystal ball was dead to my touch. I don't know if it was because my emotional well had run dry or because my body had been through hell and back again, but I didn't see so much as a blip of light. Nothing was going my way.

But as I dressed in three-quarter-length sleeves for the first time in months, I determined that today would be the day I turned the tide in my favor. Something different, something special would happen today. I had no clue as to what, but I knew who could help me figure it out.

As I approached Mike's shed, leaves from the giant elm that towered over and shaded my walled-in garden shuffled on the stone pathway, sounding brittle and lost. I paused to gaze at Mike's orange and red koi. These foot-long goldfish must have thought I was some omnipotent being, because they lunged at the water's surface, smacking their lips together like hands in prayer, apparently trusting that if they went through the motions of eating, I would provide the food. Alas, their faith was wasted on me today.

"Sorry, fellas," I said, sliding my hands into my empty pockets. "I didn't bring any bread. But don't worry. Mike will feed you later. I'll see to it."

When I circled around to the entrance of the converted carriageway, Mike's accordion, double six-pane glass doors were open. He sat cross-legged on his mat flooring next to a heating pad where he made tea.

"You promised a feast to those swimming piglets?" Mike said in his Chinese accent.

"Yes, I did." I crossed my arms and leaned against the door, smiling down at his bald head with more appreciation than I'd ever known. "You got a problem with that?"

"No. I will feed them later. I do what you ask, Baker. You now that."

"Yes, I do. You've never failed me yet."

"Come. Sit and drink tea. I went shopping very late to get ou good Chinese herbs. They make you better."

I gingerly lowered myself onto the mat, ready to be cared or by Mike. He was so tough yet so caring. My best friend as an enigma, a man of contradictions.

This thirty-something former Shaolin monk, wushu mas-r and dear friend was often surprisingly superstitious and sually expected the worst in any given situation, which per-aps was to be expected from someone who'd spent three ears in indentured servitude. But in spite of these ostensible aws, Mike always handled himself with dignity and finesse, hich he managed to do by being ready for anything, even e worst.

More important, Mike put the well-being of others first. m convinced that's why he'd had the good fortune of run-ng into me, the one person on the planet impulsive enough risk everything to help him escape from the opium plant in liet. With that chance meeting, Mike had won his freedom. od really did work in mysterious ways when He had to, if at's what it took to look out for the good guys.

Then again, maybe I was like the fish, giving too much edit to a higher power that really didn't give a squat about e. What the heck, I'd be happy with a few bread crumbs my-lf at this point.

"Drink this." He filled a small round ceramic cup with a rk, pungent tea that had the consistency, color and odor of nd scum.

I took a sniff but hesitated to actually swallow. "Is this sup-sed to kill me or cure me?"

"Either way, you will feel better." He didn't smile, rarely

did, but his onyx eyes lit with humor barely visible beneath his slanted eyelids.

"Here goes."

I knew from past experience with Dr. Mike's hideously flavored remedies that guzzling was advisable, because if you stopped to take a breath, every fiber of your being would revolt against a second swig. I swilled, swallowed, then put the empty teacup down and cut loose with a full body shiver and an ungracious gagging noise.

"Hmmm," I said, clearing my throat. "Delicious."

"Now you should meditate. Your chi is no doubt out of balance."

"My chi is so far out of balance that it's fallen flat on its back. I haven't meditated or worked out since my arrest."

"If you want things to go well, Baker, you must be in balance."

"I know, Mike. In theory, I agree completely. But I have a little time problem here. I think someone is about to murder me. And I don't particularly want to be sitting in a lotus position when it happens."

"Who?"

"The same someone who has been dating my mother, Gorky."

"Vladimir Gorky?" Mike was unusually emphatic. Then again, he had reason to be. He was by my side when I went into Gorky's northside compound last month, demanding the release of the girls. "Why does he want to harm you this time?"

"My guess is that he couldn't find the Maltese Falcon where I told him it would be."

Mike poured two cups of green tea that had been steeping in a small, brown earthen teapot. I sipped. "Ah, much better."

"I wasn't sure if he was serious when he threatened to come after you if your vision was wrong."

"I suspect he's a man of his word when it comes to threats."

nd since he's also an amoral monster, he assumes everyone lse is as well. It would never occur to him that I might have ade a simple mistake. He assumes I pulled a fast one, and e hates being bested. Or maybe he's afraid I figured out here his treasure is hidden but lied to him about it so I could ollect the fortune myself."

"You sound like Detective Marco."

"You think I'm overanalyzing the situation?"

"Maybe you can just tell Gorky the truth. You made a istake."

I shut my eyes, trying to envision having another heart-to-eart with the R.M.O. leader. I focused on Mike. "Nice idea, ut I don't think that will work. Whatever anger he holds toward e is spilling over to my colleagues. He's picking them off one y one, and the police seem to be delighted. I don't think Gorky as much motivation to stop now that he's on a roll. His *sgar-stas* can carry out his assassinations and blackmail more freely they don't have to worry about retributionists after the fact."

"Maybe it's time for a trip to China. We could bring Lin. could show you the Shaolin Temple."

"You mean run away for a while? That might solve my roblems in the short term, but I would still feel responsible or Roy's and Geddy's deaths. And I would worry about the thers. Gorky is, by all accounts, one determined and obses-ve SOB. If I hadn't attracted his attention by rescuing those irls, Roy and Getty might still be alive."

"Then you must kill Gorky."

That stunned me out of my stupor of indecision. "What?"

"Kill or be killed."

I couldn't believe Mike was saying this. "I don't want to ill him. Why would you tell me to do such a thing, Mike? uddhists believe killing is wrong. You're not even supposed squash an ant."

Mike shrugged. "Maybe the Buddha was wrong. He neve met Vladimir Gorky. You want to turn the other cheek lik your Jesus did? Look what happened to him."

This wasn't what I wanted to hear. I couldn't tell if Mik my ersatz guru, was playing devil's advocate, or if he'd gon over to the dark side. I rubbed my face with both hands, try ing to wipe away the moral ambiguity that was my life. I ha never killed anyone, but who knows what happened to the e cons I hauled in for retribution? My clients signed contrac saying they wouldn't harm their assailants during paybac time, but I didn't exactly make follow-up house calls to e force every clause in the contract. And sometimes I used bru force with a recalcitrant thug in order to make a delivery. could hardly claim to be a pacifist myself.

And yet killing someone to prevent a crime was muc more of a serious proposition, wasn't it? That would be ta ing the role of earthly omnipotent being too far. Surely, wasn't about to cross that line. Even if some colleagues ha Even if Judge Gibson had given us permission in the cases restraining order violators.

"No, Mike, I can't."

He regarded me thoughtfully. "Why not?"

"Because it's wrong. Because I'm not willing to becom like Gorky to get rid of him, no matter how much better o the world might be. And because I promised Lin that I wou be there for her, and I can't be if I'm rotting in prison for a sassinating Gorky. I'd rather be assassinated myself than vo untarily let down that little girl."

"Either way, you and Lin will lose."

"No! There has to be another way. We can outsmart Gork Mike. We've done it before."

He smiled wanly. "You always are the optimist. Such American trait."

"Actually, I think the word for it is foolhardy."

"So what will we do?"

"Like you said, I have to have another chat with my old friend Vlad. If he kills me, then you can tell Lin I died trying. But I feel responsible for my colleagues, and I have to do something before somebody else dies."

"Last time you bluffed Gorky and found out he could be bought."

"Mike, you're a genius!" I beamed like sun bursting through a dark cloud. "That's it. Gorky was willing to give me the twelve Chinese orphans he'd stolen from Mongolian Mob chief Corleone Capone. And all Gorky wanted in return was a psychic reading that would reveal the location of his missing Maltese Falcon and a promise that I wouldn't return the girls to his archrival. And that was it."

"You make it sound so easy. It wasn't. We were nearly killed when the Mongolian runners chased us down."

I nodded, not denying it, but we'd survived and that's all that counted. "Of course, Gorky considered it an added bonus that my taking the girls would rob Capone of millions of dollars that could have been made from selling them on the black market. And my vision had to be accurate, which it apparently wasn't."

"Yes, Baker," Mike said between sips of tea. "A man like Gorky can usually be bought, but frequently the price is too high."

"So, all I have to do is have another cordial meeting with Gorky, ask him to end his deadly plot and find out what his price is this time."

"Your soul," Mike said softly, looking out the open window as a wren flew by.

"What did you say?"

He looked back at me with a little start, as if he'd momen-

tarily forgotten I was there. "I said, this time the price will b
your soul."

When his meaning penetrated, an ominous chill raced ove
my flesh like a sudden frost. Murder was one way to lose you
soul, but there were others. Mike wasn't psychic, but some
times he spoke like a prophet, and all too frequently, hi
prophecies turned into realities.

Chapter 18

Date with the Devil

threatened Lola within an inch of her life to get her to set
p another meeting between me and Gorky. She knew some-
1ing big was up, but I refused to let her in on the secret. She
as infuriated to think that I would have my own secrets re-
arding her good "friend" Vladimir, but I knew she would
lab everything to lover boy if I clued her in. Like the last
me, Gorky would meet me at Rick's Café Americain at nine
'clock. Those were the only details I was willing to entrust
1y mother with at this point.

I spent the rest of the day getting ready. I meditated,
tretched and worked out with Mike as best I could, then took
pain pill. If the evening ended with a fight for my life, I
idn't want to lose because a few aching ribs held me back.

Finally, I bathed and dressed for the evening. Last time we'd

met, I wore a minimal of clothing to show Gorky I had noth
ing to hide, including weapons. But he ended up leering at m
low-cut top. It was rare that a man could make me feel tacky
but he had. I guess because he was tacky himself. This time
I would use my femininity to my advantage. If I didn't use it
he would. Like a politician, I needed to control the message

I wore a shell-pink, knee-length skirt slit up the front to my
thighs, a short-sleeved, dove-gray blouse with a high, starched
open collar that rode up my neckline to the bottom fringes of
my blond hair.

Next came the gifts from Sydney that I admired but rarely
wore—a classy pink pearl earrings-and-necklace set. Then
came matching pink lipstick and fingernail polish. Instead of
applying my usual facial tattoo, I wore a blue-and-silver
dragon bracelet that curled up my left forearm. Finally, I
climbed into gray chammy ankle boots and tucked a six-inch
dagger alongside my right ankle.

Spinning in front of my full-length bedroom mirror, I con
cluded that my presentation was perfect. I was feminine, el
egant and ready to cut Gorky's carotid artery in a pinch. In
medieval times, small daggers were used to deliver the coup
de grâce, or cut of mercy, to the enemy after a brutal and
maiming battle. Who knows? Maybe I would decide that
Mike was right about Gorky and put him out of his misery
before the night was through.

When I entered Rick's Café Americain, tropical air spin
ning from the ceiling fans, entwined with Turkish cigarette
smoke and old-fashioned French colognes, infused my senses
reminding me of simpler days when my only lover was the
club's star compubot. In retrospect, my affair with Bogart
seemed pathetic, but I still had fond memories and wondered
if I'd see him tonight.

After being greeted by the maître d', I scanned the crowd

of twenty-second-century patrons mingling with compubots dressed like film extras from *Casablanca*. The bit players wore World War II suits and dresses and always looked tense, as if they couldn't wait for an illicit passport to flee Nazi-occupied French Morocco.

I spotted Sam behind the piano. Gleaming with perspiration, he smiled and sang his heart out. Ilsa and Victor Laszlo dined in the corner. It looked like Gorky hadn't arrived yet, so I pressed through the crowd of drinking and laughing customers in search of Bogie.

I couldn't see him anywhere, but spotted a man reading the daily news—the old-fashioned kind printed on paper. His face was hidden. On the off chance it was Bogie, I sidled up to him and sat on a bar stool. If it wasn't Bogie, he'd find me here sooner or later.

"I'll have a club soda," I said to the bartender.

The man lowered the paper and winked at me.

"Marco?"

"Yes, Angel?" he said coolly.

"What are you doing here?"

"Reading the paper." He raised it again, apparently so no one could see his face.

My heart thundered into high gear. The last thing I needed right now was a complication. Was this a coincidence, or had Gorky sent Marco to scope out the scene before he made his grand entrance?

I spotted Bogie in the corner, apparently fending off the advances of a young admirer adorned in exotic body piercings, orange hair and a skirt so short she may as well have been a Skinny. I went to Bogie's rescue so I could give him a hard time myself.

"Please, Mr. Blaine," the teenager said, "just go to bed with me once so I can say I did it with Humphrey Bogart. Please?"

"I'm sorry, Miss—what is your name?"

"Belinda Mathews."

"I'm sorry, Miss Mathews, I'm not available. Now I suggest you go home and get yourself a good night's sleep."

"Hello, Rick," I said, interrupting.

Belinda looked me up and down as if I were the competition. "Go on and get out of here, lady, he's mine."

"No, he's not," I replied. "Rick Blaine doesn't go to bed with anyone who acts like a tramp."

Tears filled her eyes and she turned in a huff, tromping off.

Sighing, I said, "I guess I was a little rough on her."

"That's my Angel," Bogie replied. He always wore a slight frown, but underneath his jaded exterior was a man of humor and integrity. Or rather, a compubot programmed with those qualities. It was easy to forget when I was in Bogie's manly, unflappable presence. He gripped my elbow, saying, "Come with me, sweetheart, where we can talk in private."

He led me to his gaming room, where a few invited patrons engaged in private card games. I knew from past experience that the stakes in the games were high.

"Can I offer you a drink?"

I shook my head. "I left my seltzer at the bar. I have to have a clear head tonight."

He took out a cigarette case and lit up, each move precise and thoughtful. "So you're meeting with Vladimir Gorky tonight."

"How did you know?"

"He called in a reservation and asked for the same table you had the last time."

"Rick, do you know why Detective Marco is here? Did Gorky send him?"

"Gorky? Look here, Angel, Detective Marco may have his faults, but he's no stooge for Gorky."

I wasn't sure about that and even less certain how Bogie

would know one way or the other. Still, it was nice to hear some reassurance about Marco.

"Then why is Marco here?"

"Because I asked him to come."

I frowned. "You?"

"That's right. He's concerned about your welfare. I thought it might be a good idea to have him here in case your chat with Gorky goes awry."

"But I don't want him here."

"Why not?"

"I'm not sure I can trust him."

"Who can you trust in this world, sweetheart? But you can't let that keep you from taking a chance with someone you love. Whatever his faults, Detective Marco gives a damn about you."

"How do you know?"

Bogie raised his brows provocatively. "He told me. Now, get out there and give Gorky hell."

"Gladly." It was time somebody put the heat on Vladimir Gorky. I'd get things started and let the devil take it from there.

I headed out to the main dining room and saw Gorky being seated at our table. "Our" table. What a weird concept. Once again, I would have to give the performance of my life. Interesting how this horrible human being inadvertently brought out the best in me.

I straightened my shoulders, held my head high and headed his way, only briefly locking eyes with Marco. His dark glance spoke volumes, but I was too nervous to translate hidden text. He could be saying "Be careful," or "So long, sucker."

I quickened my pace until I reached the semicircular dais at the back of the room where Gorky waited for me in intimate shadows and candlelight.

"Hello, Mr. Gorky." I stepped up on the dais, but didn't bother to offer my hand, since I knew he wouldn't take it.

"Ah, Angel *moy*." He rose to his considerable height and gripped my upper arms. They seemed like twigs in his hands. He kissed both cheeks with flair, saying, "It is so good to see you again. Please, take a seat."

Considering his apparent plot to murder me, his warmth was patent hypocrisy, but I said nothing and slid into place, immediately sipping from the waiting goblet of water to clear my dry throat. We assessed each other silently, like two people who hadn't seen each other in half a century, with none of the discomfort that often came during pauses in social conversation.

He looked as impressive as ever, with his thick shock of silver hair, high Slavic cheeks, unusually broad shoulders and lean waist. Only the hair, his tough-as-leather skin and milky circles around his sky blue eyes hinted at his seventy years of age. Otherwise, he seemed ageless. I'd noticed that tendency with immensely powerful men. I guess it was easy to look young when you wasted no time worrying about the moral ramifications of your actions.

"So, *dorogaya moya*," he said. "You look beautiful tonight."

"Thank you." He'd called me "my dear," but he didn't seem quite as lecherous as the last time, so I allowed my demeanor to thaw a degree. He wore a traditional gray tuxedo with a Nehru collar and hidden buttons down the front. "You're dressed up tonight. Are you getting married?"

He threw back his head and let out a gruff belly laugh. "That is very funny, Angel *moy*." My Angel.

This creepy, false affection from a man who was killing my friends was beginning to irritate. But I couldn't blast him until I'd at least tried to reason with him.

"No, I am not getting married. And what did I tell you

about calling me Mr. Gorky?" He poured two shots of vodka. "You must call me Vladimir. Vlad, even."

When he held out one of the clear shot glasses to me, I took it, unlike the last time. He smiled broadly at my acquiescence and held up his shot glass. *"Za zdorovje."*

"Cheers," I replied, then tossed back the clean, burning liquid. I had to negotiate fast, because I didn't want to have to drink any more to grease the social wheels. Gorky was a prodigious drinker, and if I tried to keep up I'd soon be passed out under the table.

"So, Angel *moy,* why did you want to meet this time?"

"Because I wanted to personally tell you that I think what you're doing is despicable and cowardly." I looked askance at the bottle of Russian vodka. One shot had obliterated all discretion.

"You think I am despicable and a coward?" His thick gray eyebrows curled with great finesse as his twinkling blue eyes turned to steel. "What have I done to make you think these things?"

"Murdering two of my colleagues, not to mention the mayor's son, was a good start."

He made no move to deny it. Pouring himself another shot, he leaned back and regarded me with slightly less hostility. "I see. Is that all?"

I huffed incredulously. "That would be enough, but no, there's more. I just busted your set-up across the street from my apartment. I know you've been watching me and using my mother to get to me."

"And how have I been doing that?"

My cheeks reddened, but I refused to avert my gaze. "By seducing her, buying her clothes, making her feel attractive, just so you can find out what I've learned about your murderous plot."

"Perhaps I do find her attractive." His upper lip curled disdainfully. "You young people think you have exclusive rights to beauty and love. Wait until you no longer have the indulgence of youth on your side."

Carl, Bogie's white-haired and sophisticated waiter, came to the table. "Are you ready to order, sir?"

"What would you like, Angel?"

"Whatever you are having," I told Vladimir with uncharacteristic docility. I was too preoccupied with his last comment to care about the menu. While he conversed with Carl, I wondered if it was possible I had misread his interest in Lola. I did have a tendency to think the entire world revolved around me, and I guess that was one of the indulgences of youth he'd been referring to.

"So, what other accusations do you have, *dorogaya moya?*" he inquired when the plump waiter bustled off.

"I know you're planning to kill me next. I just don't how or when."

"And why would I want to kill you?"

Fear screwed into my chest, making it difficult for me to breathe. It was insane to remind him of his threat, but I needed to impress him with my deductive reasoning. If he didn't think I was at least as smart as he was, he'd play me like a Russian balalaika.

"You want to kill me, Vladimir, because you couldn't find the Maltese Falcon in that Chechen farmhouse I saw in my vision."

He entwined his massive fingers as he contemplated my assessment. The third finger on his right hand beamed like a headlight with a diamond so huge I wondered how he had the strength to lift it. "Well, Angel *moy,* I see you have this all figured out."

"Yes." Pride flushed through my body like an illicit and addictive drug. "Yes, I do."

"There is only one small problem with your conclusion."

"Oh?"

"I did find the Maltese Falcon. And it was exactly where you said it would be."

I blinked. "You did?"

"Yes. You should be proud of yourself."

I wanted to be, but not for that. Not now. "How do I know you're telling the truth?"

He waited until Carl placed salad plates before us and departed. Then he waved his ring finger, showing off the enormous cushion diamond. "This was one of the treasures contained in the falcon. It's the Regent Diamond. You may have heard of it."

"The Regent Diamond," I repeated, recalling something about it in the news.

"Once owned by the Duke of Orleans, the Regent of France, it was later bought by Napoleon."

"How many carats?" I braced myself.

"Just a little over 140."

"Wow." I exhaled. "I would think the French government would keep it as a historical heirloom."

"It was in the government's possession in Paris until two years ago."

"I see." Then it hit me. I remembered seeing pictures of the diamond in the news after it had been stolen from the Louvre. I didn't want to ask what I already instinctively knew. Gorky had masterminded the daring heist.

"If you found the statue and reclaimed your precious diamond, then why would you want to kill me?"

"Precisely," he said with a smug smile.

I watched Gorky wolf down his meal in a matter of minutes, poking at my food but eating little. I'd already had my fill of crow. I only half listened to his rambling stories of his childhood and youth. I was preoccupied with trying to figure how I could force him to admit his culpability now that the revenge motive had fizzled.

How do you tell a very evil human being you think they're plotting to murder you because they're a very evil human being? It wasn't easy, especially when the person in question had no apparent sense of right and wrong. And if I couldn' get him to admit his guilt, there would be no way to negotiate an end to the conspiracy.

I'd make a lousy lawyer. Thank heavens I wasn't represent ing myself in court, or I'd end up with one hundred consec utive life sentences. I glanced furtively at Marco. He eyed me intensely over the top of his paper, as if he somehow knew I'd backed myself into a corner. Though Marco couldn't help me now, I was glad he was here.

"Let's go," Gorky said abruptly, tossing his napkin on his empty plate. He stood and motioned impatiently, tossing a pay chip on the table.

"Go where?" I stood in spite of my innate reluctance.

"Come into my car. I have a limo waiting outside."

"Why would I want to get in a car with you?"

The mobster put his hand over his heart. "It hurts me to think that Lola's daughter doesn't trust me. I wanted you to think of me as an uncle."

Okay, I thought, that's a new one. "Look, Mr. Gorky… Vladimir…I think I've done a really bad job of communicat ing here. I believe you're going to murder me."

"I'm not plotting to kill you. But I know who is. Now are you fucking coming with me or not?"

He said it with a smile. I had to give the guy credit for being the master of the unexpected.

Startled into complacency, I left with him, to my everlast ing regret.

Chapter 19

Don't Look Now

The silver stretch aerolimo sat at the curb. Two *sgarristas* climbed out as soon as they saw Gorky exit Rick's Café Amercain. I followed a step behind, knowing there was no point in attempting to flee. I'd sealed my fate when I'd set up the meeting with Gorky. But I'll admit I was shaken when I turned back for one last glance at the bar and found Marco looking at me like I was already dead.

One of them, dressed all in black with black shades and greasy black hair, opened the door for Gorky and spoke in a language that wasn't quite Russian. I assumed it was Chechen. He was apparently fluent in both languages.

"Please, step in," Gorky said, allowing me to enter first. I slid across the long seat, straightened my skirt and plastered myself against the far door, trying not to wince from the pain in my ribs. He climbed in and his assistant shut the door. He reached for two glasses of champagne that fizzed, awaiting our palates, handing me one and raising the other. "May this be the beginning of a long and trusting friendship."

Instead of raising my glass, I brought it to my lips and drank. By now, I really did need a drink. The limo hummed to life, lifted a few feet off the ground, then began to cruise at a slow speed.

"So who is killing off my friends?" I asked point-blank.

Gorky rested his champagne flute on one of his big knees that seemed cramped in spite of the spacious, private compartment we shared. "It amuses me that you would suspect me, Angel *moy.* After all, I am the one who set up the operation across from your apartment to track your moves and insure your safety."

I gave him a long, hard look. "You're spying on me to keep me safe?"

"Yes. The person who is responsible for these murders ran his plan by me, asking me not to interfere. I'm afraid, Angel *moy,* that I was not exactly heartbroken to hear that Chicago would soon be missing a few retributionists. But I made it clear that you were not to be harmed."

I felt a momentary flash of gratitude, then a flush of shame. How could I be grateful for my own survival when others were dying? "Why? Why did you care what happened to me?"

"Because you found my treasure for me." He took another sip of champagne and regarded his ring finger admiringly. "Besides, how do you think your mother would feel if I allowed her only daughter to be assassinated? She saved my life once. Vladimir Gorky never forgets a favor."

Or an insult, I suspected.

"Who is behind the plot?" I asked in a strident voice.

He frowned at me. "You do not expect me to tell you that."

"Yes, I do. How can I defend myself if I don't even know who the enemy is?"

"I will protect you."

"I don't want your protection."

He blinked slowly and took another sip. "I like your attitude. But I cannot divulge the name. There is a code of honor among thieves."

"Vory V zakone," I suggested.

"Yes, thieves of law."

It was a concept that came into vogue after the fall of the Soviet Union more than a hundred years ago. When the government folded, former KGB agents and mobsters rushed in to fill the power void and established their own rule of law.

"Does this mean that the mastermind of this plot is part of the R.M.O.?"

"Not necessarily. A thief is a thief by any name or association."

"Then don't protect this SOB. I'm not going to sit by and let others be killed, Vladimir. You know I'm going to stick my nose in the middle of every murder that happens to my colleagues. You can't shield me from that. And if I get killed, you'll have to explain that to my mother."

He seemed genuinely displeased by the notion. "Don't be difficult, Angel. I could have you imprisoned in Emerald City if I wanted to keep you out of harm's way."

"Just like you imprisoned Lola?" I laughed cynically. "You're unbelievable. She would have rotted in Cyclops's prison if I hadn't rescued her."

"That's not true."

"He's after me now. Did you know that?"

"Yes. Don't worry about him. I can take care of Cyclops."

"No!" I struggled to keep my cool, but talking to this man

was like conversing with a brick wall. Nothing got through to the other side. "I don't want your protection."

I realized we'd been driving a square pattern around my block. For some reason, the car pulled over in front of my two-flat. I glanced out the window and did a double take when I saw Brad standing on the curb.

"You didn't seem to mind my protection when it came in the shape of a handsome young retributionist from New Orleans," Gorky said, his wide, firm mouth pulling into a smirk.

I turned my gaze slowly from Brad to the great and powerful Oz sitting beside me. "You mean that Brad—"

"I had him flown to Chicago on one of my private planes to look after you."

I sank back against the seat, stunned into silence as I tried to recall the day I'd run into Brad on the street. God, what a fool I'd been. "Why Brad?" I asked hoarsely.

"I've hired him before for special projects. I heard about him from one of my business partners. I liked that he called himself Vlad the Impaler. And he was highly recommended."

And easily bought. I reached for the door, ready to belt Brad in the jaw.

Gorky must have seen my tightened fists. He pressed a button and the doors locked.

"Don't go, *dorogaya moya*. Not yet." Gorky motioned to the driver via the rearview mirror. The car pulled away from the curb and continued to cruise in a meandering pattern through the Lakeview neighborhood. "There is one other matter I wish to discuss."

I tried to wipe the visible signs of rage and dismay from my face with one hand. "What is it?" I mumbled into my palm.

"Riccuccio Marco."

My hand dropped to the seat and I caught my breath, unable to feign a disinterested reply.

"I think you should avoid further contact with Detective Marco."

"Yes, I know."

He raised a brow in query, and I felt a small ping of victory. It wasn't easy taking this guy by surprise.

"How did you know that?"

"I saw you two talking about me in a vision."

He shifted his weight. The leather seat protested. "What did we say?"

"I couldn't make out much," I answered honestly, "other than the fact that you warned Marco to stay away from me."

"That's right."

"Why?"

"He is not the man you think he is. I used to trust him, but now…"

I listened to the hum of the limo, inhaled the scent of popped champagne bubbles, and waited for the other shoe to drop. When Gorky coyly refused to continue, I was forced to connect the dots he'd laid out.

"You think Marco is involved with the plot to kill off Certified Retribution Specialists?"

He raised his broad shoulders in a calculated shrug. "Detective Marco has infiltrated the Chicago Police Department on my behalf. He does work for me, but not like in the old days. I think he may now be serving another master as well."

"I don't believe you," I said flatly, clinging to my memories of the man who had made love to my very soul. "You want me to distrust him. You want to isolate me from anyone who is not connected with you so that you can control my opinion of you. I don't know why. Maybe because of my mother. Maybe because you just like to control people."

"Detective Marco is a bad man, Angel."

I laughed incredulously. "Oh, well, that is certainly the pot calling the kettle black, isn't it?"

He smiled humorlessly. "I knew you would say that. I didn't expect you to take my word for it. So I brought these."

Gorky reached into a leather briefcase I hadn't noticed in the dark interior. He touched a control panel in the door and a dome light came to life, casting a yellow spotlight on the empty space between us. He tossed down a stack of aging 8-by-10-inch photo printouts.

"Riccuccio Marco was an assassin for me years ago. I am no stranger to murder, but this disturbed even me. Some madness overtook him and he went far beyond the role of professional assassin."

Unwilling to absorb the word assassin in connection with Marco, I shut my eyes, as if Gorky would actually let me leave this vehicle without looking at the photos. I was like a child who thinks she can't be seen if she can't see.

Yes, I'd feared—even suspected—Marco had blood on his hands. But I wasn't ready to accept hard evidence.

"Don't do this to me," I whispered, my voice raw with vulnerability I despised. "Please. I don't want to see."

"You must."

His emphatic voice rang with a truth that forced me to slowly open my eyes. I had my share of faults, but being an ostrich wasn't one of them. Resigned and businesslike, I picked up the stack and flipped through it.

One photo showed a man on the ground, reaching toward the camera for help, a look of agony etched deep in his Slavic features, while the hand of his assailant plunged a knife in his shoulder. Who on earth would photograph something like this? I thought. And who was wielding the knife?

The next photo was a blur of motion, presumably a stab

caught in action. The victim no longer pleaded. He was prone in a large pool of blood.

The third photo was taken from the waist down. The victim's legs were wide, naked, covered in pageant red. It took me a moment to realize why this close-up had been taken. The man's genitals had been cut off. Whoever had killed him had also castrated him.

A wave of nausea sent heat rushing to my head just as a chill froze my intestines. I broke out in a cold sweat. Tossing the photos down, I pleaded, "No more."

"Ah, *dorogaya moya,* you have one last photo to see. The best one of all."

I loathed Gorky as he rustled eagerly through the photos, uttering satisfaction when he found his pièce de résistance and placed it on my lap. Through sheer willpower, I focused on the photo. There was Marco standing over the body, covered in blood, holding the knife like a proud hunter showing off his kill. Except he didn't look proud. With a wild grin and feral eyes, he looked savage and insane.

I didn't know this man, and I didn't want to. Ever.

"Pull over!" I choked, tossing aside the photo. Before the limo even came to a stop, I opened the door, leaned out and vomited. With little to purge, I heaved until I tasted bile.

"Oh, my dear Angel, have I upset you?" Gorky said, patting my back.

The question was so absurdly disingenuous I wanted to laugh. He handed me a hand towel and I wiped my mouth, then sat up, closing the door, dignity restored. As the car moved on, he filled a glass of water from his bar dispenser and handed it to me. I couldn't believe he was being this solicitous. Then again, I'd read that Hitler had been kind to his dog. Before he killed it.

"Those photos of Detective Marco upset you, didn't they?"

"Too much champagne on an empty stomach," I lied, refusing to give him the satisfaction of knowing he'd swayed my feelings for my lover, perhaps forever.

When Gorky finally dropped me off in front of my two-flat, he promised me that he would call off his spies camped out across the street. Sickened and numb, though far from defeated, I climbed out of the limo, said goodbye and walked toward my front door with wobbly knees.

I was just about to open my door when Brad stepped into the streetlight that brightened the wide swath of concrete that stretched from the sidewalk to my porch.

"Hello, Angel," he said, unusually subdued. With his hands tucked in his tight, white jeans, he looked boyish and almost apologetic. That would be a first for Brad the Impaler.

"What do you want?" I practically snarled.

He tipped up his chin, a gesture that suggested arrogance but was more habitual and meaningless than that. "I want your understanding."

I whirled and got into his face. "You're a traitor, do you know that?" Just in case he hadn't gotten my point, I punched his shoulder hard enough to make us both wince. "I'll never trust you again, so pack your bags. Your work here is done."

"Gorky hired me to protect you," Brad argued as I stalked off.

I slammed my palm on the ID pad, impatient for the door to swing open so I could close it in his face. "You were hired by a murderous, evil, manipulative syndicate boss, Brad. Don't sugarcoat it."

"He's all those things, but he wanted to protect you. And I had some way cool memories of you, Angel. Surely, you haven't forgotten our week in New Orleans."

"No, but I will now." I frosted him with an icy look over

my shoulder. "I'm quite good at making myself forget the past. And forgetting you will be easy."

"I did nothing wrong," he persisted, following when I stepped into the foyer.

I turned, hands on hips, forcing him to stop at the threshold. "How do you figure that you did nothing wrong?"

He raised his hands in his we're-cool gesture. "I'll leave you alone, Angel, but I'm going to do my best to see you don't get hurt. If you need me, call. If you don't ever want to speak to me again, fine." He pointed his index finger at my chest, anger now simmering in his beach-boy blue eyes. "But just remember, I've protected you from harm. Last I heard, that's not a crime."

"I'm grateful you saved me from the Shadowman. But you also alerted Gorky's spies that you were coming to pay a little visit on my behalf, allowing them to escape."

"No, I didn't. I didn't *have* to warn them we were coming."

His peculiar emphasis caught me off guard. "What do you mean?"

"Your place is bugged."

The door finally swung open, but I barely noticed. I looked closely to see if Brad was telling the truth.

"Gorky has been tracking your every move," Brad said, sounding disgusted with himself now that his complicity was out in the open. "How else do you think Detective Marco managed to get to the crime scenes so fast?"

"How did you know that?"

"Gorky told me. He says he doesn't trust your detective friend, but he wanted to make sure Marco was at the scene of the crimes so he could make sure you didn't get railroaded by the criminal injustice system."

I waved a hand in the air. "No more. I've heard enough for one night." I'd heard too much.

* * *

Naturally, the first thing I did was comb my two-flat for signs of bugging devices. Let me paint a better picture—I ran through the apartment like a raving maniac, pulling out drawers, flipping through papers and looking under beds. I found nada.

Hearing the commotion, Lola knocked on the door. She had been playing cards with Jimmy downstairs, and he took the service elevator, joining us a few minutes later.

"What is going on here?" Lola demanded to know, her plump fists planted on either side of the cylinder that used to be her waist.

Jimmy wheeled after me. "What is it, Angel? What are you looking for? I can help."

"I'm looking for an eavesdropping device," I muttered angrily as I flashed a pin light under the easy chair.

"What on earth for?" Lola asked. "You broke up a card game I was about to win."

I growled with frustration and stood, shooing a miniature dust bunny from my hair with a swipe of a hand. "It's all about you, isn't it, Lola? It's always about you."

"Now, now, Angel," Jimmy said in his irritatingly avuncular style. "Your mother—"

"My mother," I shot back at him with seething precision, "is Sydney Bassett."

"Oh!" Lola sucked in an audible gasp of air and staggered a few steps back.

"Spare me the histrionics," I continued mercilessly. "They don't give out Academy Awards for melodrama."

"Now, Angel," Jimmy said, "be nice."

"Nice? She betrayed me to the most notorious syndicate leader in Chicago!"

"I did not!"

I slowly circled Lola, looking closer than I ever had before.

She wore a surprisingly tasteful beige and cream-colored pantsuit. Maybe Gorky had hired her a clothing consultant. Her face, though wrinkled and almost cartoonish in its expressiveness, was expertly painted with refined cosmetics. If I didn't know better, I'd think she was trying to emulate Sydney. If so, my earlier comment had been even crueler than I'd intended.

"What was your price, *Mom?*" I said sarcastically. "Was it the clothing he bought you? Or the attention he gave you? How much did Vladimir Gorky have to pay to get you to betray your only child?"

"I did not betray you!"

"My apartment has been bugged by the R.M.O.! You don't call that betrayal? I trusted you. I thought we had an agreement and were starting to have a real relationship."

"The R.M.O. was spying on you for your own protection, sweetie."

"Bullshit! Gorky has brainwashed you, Lola. If you're not going to tell me where the bugs are planted, I don't want to hear another word from you."

"But I don't know where they are!"

I grabbed two fistfuls of my hair, ready to tear it out. "They've got to be somewhere. I've searched every surface."

"M-maybe," Lola said through sniffles as she dabbed her eyes with a tissue, "th-they're planted in-inside something."

When she burst into tears, I turned my back on her. Lola had always used tears as a last defense, but I refused to be drawn in this time. Instead, I considered what she'd said.

"Maybe you're right. Maybe the bugging devices are implanted in something I'd never consider as a suspect location."

I scanned the room, looking for any object that had recently been introduced into my environment. Something that was mechanical or manufactured but didn't look like it. Something that looked natural enough that I might overlook it. My gaze breezed in a 360-degree pattern until I spotted Jimmy. Then I stopped.

"What?" he asked, regarding me with trepidation. "Why are you looking at me like that?"

"Oh, my God," I whispered as it all became clear in a flash. "It was you all along."

"Now, Angel," Jimmy said, smiling nervously, "I haven't done a thing."

I slowly stalked toward the compubot as the pieces of the puzzle fell into place. "You arrived the day that I was bonded out of the Crypt."

"It was a coincidence," he reasoned.

"And I was so busy that you moved in before I had a chance to say no. I tried to have you returned, but I couldn't get through the phone system. Now I know why. You were planted here as an operative."

"No, Angel!"

"Leave him alone." Lola came to Jimmy's defense, standing behind his wheelchair, gripping the rubber handles as if she was prepared to run me over. "Stop picking on him."

I glared at her like a gunslinger in the old west. "Back away, Lola. You don't know what you're doing. He's a compubot."

"Compubots have feelings, too."

"That's just a TV jingle from a public-service announcement. I bought into that propaganda myself." I returned my focus to Jimmy. He still wore the same tailored pajamas he'd arrived in. He looked up at me like a puppy dog caught rifling through the trash. "Now I realize that his feelings are nothing more than top-notch programming."

"But I still *feel,* Angel," Jimmy said. "And one of my feelings is loyalty. I would never spy on you."

"Jimmy, I know you believe what you just said. But this

has nothing to do with you. It has everything to do with the people who manufactured you and installed eavesdropping equipment somewhere…inside you. Probably on orders from Gorky. With my luck, I'll probably find out he's on the board of directors of AutoMates, Inc."

"No, no, he's not," Jimmy said in a nervous rush, cowering as I loomed over him.

"How would you know?" I rasped, finally at the breaking point. "You're just a pawn, like all of us in this room."

"Speak for yourself!" Lola snapped.

I held out my hand. "I need your programming chip, Jimmy. If you don't do it, I will."

"No." He shook his head almost desperately.

I marveled that his creators had somehow managed to re-create human survival instinct. Or was he simply panicked over the prospect of failing to achieve his prime directive of spying on me?

"I won't let you take it, Angel. I came here to replace Bogie. I've done nothing but try to please you."

"Give it to me."

"No!"

I grabbed his shoulders, pulled him forward, and reached between his back and the wheelchair, fumbling to find the chip.

"Leave him alone!" Lola shouted, shoving me.

"Damn it, Lola!" I tried to push her away without hurting her while Jimmy made a sneaky bid to escape. I stuck my foot between the spokes of one of his two large wheels, but he kept going. "Ow! Stop!"

I grabbed his armrest and bent over to wheedle my foot free. Pain shot through my ribs. Just then Lola whopped the side of my head with a chair cushion. Moaning and cursing, fending off her blows, I nevertheless managed to dig behind Jimmy and grab the computer chip edging out just above the waistband of his pajama bottoms. He started to fling himself out of the chair, but I yanked out what amounted to his brain which, oddly enough, was closer to his ass than his head.

That ended the struggle. Jimmy sat upright, closed his eyes and went into synthesleep mode. Lola glared at me as if I'd killed him.

"I've seen a side of you today, Angel, that shames me."

I clutched the chip in my fist. "I'm sorry. I don't like myself very much right now, either. But that's the least of my concerns. Please, Lola, go back downstairs and leave me alone for a few days. We'll hash things out when all of this is over."

At the rate I was going, that would be sometime during the next century.

Chapter 20

White Tiger, Blue Dragon

There were nearly a hundred hits on my Info-Tech system, from reporters requesting interviews to fellow retributionists who'd shaken down tidbits of information to a request for half of my liver from the Living Donor Organ Bank, which had called for the umpteenth time this month. If that group didn't stop harassing me, I was going to have to vent my spleen.

I didn't return any calls, except for a quick message to my lawyer's system. I crashed, slept fitfully and woke up just before dawn. I must have been working things out in my dreams, because I knew exactly what I had to do as soon as my eyes popped open.

I felt my way in semidarkness to the kitchen. Through an open window, I heard Mike's chanting floating up from the garden. Tranquil rose-colored light streaked across the building-etched horizon. I heaved a sigh, finally reclaiming a semblance of centeredness. I retrieved my crystal ball, which I kept on the counter, and placed it at the kitchen table.

I put my hands on the cool glass and mentally invited more details of Marco's brutal crime. As always, I was relieved when the crystal ball grew warm and sparks of orange light glowed inside. I still wasn't convinced I was a bona-fide psychic. My ability seemed too accidental. I guess I didn't trust anything I couldn't control.

This time, though, my eagerness for a vision warred with dread that I might actually have one. Did Marco have even more dark secrets? Could I take any more?

I focused on the vision, surprised that it was not at all what I had expected. Marco was walking arm-in-arm with a beautiful young woman. He was young, too. And there was a child tagging along behind them, maybe three years old. The woman laughed at something he said. He stopped, stroked her cheek, laughed himself, then kissed her deeply.

They're in love. The certainty hit my heart like a wrecking ball. Marco scooped up the child and they walked on.

"Oh, Lord," I whispered, "is Marco married?"

As soon as I voiced the question, the vision disappeared. The glass grew cold. The session had been successful. I had more answers. Unfortunately, they were answers to questions I hadn't even thought to ask.

Marco arrived at the mayoral mansion just as the streetlights flickered out for the day. A rosy hint of sunrise tinged the white fog, hovering over the lake on the other side of Lake Shore Drive and hugging the chimney tops of the impressive Gold Coast historic manses, tightly spaced on a tranquil street that was quaintly crowded with trees.

The mayor's limo and liveried driver waited for him curbside. Marco nodded to the driver and jogged up the steep brick stairway to the second-story entrance. An undercover cop he recognized but didn't know came out of the front door to check him out and politely tell him to get lost. The mayor was under tightened security and wouldn't see anyone at home.

"Call him," was Marco's terse reply. "Tell him Detective Marco knows who killed his son. And it's not Angel Baker."

This astounding statement was met with a dubious scowl, but the cop knew Marco had him checkmated. He couldn't blow off anyone who might have new information on Victor Alvarez's murder. And Marco's forthright approach worked. Moments later, to the cop's obvious resentment, the mayor's personal assistant escorted Marco to a lush and stately library.

He sat in one of two dark red leather winged-back chairs and waited, scanning the twelve-foot-high bookcases filled with classics that looked as if they were there more for show than pleasure. There wasn't a hint of Alvarez's Hispanic roots in the room. Rather, Marco felt like he'd stepped into a British drawing room.

The heavy wooden library door opened fast and Alvarez, somewhat stocky but dapperly dressed in a conservative suit, filled the room with his presence. He walked purposefully across the room to shake hands. "Detective Marco, good to see you."

"Likewise, sir."

The two men had developed a cordial relationship while working together on the mayor's top-secret Mob Termination Committee. Alvarez motioned for Marco to sit, then took the winged-back chair next to his.

"Tell me what you know."

Marco settled at the edge of his chair. "Angel Baker is innocent."

Alvarez looked back and forth between Marco's eyes, pursing his full, small mouth thoughtfully beneath his thick, dark mustache. "What are you saying?"

"I'm saying that Angel was set up."

The mayor's attentive gaze gelled into a condescending sheen. "You're in love with her. Lieutenant Townsend told me everything."

"She's been set up by Vladimir Gorky. His *sgarristas* killed Victor and Roy Leibman and Getty Bellows."

The mayor listened, then slammed a hand unexpectedly on a leather arm of his chair. "Damn it, Marco!" He jumped up, smoothed a hand over his carefully coiffed brown hair, then began to pace. "I don't want to hear this. I hate Gorky as much as you do, but he didn't kill my son."

"How do you know he didn't?"

The mayor's sleek, black dress shoes slid an inch to an abrupt stop on the thick carpet. He jabbed a finger in the air. "I know what you're doing. You're playing all your cards for your girlfriend's benefit."

"No."

"You're trying to play on my conscience because I decided to give Gorky a pass until after the next election and you didn't want to wait to take him down."

"I wouldn't play games with you like that. I'm here because I know Angel is innocent, and as long as you allow the police force to use her as a quick fix to their public-relations problem, you're letting the real killer go free."

Alvarez studied Marco, assessing him with a jaundiced eye and the political acumen that had kept the mayor in power for three terms. Only now a bit of the passion and zest Alvarez had worn like a bright suit of armor had tarnished. Marco suspected the man would never fully recover from the death of his son.

"I'm so sorry about Victor. But you can't let your pain blind you to the truth. Bring Gorky in and question him about Victor's murder."

"Bring Gorky in for questioning? Talk about a fucking public relations disaster," the mayor said disparagingly. "Marco, you know if I thought for an instant that Gorky killed my boy, I'd hang him by the balls from the Sears Tower. But you're wrong. You're letting your emotions cloud your judgment. What in God's name did Gorky do to you to make you despise him so much that you'd try to lay every crime in this city at his doorstep?"

Marco leaned back in the chair and shut his eyes, sighing as the memories clawed painfully to the surface. Some wrongs were so heinous they couldn't be righted. They could only be avenged.

"I lost two of the people I loved most in the world."

After a long pause, the mayor said, "I'm sorry."

Marco stood with weary resignation and walked to the door, turning back to say, "I'm not going to lose another. You'll be wrong on this one, Alvarez. You'll wish you'd backed me. Just wait and see."

"I had a dream last night, Angel," Mike said.

"Really?" I replied offhandedly.

Normally I hung on Mike's every prophetic word, but I was preoccupied with watching the Bassetts' front door. After seeing that child with Marco in my crystal ball, I'd been overcome with the desire—no, the need—to see my foster daughter. So I'd talked Mike into driving me up to Evanston in his new used car. It was a beater that shook and rattled as if it would fall apart at every stoplight, but we made it in one piece. And we did it legally. Mike had finally gotten his driving license.

We'd parked across the street and a few cars down from

the house. If I got caught even trying to talk to Lin, my bond would be revoked. So I'd have to be content with a good look as she passed by. If she didn't come out of the house soon, I'd call Sydney and ask her to contrive some errand for Lin.

"You do not want to know what my dream was about?" Mike prodded when I did not nibble at his bait.

"I'm sorry, *sifu*," I said, grinning his way, "you're not getting enough attention from your devotee?"

He shrugged indifferently, looking very western in his jeans and button-down shirt. "It does not matter to me. The dream was about you."

"Great." I turned my attention back to the front door of the stately gray-stone Tudor house I'd once called home, looking for Lin. "Whenever you dream about me, something really bad usually happens."

"At least you know about it ahead of time."

"That doesn't count if there's nothing I can do to change the course of events."

"So I will not tell you about the dream."

"Go ahead. I can take it. I'm tough. I'm desperate. My life is for shit. What's a little more?"

"It was also about Detective Marco."

My stomach tied itself into a knot over that one. Feigning disinterest, I said, "Oh?"

"You were both visiting the Shaolin Temple in China. You came to see the monks perform kung fu for the tourists. Marco had come with you. He said something and you laughed. Then he stroked your face and kissed you."

My head pivoted sharply. This was starting to sound too much like my vision. "Was there a kid in the dream? Maybe a three-year-old?"

Mike shook his head. "Just you and Marco and the performing monks."

"What happened next?"

"Marco went away to talk to a friend, and while he was gone he turned into a white tiger."

"What does that mean?" In China, animals were significant symbols of human conditions or traits. Everything had a hidden meaning.

Mike stared at the Bassetts' house a moment before answering. "The white tiger is a predator, a symbol of war. Very powerful."

"More powerful than a blue dragon?"

He didn't answer, but his gaze slid nervously my way. I regretted posing the question. If I got into a power struggle with Marco, we'd both lose. At this point the stakes were way too high for silly games.

"What happened after he turned into the white tiger?"

"You touched him." Some sort of inner disturbance wrinkled his smooth brow. "And he killed you."

Before I could reply, I heard the distant sounds of a door opening and laughter.

"It's Lin!" I leaned my head out the passenger window as far as I dared, greedily consuming every detail of the lithe little seven-year-old girl. Her mahogany hair bounced around her nimble shoulders as she bounded down the front steps to the sidewalk. She had on a new outfit—a red plaid skirt and white doily blouse. I didn't recognize it and felt a pang of jealousy that she'd been shopping with Sydney. I should feel grateful, and I was. But I had so wanted to be there for Lin in every way.

"Isn't she beautiful, Mike?"

"Yes."

"I'm so glad she's happy. I feel like I haven't seen her in a year, but it's only been a few days. She wouldn't forget me in that short time, would she?"

"No one could forget Angel Baker."

His tone was slightly sarcastic, but I felt reassured nonetheless. Mike and I had an unspoken agreement that we would never gush about our mutual affection.

"I wonder what she's doing outside." I had my answer when my older foster sister made her grand exit, giving a ta-ta wave to Sydney, who watched their departure through the glass door.

The very sight of the ultraperky, ultracoiffed Gigi put me on edge. I had barely thought about the fact that she would be interacting with Lin in my absence. The extent to which she would exploit the situation became clear when Lin trotted back up the sidewalk and took Gigi's hand.

I literally gasped at this evidence of their quick bonding. Then my jaw dropped when I realized they were dressed like twins. Gigi wore an identical plaid skirt and white blouse. If I didn't know better I'd think Getty Bellows had risen from the dead.

"Unbelievable! I think I'm going to be sick."

"I see double," Mike said.

Gigi squatted until she was eye level with Lin. She stroked Lin's bangs, smiling wide as if she were a model in a toothpaste commercial, then pointed to her own cheek, demanding a kiss. I watched in horror as Lin obliged. I couldn't see whether she was happy about it or not, but it didn't matter.

"That's it. I can't take any more." I pushed the exit button and my door whooshed skyward.

"No, Baker, stay." Mike reached for my arm, but too late. No sooner had I stepped out of the vehicle than my lapel phone rang. I was torn between answering it and running after Gigi before she and Lin drove off for another shopping spree. I popped the phone in my ear, mumbling, "Who is it?"

"It's Sydney."

At the rich and dignified sound of my foster mother's voice, I abandoned all thoughts of Gigi and looked toward the house. Sydney watched me through the glass door. She had spotted me and was giving me a look of motherly warning.

"You can't go after them, Angel. The police have been keeping an eye on our house. If they drive by while you're talking with Lin, you'll have to go back to jail."

"I know," I said raggedly, watching Lin climb into Gigi's car.

"At least I know you're back on your feet after that vicious attack. You're feeling okay now?"

"Sydney, how could you let her do this to me? She's trying to steal my daughter from me, just like she tried to steal you and Henry from me."

My foster mother paused, and I could almost hear the pain crackling between us. "Lin needed to get out of the house. I've told her that you're coming for her soon. And I believe you will, darling, but until then, Lin needs to live as normal a life as possible. Think of the trauma she's been through already."

Her sound logic chastened me. "I'm sorry. It's just...do they have to dress alike?"

Sydney chuckled softly. "It's pathetic, isn't it? They went shopping and that's what Gigi brought home. I tried to talk her into taking her outfit back, but she convinced me that Lin was amused by the idea of dressing like an adult."

There was another long pause as I tried to gulp back the emotion that swelled in my throat. "Sydney...Sydney do you think Lin will want to come back to my house when this is over?"

"Oh, sweetheart, of course she will. She asks about you every night when I put her to bed. You know, Angel, there were many times when you were young that Henry and I thought we were going to lose you. It seemed we were constantly battling the system to keep you in our home."

"You guys were terrific."

"And it all worked out for the best. But even if it didn't, if the worst had come to past, and we had lost you, I would have known that you carried a part of us with you. Even if one day you were to forget all about us, I would have known you were a better person for having been loved by us."

"And for loving you," I said in a half-voice as tears swelled in my eyes.

I heard Sydney sniffle, but she didn't admit to tears, and I didn't see her wipe her eyes.

"Go home now, sweetheart. Henry and Hank are doing everything they can to help your attorney build his case."

"Do you think Henry has forgiven me?"

"I'm sure he has. He's going to call later today and tell you the courtroom strategy he and Berkowitz have hammered out."

"Has Henry found a rabbit to pull out of the hat? I'd settle for a dwarf bunny."

"You don't need magic, Angel. What you need is another viable suspect."

I leaned back in the passenger seat and stretched out for the ride back to the Lakeview Neighborhood. Shutting my eyes, I replayed Sydney's comments in my head. *A viable suspect.* She was right. I needed a sop to throw the prosecutors who would otherwise be loathe to admit I'd been mistakenly arrested. And funnily enough, I did have a viable alternative murder suspect—Marco.

There was no reason to believe that Gorky could have fabricated the realistic images in those horrific photographs. So how could I love a man capable of such brutality? And how could that man be the same one who had made love to me so sweetly? But he had and I did and the knowledge of both these facts rammed my heart like a burning ember. It was paralyzing pain. Yet my mind still worked and sought some order and analysis of the evidence.

Perhaps Marco had become a cop to make amends for heinous crimes committed in his youth. Then again, maybe he was a sociopath using the perks and authority of his profession to stalk his victims.

He'd first appeared at my door a few months ago out of the blue, claiming that he had just graduated from a detective training program after serving for years as a psychologist in the police department. He said he was reopening the investigation into his half-brother's murder, who'd been gunned down in a drug deal gone awry, which I had witnessed.

When that excuse for making my acquaintance proved misleading, Marco claimed he was using me to learn more about Gorky via Lola for the mayor's secret committee. Obviously, that too was a lie, since he knows Gorky as well as, if not better, than my mother does.

So what was Marco's real reason for knocking on my door? Perhaps he was casing the joint for his planned attack against Certified Retribution Specialists. Gorky had said the murderer wanted to discredit my profession, and that would certainly fit in with Marco's disdain for retributionists. He once called me a vigilante.

Oh God, was that the real reason he had asked me to give up my work? Had he unintentionally fallen in love with me and then needed a way to protect me from his own murderous plot?

A white tiger indeed. It was time that Detective Marco and I had a little chat.

Chapter 21

Blast in the Past

When I trudged up the stairs to my apartment, I found myself disappointed to see that Jimmy was still deep in permanent synthesleep. I guess I'd gotten used to having him around. The AutoMates pickup service was supposed to come for him today. I'd finally gotten through the voice-mail system. That was probably because whoever planted the bug in Jimmy's system realized it was no longer working.

While I was pouring myself a glass of iced tea in the kitchen, my phone beeped. It was Henry, who wanted to update me on trial preparations. I plugged the earpiece in and wandered out to the living room while we chatted.

According to Henry, it was time I stopped gallivanting around the streets in search of evidence and started huddling with my lawyer. When he asked what my investigation had uncovered, I shared the information gathered by some of my colleagues and their PIs. I did not share with him my suspicions about Marco, but nevertheless his name came up in the conversation.

"Angel, Berkowitz thinks he might be able to get the case thrown out of court on a technicality."

"No!" I sat upright in the armchair. "You're kidding. How can that be possible? I chose the Diva. I thought I was screwed."

"Well, he didn't say he could settle it before you went to trial. But he thinks the judge might dismiss the case once Berkowitz makes it clear that you were involved with the arresting officer."

I took a long moment before responding. "How did you know that I was seeing Detective Marco?"

"Hank told me. We both thought it might cast doubt on the legality of your arrest."

"It won't."

"How do you know?"

"The public defender assigned to me in the Crypt told me that judges ignore that kind of thing in their haste to keep the wheels of justice cranking and groaning."

"Well, he was wrong, if Berkowitz is to believed. And I'd trust him more than a public defender. How did you get him, anyway? There's always a long line of suspects waiting for free representation."

"He had his arm twisted by Marc—" I stopped midsentence. Once again the dots of this ugly little picture were connecting back to Marco. How convenient it would be for him to have me misunderstand my rights so that I wouldn't bring his name into the case.

"Detective Marco set you up with this bozo?" Henry said. And I didn't need to see his distinguished gray eyebrows raise nearly to his thinning hairline to get the gist of his incredulous question.

"Yes, Henry. You know, I'm starting to feel like a gullible...ditz."

"A ditz you are not, my dear. But your boyfriend is a son of a bitch."

I gasped. "Henry!"

"You need to break with him, honey. Publicly and personally."

"No, Henry—"

"He's not worth your loyalty."

"I just need to talk to him one more time. There is something I need to ask him. Then I'll make a clean cut."

"The sooner the better, Angel."

"Okay," I said reluctantly.

We made arrangements to meet the next day at Berkowitz's downtown office, and said our goodbyes.

When our conversation ended, I sat a moment, torn between joy over the possible resolution of the charges against me and regret that it would depend on making Marco the bad guy. Even if Marco was innocent of all the crimes I feared he had committed, his reputation would be badly damaged.

And most upsetting of all—I knew Henry was right. I had to cut Marco off at the knees. But I didn't want to. I'd almost rather go down than lose what he and I had together. How pathetic was that?

Frustrated, I looked around the room and found my Personal Listening Device looking at me, eyes open. Her face was an inexpensive blend of synthetics that didn't feel much like skin but allowed for movement of the jaw and eyelids. With her puffy blond hair and permanent hot pink lipstick, her resemblance to my foster sister had never seemed so strong.

"What are you looking at?" I demanded to know. "I thought Jimmy had turned you off."

She blinked. "Hello, Angel. Would you like to talk?"

"Oh, yeah," I said, dripping sarcasm. "I'd *love* to talk with you, *Gigi*. I'd love to tell you how much I want to strangle your pretty little neck."

"That's nice," she replied, dripping sugar.

"I'd love to tell you that there's something I've wanted to do for a long, long time," I said, putting down my glass and stalking her like an animal in the jungle. I picked her up by the neck, which was made of a porcelain-like substance with a rotating joint at the point where her head was attached.

"What is it you want to do, Angel?" She tried to hold my gaze, but it was difficult when I started marching toward the back porch with her cradled in my arms. Her glassy eyes moved herky jerky every time my stride threw her out of balance.

"What are you doing, Angel?" she asked when I shoved open the screen door and walked to the porch railing overlooking my garden.

"You'll see." I held her up in front of my face for one last good look. "Goodbye, Gigi, it was nice knowing you."

"Goodbye, Angel."

With that, I let go and the robotic device fell to the patio below. The sound of breakage was music to my ears. I wanted to gloat over the mangled mess, but the doorbell rang. I ran inside, found out it was the AutoMates pickup service, buzzed them up, then ran back outside and down to the garden to make sure Gigi was as destroyed as she looked.

I picked up the cracked device, delighted that one of those creepy blue eyes had shattered, then turned it over to examine the guts of the computer system, which hung from the bottom by a wire. That's when I saw it.

"Oh, no," I whispered to myself. Attached to the matchbook-size black smart box that housed the device's central brain was a button-sized red eavesdropping device. "Just one more reason to hate you, Gigi."

I ripped out the bug and ran upstairs just in time to see a lanky young man in a white jumpsuit wheeling Jimmy out my door.

"Wait! Stop!"

The deliveryman looked at me as if I were crazy.

"You can't take him," I pronounced. "He didn't do it."

"Didn't do what, ma'am?" He scratched his head, clearly not in the mood for a change of plans.

"He didn't sp—" I caught myself. "There's a misunderstanding. Jimmy has to stay."

"I have orders."

When he started to pull out an e-tracker, I ran to my stash of money chips and returned, pressing one into his palm. "I'm sorry for your trouble," I said glibly. "Have a nice day."

He looked at the amount I'd given him and nodded agreeably. "Don't mention it, ma'am."

When the delivery truck zoomed off, I wheeled Jimmy to the middle of the room and reinstalled the program in the small of his back. A few computer beeps later, his eyes opened, his body came back to virtual life, and he looked at me.

"What's wrong, Angel?"

"Nothing, you dear man!" I kissed him full on the mouth then tousled his hair. "Nothing is wrong. You didn't spy on me. It was that stupid Personal Listening Device."

"Gigi? Where is she?"

"Where is *it*," I corrected. "I destroyed it." I ran both hands through my hair and paced in aimless circles, full of giddiness and relief.

"Why are you so happy?" Jimmy asked.

I turned on him with a brilliant smile. "Because you didn't betray me. Oh, I know your loyalty doesn't matter because 're not...real. But still, I never suspected you, and my trust you turned out to be justified. I'd always hated that PLD, my suspicions proved valid in that case as well. And Lola right, as well. She had predicted these murders were con-ted to a woman who had no heart."

"That's right," Jimmy said, agreeing as far as it went, but arly he didn't understand why being right meant so much ne in this instance.

But my heart understood, even if my brain wasn't quite dy to agree, that if Jimmy hadn't betrayed me when I ught he had, maybe Marco hadn't, either.

Two hours later, I stepped off of busy Clark Street on the r northside of the city into what used to be the Biograph eater. Now called the Tommy Gun Interpretive Center, it half a block of connected buildings filled with games, es, shops and displays celebrating Chicago's long history gangs. Basically, it was a glorified tourist trap. The Bio-ph was the place where cops arrested John Dillinger, Pub-Enemy #1, in 1934.

walked into the movie house, which showed antiquated vs footage detailing the war between South side gangster Capone and his North side rival Bugs Moran. I picked up ap of the arcade. Popping corn sounded like the muted rat-t of a machine gun, and the buttery smell made my stom-gurgle. When Marco called saying he wanted to meet me e, I'd dropped everything, including lunch.

wasn't sure why he wanted to meet in a public place, and h a surreal one at that, but this was probably the best for it I suspected would be our showdown. If we weren't ne, we'd have to keep the melodrama, not to mention dly assaults, to a minimum.

skirted a crowd as it exited the theater at the end of a

showing and moved on through a virtual arcade, where do
ens of people stood on small platforms, wearing comp
glasses, swinging their virtual Tommy guns this way and th
as they played out scenes from the gory days of Al Capon

I passed by kiosks selling Elliot Ness FBI badges and ca
puccino. I took a pass on the badges but bought a coffee to ti
me over. Heading toward the museum in the back of the co
plex, my chest began to constrict with nerves. Or was it exci
ment? Or the caffeine narrowing my arteries? In truth, I could
wait to feast my eyes on the swarthy, muscular Riccuc
Marco. I actually felt a twinge of desire just thinking about hi

You need therapy, Baker, I told myself as I took anoth
slug of enervating caffeine. I'd always known that a childho
of neglect had made me a master of disassociation, but th
was ridiculous. In my mind, there was a good Marco an
bad Marco. I couldn't wait to make love again with the go
one, all the while hoping the bad one wouldn't slit my thro

For some reason the back of the building was empty. I w
to the ticket booth, but no one was there to charge admissi
to the museum. This wing of the arcade must have been s
down, yet I'd managed to wander back here unnoticed. Si
I hated crowds, I was happy to go it alone.

"Marco?" I called out when I entered the oblong, high-c
inged brick building.

When I didn't get an answer, I wandered around the la
exhibition hall. With shiny wooden floors and walls ma
from the bricks of the garage where four of Al Capone's
sassins, dressed like police, gunned down seven of Bu
Moran's men in the infamous 1929 Valentine's Day Mas
cre. Moran was the rakish, hot-tempered leader of the No
Side "Irish Gang" that competed with Capone for dominar
in illegal liquor sales.

This wing was a pleasing blend of old and new. A bull

lden black Ford was parked in one corner. In another was
ile of wooden liquor barrels from Capone's bootleg oper-
ons. I was particularly taken with a life-sized robotics dis-
ay of a Capone and Ness argument.

And then there were the wax figures of the men who had
en slaughtered execution style. Fake blood had been splat-
ed on the brick wall behind their crumpled and bloody
dies. It was too realistic, and I stifled a gag as a wave of
dness, nausea and thwarted anger over the death of my
ends threatened to undo me.

"Angel."

I gasped and jumped, whirling. "Marco!" Coffee splashed
d burned my hand. "Ouch." I dumped the two-thirds-full
p in a nearby waste bin.

"Let me see your hand," he said intimately, grasping my
ist. He pulled out a cloth handkerchief—who had those
ymore?—and wiped the milky coffee from my fingers,
ning my hand over with care to make sure he'd dabbed
ry drop.

Satisfied, he tucked the kerchief in the pocket of his tai-
ed, pleated sea-green pants, pushing back the flowing folds
his aquamarine, knee-length Renaissance coat. The light
at was made of smart fiber and the weave had widened to
commodate the heat of the museum. Underneath he wore
oose white linen shirt. With his dark hair coiled just above
high collar, he reminded me of Mozart.

"You look like a composer."

"Can't play a note." A skylight cast a rectangle of sun on
brown eyes. They looked like caramels, slowly melting in
heat that passed between us. "But I am a painter. Strictly
ateur."

"You'll have to tell me more about that sometime." I found

myself moving toward him, unable to deny my attraction.
was surprised to see the paintings in your apartment."

"I was surprised to see *you* in my apartment. That day s
off a long, crazy chain of events. But I'd do it again, Ang
I'd do anything for you."

"I've missed you, too," I said, the truth winning out ov
conscience.

His hands slid around my waist and moved, smooth a
hot, like the sun up my back as he pulled me close. I slid n
hands up his strong arms, over broad shoulders and arou
the back of his neck, where heated skin met the fringes of l
unruly, dark hair. We needed no words. Our lips connecte
brushed, caressed, then fused. I breathed in his luscio
breath. Like a shot of pure oxygen, it made me high.

Locked in a deep, full-bodied kiss, I was on anoth
planet. The world could have exploded around us and
wouldn't have noticed. I wasn't sure if this was hello
goodbye, right or wrong, but since the moment seemed
be all I had left in this world, I was going to live in it as lo
as I could.

Marco's tongue rotated intense and deeply around my ov
Who needed to make love when you could kiss like this?

But all good things must come to an end. When we fina
detached ourselves, both gasping in wonder, trying to find b
ance as we came down to earth, I searched his eyes a
stroked his cheeks. He gave me such pleasure, but still the
was so much pain.

"Marco?" I rasped, knowing I had to speak. "Are you t
killer?"

His face went dead, though he still clung to me as if I we
a life raft, just as I still held him.

"Did you kill Roy and Victor and Getty?"

He frowned. "Is that why you asked me to come here?"

I took in a breath, held it, then released it, saying, "But I didn't. You called me."

We looked at each other as realization set in.

"Oh, my God," I said.

"Let's get out of here!"

He grabbed my hand and ran for the exit just as the building exploded around us.

Chapter 22

Falling Water on the Lake

Just before the blast propelled deadly slivers of bricks, concrete and glass like missiles into the ticket area, Marco and briefly fought each other, both trying to be the one on top— the protector. We quickly compromised and rolled togethe behind a giant steel bank vault that Capone's goons had onc robbed. It saved our lives.

Scratched, bruised and disoriented, but otherwise miracu lously fine, I climbed to my unsteady feet while Marco leane against the steel vault and made a call on his wrist phone. assumed he was calling for help.

I stumbled toward the burning rubble of what was now a open-air museum with obliterated displays. Wind blew smok my way, and I coughed, covering my mouth with a forearm Sirens wailed in the distance.

Museum officials, who had been so suspiciously absent before, now came running, shouting in disbelief, dispensing panicked orders. Keeping my nose out of it, I staggered back to the bank vault, gripping it for support.

Marco, now standing, looked like rage incarnate. He held his wrist up to his mouth and hissed, "You bloody bastard, you almost killed Angel."

There was a pause.

"She's here. At the museum. With me. We're coming to see you. Make sure the gates are open."

Marco and I said little as he zoomed his hydrocruiser northward along the lakefront. I didn't have to ask where we were going. Nor was I surprised when he pulled into Falling Water on the Lake, Gorky's lakeside compound. The gates, as Marco had requested, opened as soon we pulled onto the private drive.

"Marco," I said as the safety belts released me, "why are we here?"

He reached over and took my hand, squeezing hard, a world of regret and anger swirling in his deep eyes. "It's time we stopped the game."

"Is that what this has been? A game?"

"There are things you need to know, Angel, and you need to hear them from the original source."

"Why?" I inquired in a small voice. "I'd rather hear it from you. Why can't you tell me?"

His handsome mouth creased with an empathetic smile. "Because you'd never believe me."

I nodded, swallowing my trepidation, and we walked hand-in-hand to Gorky's front door. It was déjà vu all over again. I was glad to have Marco at my side this time. He may be a bad guy, but he ranked low on the bad-guy scale. I guess even evil could be relative.

As the housekeeper led us down the circuitous hallway toward the back of the house, I only peripherally noticed the opulent rooms we passed, each decorated in different styles that spanned the centuries—a Greco-Roman indoor swimming pool room, a Victorian sitting room, a jungle atrium, and an ultramodern home theater, to name a few.

Blood pounded in my ears so loudly I thought I was having a stroke. But I was too young and fit for that. Or was I? Scientists had proved a person could die from a broken heart. Could too many unpleasant truths congeal like a clot in the brain and kill you on the spot?

My morose ruminations came to a halt when we entered the upper level of Gorky's spectacular study, which stretched across the back of the house, the room for which the house had been named. Designed in a style reminiscent of famed twentieth-century architect Frank Lloyd Wright, it loomed over the lake in triangular fashion, with steel beams jutting out at a slight angle from the floor to the ceiling, plated in fantastic sheets of glass. When I briefly faced the lake, I felt as if I could just step through the glass and walk on water.

I turned and saw that Marco had joined Gorky on the sunken main floor by a fireplace made of giant stone slabs. The floor, too, was an uneven but intriguing patchwork of polished, natural stone. Being here was like being in nature and being indoors at the same time.

In fact, nature was all too close. I glanced anxiously at the open stairwell on the far side of the room. You could actually walk down a short flight of stairs, open a door and dive into oceanic Lake Michigan. Gorky had apparently created this unusual feature to pay homage to Wright. The architect's unsurpassed masterpiece, named Falling Water, had been built over a Pennsylvania waterfall and included a watery back exit.

"We'll talk about that in a moment," Gorky said sternly to

Marco, who was so in his face I feared Gorky might knife him at any moment.

"No, damn you, tell her now!" Marco insisted.

Gorky disengaged without reply and stepped toward me, assuming a host's magnanimous smile. Dressed in sleek white silk pants and a collarless white silk shirt, with silver chest hair peaking out, he looked almost elegant. "Angel *moy,* please come join us. I have espresso waiting."

If he'd said vodka, I would have refused. But espresso was my lifeblood, and I needed to be as clearheaded as possible, so I took the three short steps to the sunken circular main floor and accepted the minuscule coffee cup Gorky offered.

"Thank you," I said, but didn't look at him. I glanced at Marco, who watched me carefully. A thought suddenly occurred to me. "This isn't poisoned, is it?"

Why I expected a straight answer, I didn't know. But I trusted Marco's judgment, and he helped himself to his waiting coffee, albeit unenthusiastically.

"Dorogaya moya," Gorky admonished, putting a hand over his heart and sinking down into a Stickley lounge chair as if he was too weak to stand. "You wound me. Why would I poison you?"

The shock of the explosion was beginning to wear off and my hand began to shake, rattling my espresso cup and saucer as if an earthquake had struck. I gripped the saucer with my other hand and tossed the acrid caffeine essence to the back of my throat, swallowing all at once, then put the china on a side table.

Fortified, I widened my stance, squaring off for an honest confrontation.

"Why would you poison me?" I repeated, anger replacing trepidation. "Lots of reasons. Chief among them, however, is the fact that you just tried to kill me and Marco in an explosion at the Capone museum. But you failed. I knew all along I was the next victim in your cold-blooded plot, Gorky, but I didn't know how far you would go to do me in."

Gorky rubbed his chin with an open palm, as if testing to see if he needed another shave. Then he rested his elbows on the arms of the chair and regarded me seriously. "You have a right to be upset. I was furious when Marco called and said you were at the museum. I never intended to hurt you, nor was I responsible for that explosion."

"I suppose you're going to try to tell me it was Marco's fault. He was there, Gorky, he wouldn't have risked blowing himself up. Someone called us both, somehow managing to mimic our voices, and directed us to what was supposed to be a last, deadly rendezvous."

He grimaced, his silver, broom mustache moving beneath his prominent nose. "You are quite correct. It was not Marik."

"Then who was it?" Marco put down his coffee cup with a thud on the mantel. "We want evidence. Names. It's time to stop this deadly game of craps."

Gorky looked back and forth between us, weighing consequences only someone from his high altitude could reckon. Then he called for Alexia and told her it was time for their restricted guest to make his entrance.

Marco and I exchanged wary glances. Restricted guest? A prisoner?

My speculations came to a screeching halt when two R.M.O. thugs entered the upper level pushing in a rectangular container on rollers, stopping in front of the three steps to the lower level.

"Step aside," Gorky ordered his men and they made themselves scarce.

The container, roughly three feet squared in width and

five-feet tall was made of vertical metal bars, like an anti-quated animal cage at the zoo. Except this one contained a man.

"Lieutenant Townsend," I said. It was more a horrified whisper. I could hardly believe what I was seeing.

"Marco," Townsend said after spotting us. He reached a hand through the bars. "Help me! He's going to kill me. Get me out of here."

"Townsend," was all Marco could manage in reply, the throaty word rife with shock and dismay.

Townsend's thinning gray hair, usually combed neatly back, sprouted in limp tufts. His long, gray face was smudged with dirt and blood. His black, military-esque Q.E.D. uniform was in tatters. He tried to stand, but couldn't. And though he supposedly could feel no emotions, I thought I recognized humiliation and fear in his once-placid, now darting gray eyes. Surely the surgeons had not been unable to extract Townsend's survival instincts.

"Help me, Detective," he pleaded in a still commanding voice. "Save me from this madman."

"This man," Gorky said, rising to his full six-feet-four height, repeating for dramatic emphasis, "this man is the one who is responsible for the deaths of your fellow retribution-ists, Angel."

"That's a lie!" Townsend shouted, more for emphasis than out of anger. "Don't listen to him, Marco. He'll say anything to avoid responsibility for his own heinous crimes."

I looked at Marco. His easygoing confidence had given way to a terrible struggle between truth and lies, law and dis-order. His handsome face was now a mask of grim hatred, for whom I couldn't tell.

"I could say the same thing," Gorky said, ambling toward the cage, stopping without climbing the stairs. He motioned toward Townsend like a docent at the zoo. "The lieutenant will say anything to avoid his responsibility for the murders of Roy Leibman, Victor Alvarez, Getty Bellows…and what would have been the murder of Angel Baker and Riccuccio Marco, if fate hadn't intervened. When I heard about the explosion, just before you called, Marik, I had my men capture this piece of shit. He arrived here just before you did."

Marco turned to Gorky like a man preparing for a duel at dawn. "Explain," he ordered.

"Consider," Gorky said, leaning on the upper-level railing, "that Townsend was at both murder scenes."

"He's a cop!" Marco shot back.

"No, he's Q.E.D. There's a difference. They aren't usually the first responders. Am I wrong?"

Marco's grudging silence was answer enough.

"I have been following the investigations in the news," Gorky said, leisurely folding his powerful arms over his chest.

I doubted he needed to watch the news to get the inside story on any criminal investigation, but kept the thought to myself.

"Who else would have powerful enough connections to steal darling Angel's gun from a bank safety deposit box?" Gorky said with disingenuous dismay. "Who else would be powerful enough to change her phone records?"

"You," I said.

He held out his hands in a gesture of abject innocence. "Yes, Angel *moy,* but why would I do it? I already told you I have the greatest respect for your mother, and I am grateful to you for finding the Maltese Falcon. What possible motive would I have?"

"You don't like retributionists hassling your assassins and *sgarristas* on the street."

He nodded and wagged a finger at me. "You are right on that point. And that is why Lieutenant Townsend came to me and told me what he was going to do and asked me not to interfere. I agreed. But I determined that if he was going to kill Certified Retribution Specialists, he was not going to kill Angel Baker. And that is why I hired Vlad the Impaler, and that is why I set up the crew across from your apartment, to keep an eye on you and track your movements. To keep you safe."

He sat down again and folded his hands in his lap, smiling contentedly like Santa Claus after a long night of benevolent work on Christmas Eve.

Marco and I looked at each other. Nothing that Gorky had said rang false. In unison, we turned our discerning gazes, now suspiciously, toward Townsend.

Since he could not stand in the small cage, Townsend had been kneeling, and sank back on his heels in defeat.

"Very well," he said calmly, logically. "I will not try to deny it any longer."

"What?" I had so convinced myself that Gorky was responsible for the deaths of my friends that I almost couldn't accept a confession at face value. It made no sense.

"Why?" Marco asked Townsend. "Why in God's name would you do such a thing?"

"It seemed the logical thing to do," Townsend said, regarding Marco calmly. "You yourself, Detective, wanted politicians to rein in the growing presence of Certified Retribution Specialists. You head the police committee lobbying on that issue, and with good reason. Retributionists are usurping the traditional role of law enforcement. They are not sanctioned by any official covenant or law. To allow such a force to exist will lead to social anarchy."

"You cold-blooded bastard!" I shouted.

Ignoring me, he held Marco's angry gaze. "But you and the politicians were inefficient. You listened to constituents who considered retributionists heroes. You allowed yourself to delay action, when clearly action needed to be taken."

"And so you took this matter on yourself?" Marco asked.

"Q.E.D. decided it was in everyone's best interest. Well-meaning cops are too influenced by emotional considerations. The police chief was afraid of a public backlash if the CRS movement was suddenly outlawed."

"So you just planned to murder us all, one after another?" I asked as calmly as I could. "Weren't you worried about getting caught?"

He allowed his steady gaze to slide my way. "No. We wanted the public to think that your kind had morphed from vigilante protectors and avengers into assassins. The timing was propitious, since Judge Gibson had recently and obligingly crossed over the legal line by giving you warrants to terminate repeat restraining order violators. It was not a hard leap of logic, even for an ignorant public, to assume that you might get carried away and start assassinating whomever you pleased. I concluded that if I staged a few more unwarranted assassinations, the tide of public opinion would turn against you, and the gutless politicians would finally take action to outlaw your profession."

"You're good, Townsend," Gorky remarked, bobbing his head in admiration. "Very good."

Marco gave him a scathing look over his shoulder. "Depends on your definition of good." He walked closer to Townsend's cage, staring at the lieutenant as if he was, indeed, a strange animal not seen on this continent. "What about right and wrong, Townsend? How could you possibly have logically justified murdering innocent people?"

"That part was easy. Our society has always sanctioned killing for a good cause. It's called war, whether it involves defending our country or freeing the oppressed. For wars, even religious fundamentalists are willing to abandon their God-given creeds against killing. So I did not have to wrestle long with morality to conclude that the death of a few retributionists was a small price to pay for civil order and the resurgence of the government-sanctified police force. Surely, Detective, even you can see the logic in that."

"No, I don't. A death by any other name is death," Marco growled. "And justify it as we may try, we'll still have to answer to God for every life we take."

Townsend smiled wanly. "That doesn't worry me, Detective. I've logically considered the matter of a divine being and concluded that there is none."

"Then you won't have to say your prayers when I kill you," Gorky said in a merry tone. "Boys, take him down to the lake."

The two thugs, who had been lingering in the doorway, came into the room and started to roll the cage toward the flight of internal stairs that led down to the surface of Lake Michigan.

For one long moment, no one said a word. Townsend, Marco and I all seemed to realize in the same instant what Gorky was planning to do. He was going to drown Townsend by dumping the cage out of the door that opened to the lake. The cage would sink instantly.

"You can't get away with this," Marco hissed, turning on Gorky. "Authorities will dredge the entire lake if they have to to find the head of Q.E.D. And when they do, you'll go down, Gorky. I don't care how many politicians you've bought, you won't get a pass on this one."

Gorky smiled coyly. "Marik, you have no imagination. We will lower the cage into the lake until he drowns, then we will hoist him up, like a deep sea diver, extract the body and dump it somewhere else. No one will ever tie the crime to me. Townsend, you weren't stupid enough to tell anyone else about your plot, were you?"

The lieutenant, gripping the bars, tersely shook his head.

"See?" Gorky said. "It's a done deal."

"But we need a confession from Townsend in order to clear Angel of suspicion."

"Already done," Gorky replied. "He signed it just before you arrived. I'll send it to the media. Townsend has served his purpose."

"But why kill him?" I cried out, sickened by this perverse carnival of violence and amorality. "Let him spend the rest of his life in jail."

Gorky stood and came toward me, so serious and quietly furious that I actually began to tremble. "Because," he said, "he tried to kill you."

"Me?" I repeated. "What difference does that make? He killed lots of people."

"You, Angel *moy,* he tried to kill *you.* Today. And he almost succeeded."

"It wasn't personal!" Townsend shouted. "I was trying to kill Detective Marco because he was snooping around, talking to people he shouldn't. I was afraid he'd connect the dots and expose my plans. The only way I knew to get him to the museum was by using his lover."

"You mimicked our voices," I said.

"Yes," Townsend readily admitted.

"And Roy's as well. And Victor's."

"Yes."

"How?" Marco said. Townsend had the audacity to stare at him with a smug I'll-never-tell look. Marco lunged at him, grabbing the bars and rattling the cage. "Look, you inhuman SOB, you'd better start talking or I'll throw this cage in the water myself. You have no hope of survival with Gorky. But I just might have mercy on you. *If* you talk."

Townsend cleared his throat. "I had your voices recorded,

analyzed and synthesized for pliable audio reproduction. Quad techs recorded your phone calls at the station, Marco."

"And you recorded mine through my Personal Listening Device," I said.

He nodded. "Q.E.D. purchased a large order of PLDs wholesale and donated them to the Victims' Rights Association on the condition that they be given out at the CRS convention last year."

"So you've been planning this for some time," Marco remarked.

Gorky waved a hand impatiently. "Forget this. It is unimportant. What I want to know is, didn't you know that if you killed Marik in that blast that Angel would die, too?"

"Of course, but I didn't know she was important to you. If you had only told me—"

"Bastard," Gorky muttered.

"Why!" I cried in frustration. "Why am I so important to you?"

"My biggest mistake," Townsend continued, looking at no one in particular, "was involving Angel Baker in the first place. But I thought she needed to learn a lesson. I thought it appropriate that she had taken the law into her own hands and rescued those kidnapped orphans. And I thought it was the height of poor taste for her to brag about it on the nightly news. Her success weakened the morale and reputation of the police force."

"I didn't brag," I countered. "The press hounded me. Besides, people needed to know what happened to those poor girls and just how cancerous these crime syndicates are."

"I wanted to bring you down," Townsend said, his eyes finally gleaming at me with something akin to genuine emotion. If I had to guess, I'd say it was hatred. "I wanted Q.E.D. to be the saving grace of this great city. At the last minute, I changed my plans and called you to the Cloisters so that you would be charged and humbled in the public eye."

"That decision doesn't sound very logical to me," Marco said slyly. "Sounds downright emotional."

Townsend gave him a droll look. "Pride is the hardest emotion to extricate. It burrows deep in the human heart."

"I didn't know you still had one," Marco replied.

"Pride is also one of the seven deadly sins, if I recall my Bible lessons," Gorky said. "Lower the cage, boys. It's time for the lieutenant to drink his fill."

One of the bodyguard-thugs—the shorter and stockier of the pair—pushed the cage toward the inner stairwell while his sinewy cohort pushed a button on the railing surrounding the stairs. With a hum of hydraulic motion, the steps flattened into a ramp.

"No!" I hurried to Gorky's side. "Please, Vladimir, don't do this. I have more reason than any to want vengeance against Townsend, but I can't let you do this."

"You can't stop me," he said, clearly amused.

"But I can," Marco barked. He dashed to the upper level and punched the guard who guided the cage hard in the liver. When the guard doubled over, his partner pulled out a large ballooned-shaped pistol from the storage pockets on his Army-green pants, pointing it at Marco's heart.

"Freeze!" the thug said.

I recognized the weapon immediately. It was a smaller version of the Radioart Marco and I had confiscated a month ago outside Lola's apartment. Instead of shooting bullets, it dispensed deadly radiation. Hence, the name, which was short for radiation artillery.

"Don't move, Marco," I called out.

I could see the choice warring in his tortured expression: save Townsend or myself.

"Go ahead, Marik," Gorky said. "Try to save the lieutenant. If you die of radiation poisoning, that can't be traced back to me, either."

I whirled on Gorky. "You are a horrible, evil person who doesn't deserve to live. Why are you doing this? Is it just because my mother saved your life? Is this your creepy, perverse way of paying her back, by gruesomely killing anyone who tries to hurt me? Do I have to suffer because she made the mistake of rescuing a despicable human being?"

"No, Angel *moy,*" he said, tears filling his eyes. He lurched forward and clasped my upper arms in his massive hands, overwhelming me with the force of his emotion and presence. "I do this because you are my daughter. And I always protect my own."

Chapter 23

Do or Die

This revelation hit me like a mallet in the stomach. I was Vladimir Gorky's daughter. He was my father.

"You and Lola…." I couldn't complete the sentence.

"Yes, Angel." He swallowed loudly and blinked back his tears. "We were lovers in those days. Later she told me she'd had a child, but she insisted the father was someone else."

I vaguely heard the clatter of the cage being wheeled down the ramp. The guard must have recovered from Marco's blow. I tried hard to catch my breath, but my entire system was rigid with shock. *Breathe deep, Angel,* I told myself. *Breathe.*

I slowly but firmly pulled my arms from his hands, stepping back and hugging myself. "She told me that my father abandoned us shortly after I was born," I whispered, not looking at him. As if I were quickly laying out the cards in a game of So itaire that I already knew I'd won, my mind raced through the past, sorting my life in light of this stunning revelation. "She must not have wanted you and I to have a...relationship."

"And that made me angry," he said. "When I found out—"

I looked up at him. "When did you find out?"

"Last month. When Lola called to tell me you wanted to meet me to discuss the missing girls, she told me that you were mine. She was afraid I'd figure it out on my own once you and I met face-to-face."

"Angel!" Marco shouted from where he stood by the stairwell, still being held at gunpoint.

I tore my gaze from Gorky and looked at Marco.

"Save him!" Marco shouted. "They can't kill us both at the same time."

Trusting that Marco had scoped out the other thug for weapons and found him lacking, I made a mad dash toward the stairs.

"Angel!" Gorky yelled. "Stop!"

When I reached the top of the ramp and saw that the stocky guard had hooked Townsend's cage and was hoisting it over the water, I forget about my own dismay.

"Leave him!" I shouted. But before I could scramble down to Townsend's rescue, the guy holding Marco turned the Radioart on me.

"Don't aim that at her, you idiot!" Gorky roared.

Marco took advantage of the confusion and socked his lanky opponent hard in the jaw. The weapon fell to the ground as the two men embraced in hand-to-hand combat. I ran down the ramp, ready to knock the hoist operator out the door and into the murky depths of Lake Michigan, but by the time I reached him, he'd already pushed a button and the chain dangling Townsend a foot above the choppy water was suddenly loosed.

The cage dropped like a ton of bricks, splashing into the cold lake.

"Help me!" Townsend cried out as the water swirled into his cage, reaching for my hand through the bars.

The guard who'd pushed the button lumbered back up the ramp, apparently content that he had done his job. I knelt in the doorway, barely aware of the waves lapping up on my knees, and stretched out my hand to Townsend, clinging to the door frame so I wouldn't go over.

"Take my hand!" I shouted. It was a fool's quest. Neither of us would be strong enough to resist the weight of the cage that was quickly dragging him down.

"Angel!" Gorky shouted from the top of the ramp. "Come away from there. You might fall in."

Like a many-faceted diamond, my mind raced with dozens of hard-cut realizations—that Gorky sounded genuinely, almost touchingly afraid for my well-being, that Townsend's only hope of survival rested with me, that Marco might be dead by now, that my life would never, ever be the same regardless of how any of this turned out.

All this I realized in the instant it took for me to turn toward the hoist's control panel. I jabbed my fingers at every button I could find, but nothing worked.

"Come on, damn you!" I cursed. "Lift up. Lift!"

This last word was muted by the sound of bubbles bursting up from the water as the cage sank well below the surface. Desperate, I still tried to work the hoist, finally punching the panel in frustration.

"Angel," Gorky called down, not without sympathy, "give up. You cannot operate that hoist without a special code."

I stopped, still not wanting to accept the reality. I looked at the chain that fed into the water, knowing that in anothe minute—maybe two—Townsend would be dead. Then I looked up at Gorky. "Please. *Father,* please raise him up."

Gorky stared at me a long time, as if seriously considering my request, then shook his head slowly. "No. Not even for you."

I collapsed in the doorway, knowing that Townsend was already dead. *What a horrific way to die,* I thought, and I imprinted the moment deep in my psyche so I would never, ever forget just how wicked my own father really was.

By the time I had recovered the ability to ascend the ramp with some semblance of composure, Marco was once again being held at gunpoint, though this time the thin guard wielding the Radioart was, like Marco, panting and half doubled over in pain after their bruising tussle. The guard held the gun steady in one hand and with the other nursed his nose, which was spewing a copious amount of blood.

"Get out of here," Gorky barked. "You'll ruin the wood floor. Take the detective with you."

In an instant, I knew what that meant. Marco would die, perhaps not as horribly as Townsend just had, but he would see no mercy from this monster who called himself a human being.

I saw my chance and with sharpened focus noticed something that Marco had earlier overlooked—the flash of a traditional metal pistol sticking out of the back pocket of the stocky guard, who bent over to clean up the blood. I reached for his gun, faster than a State Street pickpocket, and when he shot upright, grabbing at his empty pocket, turning to retrieve it, I pressed its snubbed nose to his forehead.

"Drop the Radioart or your friend dies," I hissed at the guard holding Marco, though my eyes never left the repugnant ape who had lowered Townsend into the water. We were so close I could smell putrid sweat, which began to pour from

his temples. He scowled at me like a bulldog who had just been
pissed on by the neighbor's poodle, but he didn't dare move.

"Boss?" asked the guard holding the weapon. "What
should I do?"

My heart pounded so hard I thought it would explode. This
was do or die time. I knew it. And I was ready. If Gorky didn't
give orders to disarm, I had to act.

"I don't think she will kill him," Gorky said, like someone
speculating on whether the stock market would make a gain
on any particular day.

I pulled the trigger. Townsend's killer dropped to the floor,
flopping on his back. His lifeless eyes stared at the ceiling. A
clean, red bullet hole marked his forehead like a caste mark.
I aimed the pistol at the remaining guard.

"You're next," I said savagely. "Drop the Radioart."

Both the guard and Marco were staring wide-eyed at the
man I'd just killed, then they looked at me in a way I'd never
been regarded before—with a weird combination of awe and
dismay.

"Boss?" the guard said nervously.

"Leave us," Gorky said. "Take the Radioart with you."

The guard hightailed it out of the room and Gorky turned
to his fireplace, leaning with one hand on the mantel, the
other tucked behind his back. Facing the flickering flames, he
looked as if he were carrying the weight of the world. I sus
pected he was trying to find an appropriate way to punish me
The question was, how? And how would I respond?

I didn't think Gorky was armed. But likewise, I wasn't sure
I was ready to shoot my own father. No matter how much
hated him, this was the man I had been missing my whole life
Could I find this lost figure and kill him on the same ill-fated
day?

Marco came to my side and bolstered me with an arm

around my shoulder. Apparently sensing my ambivalence, he took the small pistol out of my hand and aimed it at Gorky.

The strapping older man's shoulders began to shake, then a rumble sounded in his broad chest, then he turned and I saw that he was smiling, laughing. He raised his arms up in a welcome gesture and came toward me, his gravelly voice booming with mirth and joy.

"You make me so proud, Angel. You killed him! I didn't think you had it in you, but you did it! Good girl!" He clapped his hands together and collapsed into his favorite chair, wiping the joy from his eyes. Quieting, he regarded me more soberly, but still with great pride. "You're a killer now. Just like your old man."

If I'd still had the pistol in my hand, I would have shot him then and there, I despised him that much. I would gladly have burned an eternity in hell just to have the pleasure of pulling the trigger. But when Marco said, "Do you want me to kill him?" I shook my head.

"No," I replied. "You already have enough blood on your hands."

Marco looked down sharply, trying to read the meaning in my closeted, grim features. Realizing that Gorky had shown me the photos of Rayenko's butchered body, Marco paled.

"Yo!" came a loud, dissonantly chipper voice from the bottom of the stairwell, which was followed by the jangly clamor of metal spurs and boots sounding on the aluminum ramp. The sound grew louder until Brad suddenly appeared.

He was a blinding sight, with his spiked, bleached white hair, white sunglasses, white facial scar, white everything—including a white floor-length Victorian smoking jacket that traipsed elegantly around his pointy, white snakeskin cowboy boots. It was John Wayne meets the Scarlet Pimpernel. And I'd never in my life been so happy to be greeted by such an incongruous sight.

"Hey, Vlad," he said, tipping his forefinger and thumb a Gorky as if his hand held an invisible gun.

"Hello, Brad," Gorky said dubiously. "What are you doing here?"

Brad shrugged, as if his flowing jacket was too tigh around the shoulders. "Just happened to be in the neighbor hood." He reached into his tight, front pants pocket and pulle out a money chip, then tossed it toward Gorky. "Catch."

Gorky caught the chip in midair, impressing me with hi quick reflexes. "What's this?"

"The money you gave me to watch over Angel. Eve though my job was to keep her safe, I started to feel lik Judas, so I'm giving back the blood money."

He turned to me with a punky grin. "Hey, babe, you read to book? Is this your boyfriend?"

"Marco," I managed to spit out, "meet Brad."

"Hey, Marco," Brad said, slapping his palm into Marco' in a fluid move. "I'm Brad the Impaler."

"Great." Marco grinned, knowing a good——albeit incom prehensible——thing when he saw it. "That's great."

"Let's go." Brad motioned us toward the ramp. "I have boat waiting downstairs."

"Brad," Gorky said, shaking his head sympathetically, "yo poor dumb shit, don't you know you'll never escape? I have thre men whose only job is to patrol the water around my house."

Brad shrugged apologetically. "I'm afraid I had to tak them out, Mr. Gorky, I'm sorry." He pulled open both side of his jacket, revealing an impressive array of compact sem automatic machine guns tucked into various pockets an straps. "A bit old-fashioned, I know, but damned effective He nodded toward the door. "Let's go."

As we made our escape, I looked back only once at Gork He returned my gaze with a distinct glimmer of affection. An

I knew that despite the bravo performance Brad had just given, if we escaped with our lives, it would only be because Gorky allowed it.

Psychologists will tell you that when children are infants and, unlike most other mammals, are completely dependent on Mom and Dad for food and protection, they make the false assumption that their parents are godlike—all powerful. Part of the maturing process involves coming to the realization that your parents aren't omnipotent.

But in my case, it was all too true.

With Marco and I seated in the back of the cigarette boat, along with the unflappable Keshon stretched out by our feet, Brad drove over the ragged waves far offshore like a bat out of hell, which was a comparison he'd probably find flattering. Every time the boat skipped into the air and crashed down into one of the bigger waves, a spray of cold water hit my face. It felt good. It reminded me that I was alive.

But Townsend wasn't. He'd done terrible things, but no one deserved to die as he had. Marco had once warned me that I didn't really understand the meaning, or the pain and consequences, of death. I did now. I understood more than I ever wanted to.

Marco called into police headquarters to report Townsend's murder, so by the time Brad pulled into Navy Pier, there was a hive of officials and law-enforcement officers waiting to take our statements and work the case, which they already knew was huge.

In my mind, the murder of the director of Q.E.D. would be comparable to Al Capone knocking off FBI Elliot Ness. This was a major wrinkle in the fabric of law and order. No matter how corrupt many of Chicago's twenty-second-century officials might be, they surely couldn't deny that this was a crime that had to be punished.

I think I answered a million questions by a half-dozen different detectives and agents before I was allowed to go home. Marco and I agreed that we had a lot to talk about, but that it could wait until we bathed and changed, so we set a time for a later rendezvous.

We went our separate ways, and I wandered back down to the dock just before Brad took off with Chicago PD's water patrol for a return trip to Gorky's lakeside compound. Brad was clearly enjoying his role as hero of the day. I called out to him, and he met me halfway on the diagonal boardwalk.

Mindless of time or place, he took me into his arms and pressed me close, baring his fangs with an audacious smile.

"Hello, Brad. Is that an automatic weapon in your pocket," I murmured as lustfully as I could, "or are you glad to see me?"

"This time it really is a weapon." He laughed and released me, shoving his hands in his pockets. "Hey, babe, it's been real."

"Real what?"

"I'm not sure, but I had a hell of a good time."

"Are you going back to New Orleans?"

He nodded, eyeing me up and down as if I were stark naked. "You wanna come?"

I shook my head. "No."

"Yeah, I know, you have other fish to fry. You tell Detective Marco that he's a lucky son of a bitch."

"I will."

He carefully lifted my chin with a touch and leaned down to press a very respectful, yet still exciting, kiss on my lips. Then straightened. "If he does you wrong, Angel, you know my number."

"Yeah," I said, laughing, "I've got your number."

And how, I thought as I walked away. I was sure I'd see Brad again, though maybe not for another five years. Like Dracula, Brad had a way of popping up when it was least expected.

* * *

I'd called ahead and warned Mike that I was coming home, the worse for wear. By the time I climbed the stairs to my flat, which felt like the final ascent to Mount Everest, Mike had a hot bath waiting. I sank into the jasmine-scented water and allowed the grime and the perversity from our visit to Falling Water on the Lake to slide from my skin.

If I could wash away the guilt I knew I'd soon feel for killing another human being, I would. But it wouldn't be that easy. And right now, I didn't feel guilt. I didn't feel much of anything but the need to shut out the world for a few precious moments.

After a long soak, I dressed in a comfortable, long-sleeved, pale pink warm-up suit. Comfort was definitely the new order of the day. I chatted with Mike in the kitchen while he cooked me a stir-fry dinner. He didn't say much, but listened carefully. When I told him about shooting the guard who'd killed Townsend, he looked at me for a long time in thoughtful silence, then nodded and turned back to his cooking.

He didn't have to say anything for me to know what he was thinking. Not because I'm psychic, but because I knew him so well.

Karma, Baker, you have just created so much karma. Ah, well. We'll work it out.

Since I was a latent Catholic, I figured I'd be facing the licking flames of hell as well as karma, but I couldn't worry about that now.

It was so peaceful without Lola here. I knew it would be a long time before I forgave her for hiding my father's identity. It would be a long time before I could even talk to her without bursting a blood vessel in my brain.

So, when I'd called earlier, I'd told Mike to give a money chip to Jimmy with the following instructions: take a chopper cab immediately to the nearest drive-through doc-in-a-box, have the fake plaster cast removed, buy some clothes, come back and take Lola somewhere far, far away. Wisconsin would do. California was even better. At least for a few days. I didn't want a second murder on my conscience, and that's what would happen if I had to see my mother right now.

When Mike scooped the wok's contents onto a platter and set the steaming array of bright green and red vegetables and tofu on the table, we both sat and helped ourselves in silence. I'm happy to report that his cooking tastes infinitely better than his healing remedies.

"So, Baker," he said at last, eyeing me intensely, "what will happen now for you and Detective Marco?"

"You mean what will happen between us?"

Mike nodded.

I pushed back my empty plate and sighed. "I wish I knew."

"You killed for him. Is it not so?"

"Yes." I nodded as the realization really struck home. "Yes, I did."

Mike had once dreamt that Marco turned into a white tiger and killed me. But today I was the one who ended up doing the killing.

"Like I said before, Mike, your prophetic dreams don't do me any good unless I can do something about them."

"But you did," he replied. "You are still alive."

"Yes, I'm still alive." Marco didn't kill me. But I believed he had brutally killed Rayenko. And I could not possibly imagine a reasonable explanation for that. At least not one that would make me ever again feel truly safe with him.

Chapter 24

Truth or Dare

By the time Marco arrived, all that remained of the day was copper dust in the twilight clouds that etched along neighboring rooftops. I'd been strolling through the garden, surprised at how cool the nights had become, thinking about what bulbs to plant for the spring.

I wanted to rearrange one of the beds so that Lin could plant a garden of her own. I hoped she'd be back with me before the frosts came. My lawyer had already told me he was confident all charges against me would be dropped because of Townsend's written confession. Now that my name would be cleared, there was no reason the adoption couldn't proceed as planned.

But I wasn't sure how much red tape we'd have to cut through before Lin could even move back home. Would she still want to? Or had she already become Sydney's daughter, or worse yet, Gigi's?

These were the thoughts roiling through my mind as I hugged my chilled arms, breathing in the scent of late-blooming flowers and turning leaves. That's when Marco appeared at the top of the balcony.

He took the steps at a serene pace, but as his silhouette came closer and I could make out his features in the waning light, I saw that he was anything but at peace with himself. Dressed in pressed jeans and a collarless blue-jean shirt, he clutched a bouquet of pink roses in one hand, but didn't offer them to me. He stopped an arm's length away and blinked hard as he struggled to find the right words, for what I wasn't sure.

"Mike let me in," he said at last, sounding disappointed with himself.

"I told him to."

He blinked as if someone had just stabbed him, then said, "Gorky showed you the photographs of Rayenko's body, didn't he?"

I nodded. "What was left of it. Did you do it, Marco?"

He nodded. And in some ineffable way, the air around us lightened. It didn't brighten, but we could breathe again. The truth had a way of freeing you. I'd always known that. Now we could talk.

"Let's go sit by the fire." I reached out and clasped one of his hands and led the way up the back stairs.

Mike passed us on the stairway as he returned to his shed in the back of the garden. He was finished doing the dishes and, as I discovered, preparing my apartment for a romantic interlude. Acting more like a Jewish yenta than a Chinese monk, he'd put out a bottle of wine and two glasses on the

ffee table in the living room. A fire crackled cozily in the
arth. The lights were low. Music played softly in the back-
ound. Only candles lit the room.

Too bad I was feeling anything but romantic. Still, the
ne was welcome. I poured two glasses and gave one to
arco as we settled back on two large cushions that Mike had
sed in front of the fire.

I took a sip and savored the oak tang of the wine, then said,
ell me about Rayenko."

Marco leaned on one elbow and swirled his wine in the
er hand, taking a fortifying drink before starting his story.

"When I was young," he began, staring into the yellow and
e fire, "I fell in love with a girl named Nadia. She was
y…special." He glanced at me, apparently conscious of the
t that even mentioning a prior girlfriend was hard for me to
r. "We were only seventeen at the time. Do you understand?"

Did I understand what impulsive, all-consuming young
e is? I'd never experienced it, but I could understand it, so
dded encouragingly, and he continued.

"Anyway, we fell in love. But her parents didn't want us to
rry, so I was essentially banished from her presence. Angry
ny mother's side of the family and all their friends who were
ncestuously tied to the R.M.O. in one way or another, I de-
ed to go to Italy to explore my father's roots. When I returned
e years later, I discovered that Nadia had had a child."

"Yours," I said.

"Mine. Her parents still didn't want us to marry, so we were
ermined to elope. But Rayenko, Gorky's second in com-
nd, took an interest in Nadia and determined that he was
ng to have her and my child for himself."

"How could that happen? This is twenty-second-century
erica, not medieval Russia."

"The abuse of power knows no timetables, no geographic

limitations. Rayenko was a very powerful man in the nec
Russian syndicate. Nadia tried to refuse his advances, but h
could not stand the idea that he could be outdone by a low
level *sgarrista* like me. So he kidnapped my child and m
lover and took them to a remote location where he intende
to coerce her into changing her mind."

In the golden firelight, I could see Marco's pulse punch
ing a beat in his temple. His rugged face was set like stone

"But he was unable to change Nadia's mind. She told hi
she loved me and always would, that she despised him an
everything he stood for."

"How did he react to that?" I asked in a strained whispe

He let out a pent-up breath. "He raped her, repeatedl
Then he murdered her, brutally. All in front of our child."

I breathed in his pain and touched the arm he'd proppe
on the cushion, squeezing with all the empathy I felt but cou
not adequately voice.

"When I found her body in Rayenko's cabin, he was sti
there and told me exactly what he had done in great deta
including the way her vocal cords ripped with the force of pa
that bellowed from her tortured body. I lost control…lost m
mind, really. I killed him. I didn't realize how savagely I ha
killed him until I later saw the photographs, and the mem
ries of that crime of passion surfaced."

"I'm so sorry, Marco."

He noticed my hand on his arm and looked at me grat
fully. "That helps. It really does. I've never shared this wi
any other lover."

His confidence warmed me, even as his story appalled.

"That's one of the reasons why I went into psychology
he said. "To understand my own dark, horrible crime, to u
derstand why someone like Rayenko would destroy someor
so innocent like Nadia."

"Did your studies bring any peace?"

One cheek tugged in a mirthless half smile. "Some. It gave me understanding. And it allowed me to accept the fact that the psychosis that I'd suffered was temporary. It allowed me to enter the police force and work in psych-ops."

"How did you get hired? Weren't there background checks?"

"Nadia's and Rayenko's deaths were never reported. Gorky saw to that. He didn't want an investigation involving what he called his people."

"What about your child?" I asked.

"When I regained my sanity, I found that Gorky had managed to obtain custody."

"What?"

"I've spent the rest of my life trying to reclaim my paternity rights. Not through the courts, because none of this was done by the book. But in reality. That's why I've never broken ties with Gorky. That's why I've been posing as his informant. I give him enough information about what goes on in the police department to think I'm working for him, but I'm careful not to betray anything that will harm my fellow officers."

"Oh, my God, Marco, what a nightmare."

He turned his head my way with an intensity that was spellbinding. "But not anymore, Angel. No more. The nightmare is over. Gorky will be arrested and put behind bars once and for all. There's no way the mayor will overlook his crimes now, not when Gorky was directly responsible for Townsend's death, and indirectly responsible for the death of the mayor's own son."

He was right. This would spell the end of Gorky's reign. I was happy about that, but still sad that my friends had perished so unnecessarily in the process.

"Marco, I still can't figure out how you happened to be the first one to arrive at the murder scenes."

"Gorky's surveillance team set up shop across from your apartment a few days before Townsend began his blood spree. So I knew where you were going almost as soon as you did."

"How? Don't tell me my conversations were being broadcast all over the city."

"No. But Gorky apparently knew what kind of bug Townsend had planted in your Personal Listening Device. It wasn't hard for the R.M.O. operatives to plug into the signal feeding back to Townsend's men. My cousin knew the guys running Gorky's equipment and tipped me off on the sly."

For a long moment, I just sat there and tried to remember all the embarrassing things I might have said.

"Gorky would never have told me where you were going, Angel. He thinks I'm not good enough for his daughter. That's probably why he brought in someone from New Orleans to protect you, because he could send the guy packing when the job was done without acquiring a son-in-law."

"Son-in-law. Thieves-in-law. What a mess."

Marco chuckled ruefully. "Yes, but at least we're alive to complain about it."

"How long have you known that I was Gorky's daughter?"

"Gorky told me the day after you were arrested. When he found out I was involved in the investigation, he called me to his compound. While he wanted me to keep him posted on the case, he made it very clear that I was to keep my hands off you. I let him think that I would be an obedient, albeit resentful, *sgarrista*. Since he has always preferred fear over affection, he was happy with that."

Marco put his wineglass aside, then mine, and smoothed his hand over my cheek, combing his fingers through my hair. In one easy, sexy move that was all Marco, he sat up and pulled me into his warm embrace, crushing my lips with his own, then soothing and parting them with a deft lave of his tongue.

We kissed soul-to-soul, hunger feeding on hunger. I wrapped my arms around him without any intention of ever letting go. Nothing existed but the heat that pulsed between us.

How could this be? How could all the moral ambiguities that whorled around us like a never-ending hurricane leave our need for each other unscathed?

I didn't know. Moreover, I didn't care.

About an hour later, somewhere between my fourth and sixth orgasm, Marco propped himself up in bed with his palms on either side of my head. Trying to hold still, though still pulsing inside me, with beads of moisture dropping from his dark ringlets of hair onto my already slick breasts, he stared into my eyes as if he could see the future in them.

With his arms quivering and voice quavering from the force and binding thrall of our sexual union, he struggled to ask one last, burning question of his own.

"Why...why did you pull the trigger?" He thrust deep into me once, then held still, trying hard to wait for my answer. "Why? You've never killed before."

I didn't have to think about my answer. Arching my back, I rolled our entwined bodies over until I was on top, straddling him. Placing my hands on either side of his head, I leaned down and gave him a deep, sweaty kiss. Then I looked deep into his eyes and said, "I pulled the trigger to save you. And I'd do it again in a heartbeat."

"But at what price?" he said, his voice hitching, his eyes wreathed with sadness. "You'll never be innocent again."

"If I have to give you up to keep my innocence, Marco, the price of innocence is way too high."

He really took in my answer, and his sadness was transformed into a strength and determination so awesome I can only describe it with a metaphor.

In Chinese mythology the white tiger, the god of war, ruled the west. Like the dragon, who ruled the east, the tiger was one of the four great celestial beings.

"If you find the azure dragon," Mike had once told me, "you will find the white tiger nearby. And when the two entwine as one, the earth will be in balance."

Balance was good. But first, I hoped we would make the earth move.

The next morning, after Marco went down to P.S. #1 to help clear up any confusion that might be lingering over my convoluted case, I enjoyed a leisurely breakfast by myself. My slate had never been wiped so utterly clean, and it felt good. Life was suddenly full of radiant and infinite possibilities. But first came the many chores ahead of me.

My lawyer had set up a press conference for me at 9:00 a.m. I didn't relish giving a command performance at a hotel podium bundled with a hundred different television and radio microphones, but there was no way I could avoid talking to the press about yesterday's dramatic events. It had made international headlines. Hank and Soji had convinced me that setting up a press event would be relatively painless and far better than having reporters camped outside my door.

Shortly after 8:00 a.m. I headed toward Southport to catch a train, enjoying the crisp breeze and mellow autumn sunshine. But I'd only walked half a block down the leaf-strewed sidewalk before I slowed, then stopped, captivated by the familiarity of an approaching aerocar heading westbound on Paulina.

"Henry," I murmured to myself when I recognized the gold sedan, feeling buoyant enough to add with almost childish glee, "It's Henry's car!"

Henry was behind the wheel, and Sydney sat beside him

in the front seat. I waved and the car pulled over to the curb. My foster parents stepped out of the car, grinning at me with relief and joy. They looked ten years younger than the last time I'd seen them.

"Hey, you guys!" I shouted, running to embrace them. We hugged and laughed and hugged again. Then we sobered, all at once, for it seemed too much of man's inhumanity to man had come to pass in recent days. How could we celebrate so much death and destruction? But I was free, and the Bassetts would get to keep their house when my bond was settled.

I wasn't ready to talk about what had happened at Gorky's compound, but I knew they'd already learned quite a bit from the news.

"What are you doing here?" I said, touching up my hair. "I'm heading downtown for a press conference. Can you come with me? I know Hank will be there."

"That can wait a few minutes, can't it?" Sydney said, her genteel eyes bright with anticipation.

"What for?" I asked.

She turned back toward the car, then motioned for someone to join us. I realized in an instant who it was. The door opened, seemingly by a ghost, because Lin wasn't visible until she stepped up on the curb and pushed the door closed with both hands and all her might.

She stood uncertainly, folding her hands in front of her stomach, as if she didn't know what else to do with them. Her straight, dark bangs hung over worried, almond-shaped eyes. She was as thin as ever, cute and girlish, but thankfully she wasn't wearing the plaid skirt and white blouse Gigi had purchased. In fact, she wore the same casual, almost boyish little pants set that she wore when I'd sent her away.

The only remnant of the life of luxury she'd enjoyed, or perhaps endured, at Gigi's bidding was a small patent-leather white purse. It hung by an oval strap around one arm. I was quite sure it was empty.

I took in a skipping breath as the sweetest, most unconditional love I had ever known surged up in me for this perfect, lonely, beautiful little girl who was utterly and completely alone. But was she still mine?

"What should I do?" I whispered, clutching Sydney's wrist.

"Hug her," she said. "Just hug her."

I released my death grip on Sydney's arm and started forward, my feet doing what Sydney had ordered, ignoring the fearful braying of my heart. After two steps, I saw Lin take one of her own, then stop. She still frowned at me.

Why did you send me away? I imagined her thinking. *And will you do it again?*

No, I replied with my footsteps, each one faster and wider. Soon I was running, and she ran, too. Straight into my arms. I scooped under her arms and lifted her high over my head like the prize she was.

Her reserve broke, and she grinned. Then cried. I pulled her down into my bearish embrace.

"That's my girl," I crooned into her hair. "That's my daughter."

There's more Silhouette Bombshell coming your way!
Every month we've got four fresh, unique,
satisfying reads that will keep you riveted....
Turn the page for an exclusive excerpt from
one of next month's releases

FINDERS KEEPERS
by Shirl Henke

*On sale October 2005
at your favorite retail outlet.*

Samantha Ballanger wore a sprayed-on pair of jeans and a halter top that revealed her assets like an Excel spreadsheet. She watched her target vacillate while she struggled to load an oversize box into the back of her white Ford Econoline van.

Chivalry won out, just as she'd hoped it would. Casting a quick glance at his watch, Matt Granger crossed the deserted pavement. She knew this wasn't the best of neighborhoods for any woman alone, especially an attractive one whose least provocative article of apparel was the fanny pack strapped to her waist.

The big brick complex of apartments where Granger had taken up residence was called Samaritan House, a haven for people hiding from their pasts, or running from their futures. Not all of them were exactly hospitable to strangers.

"Need some help?" he asked, his six-foot-six-inch frame

crowding her. He turned on a Tom Selleck smile and nodded at the box, half in, half out of the van.

"Yeah, I could use some," Sam replied with a bright grin, stepping back so he could take the box in both hands. *Predictable as snow in Boston.*

"What've you got in here, rocks?" As he bent his knees to put some muscle behind shoving the box across the carpeting of the van, she moved in close behind him. Her breasts brushed against his shoulder.

When he shoved the box across the van floor, Sam shoved the barrel of her gun sharply into his right kidney. Granger grunted in surprise as she said conversationally, "It's exactly what it feels like, so don't get cute."

"You're the one who's cute, honey, or I wouldn't have walked my stupid butt across the street to be mugged," he replied.

"No mugging, honey, but this will be a prelude to a funeral if you don't spread your legs and lean forward into the van. Put all your weight on your palms."

"If you're a kidnapper, I have to warn you there's not enough in—"

"Just do it," she snapped curtly, pressing the gun muzzle harder into his kidney to emphasize her point.

"Ouch," he muttered with an oath, leaning forward and spreading his long legs.

Sam tossed a small plastic nasal inhaler next to where his left hand pressed into the plush carpeting. "Squeeze a spray into each nostril, then snuff it up—good and hard," she instructed.

When he hesitated, she cocked the snub nose. She knew he'd done a stint as an army MP. He was probably familiar with that sound. He picked up the bottle and squeezed.

"Hey, you're choking me," he protested.

Sam had grabbed the back of his shirt and balled it up

tightly between his shoulder blades. She ignored him. No time to fool around now, she thought, eyeing the deserted street again. "Drop the bottle and put your hand back on the van floor."

"Now what, lady? You're calling the shots." He coughed as she clenched his shirt collar into the sides of his throat.

"We wait," she said, once more conversationally cheerful. Frankly, she was relieved. This was her first use of the new inhaler. Just her luck to have to use it on a guy as tall as a skyscraper.

He coughed again. "Shit, that stuff wasn't Vicks, was it?" he muttered thickly as his right arm buckled. He straightened it and shook his head.

Sam heard the slight slurring in his voice and swore silently. Jules had told her the nasal delivery system worked fast, but with a guy this big she'd never imagined it could work quite this fast. Damn! He was starting to puddle up really quickly. Distracting enough that the man was drop-dead gorgeous, but did he have to be twice her size to boot? If he oozed beneath the van, she'd be screwed. There was no way she could heft over two hundred pounds of male muscle from the pavement into her vehicle.

When his knees suddenly started to buckle, she hissed, "Lock your knees. Stiffen your legs, for God's sake." A little panic was not all that unprofessional.

"Stiffen...stiff... My ass." The sibilant sound hissed between slack lips. "I cudn' get stiff for Julia Roberts."

Sam uncocked the .38 and slipped it into her fanny pack so she could have both hands free to work. She reached up between his legs to grab the front waistband of his Levi's.

"Doan get fresh!" It came out "fesh." He grunted as she levered her forearm up against his crotch. It was an old jujitsu move guaranteed to turn any man into a toe dancer. Any man not already higher than a satellite. His knees continued to wobble like Jell-O as he muttered, "Hey, hey, that's m…m' fam'ly jew'ls."

"Either you help me get your ass in that van or I'm going to liquidate a couple of the family assets right now. Got it?" Braced behind him, Sam cupped her left hand under his knee, trying to get him to lift it onto the floor of the van. She revised her estimate of his weight. He was the size of her uncle Declan's semi carrying a full load of sheet steel.

She tugged at the knee again, cursing as she became truly desperate. "Come on, throw your friggin' leg up there!" A quick glance up and down the street revealed no spectators, her only break so far. Finally, using her body weight against his rump, she bumped him hard several times until she was able to lever his knee high enough to slide it onto the van floor and roll him inside.

He collapsed, giggling in baritone as she flopped on his back. One long leg and arm dangled out the door.

"Ya got a great…ash," he murmured as his hand groped clumsily around her hip.

Quickly she bent his leg and shoved it inside, then threw the offending arm across his chest and slammed the door before it flopped out again. Sam could hear the crack of his elbow hitting the door panel, but he was feeling no pain. The giggling continued, a side effect of the drug Jules had not warned her about.

"Crap, 'happy hour' at ten in the morning," she muttered to herself. Relief made her almost giddy enough to giggle in return as she once again scanned the street. No so much as a window shade moved in any of the buildings. Southern California. It figured. "I could've gone after him with a net and trident and nobody would've noticed a thing."

Sam climbed into the driver's seat and turned the ignition, then placed the .38 in the glove compartment before pulling out and driving away slowly. In the back of the van she could hear soft male snoring as her retrieval settled in a deep, drugged slumber.

"Well, handsome, we sure as hell gave added dimension to the term 'tailgating,'" she said, turning the corner of the street and heading for a deserted strip mall next to the freeway.

Pulling into the back of the parking lot beneath a cluster of blue gum trees, she shifted to Park, keeping the engine running while she climbed over the seat and quickly changed into a loose set of green hospital scrubs. After exchanging her slides for a pair of crepe-soled lace-ups, she climbed out the side door of the van and opened the back.

Changing his appearance took a bit more work, but she'd had lots of practice. Still, her usual snatches weren't built anything like this specimen. It took her twice the average time to get his big body trussed up in a lightweight straitjacket concealed by a large institutional-looking terry robe. The faintest hint of a raspy black beard gave him a piratical look. *More eyelashes than Liz Taylor.* She shook her head in aggravation and slipped a sleeping mask over those wonderful eyes, then taped his mouth shut.

By the time she swathed his head with gauze bandages, Sam felt her confidence return. She replaced his shoes with bedroom slippers, then used the custom seat-belt straps attached to the floor to secure him safely for the ride. The belt would also minimize any thrashing when he woke.

So far, so good, she thought as she climbed out of the van carrying two oblong magnetic plates. After locking the rear door, she attached the signs to the sides of the vehicle. They read "Fairview Hospital" and gave a bogus address about five hundred miles northeast on Interstate 15. When they neared there, she had other sets for the rest of the highways to her destination. Boston.

"Sweet dreams, Gorgeous." Humming softly to herself, she pulled out of the deserted parking lot and hopped on the freeway.

With any luck they'd make Utah by nightfall.

It takes a certain strength to practice medicine in a war zone—especially when the enemy is someone you once trusted and loved...who betrayed you.

STRONG MEDICINE
by Olivia Gates
October 2005

Author and doctor Olivia Gates brings you an unforgettable heroine in an exciting new medical thriller. Don't miss it!

Available at your favorite retail outlet.

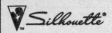

INTIMATE MOMENTS™

From *New York Times* **bestselling author**

Sharon Sala

comes

RIDER ON FIRE

SILHOUETTE INTIMATE MOMENTS #1387

With a hit man hot on her trail,
undercover DEA agent Sonora Jordan
decided to lie low—until ex Army Ranger
and local medicine man Adam Two Eagles
convinced her to look for the father she'd
never known...and offered her a love she'd
never known she wanted.

Available at your favorite retail outlet October 2005.

Where love comes alive™

BOMBSHELL™

COMING NEXT MONTH

#61 FINDERS KEEPERS by Shirl Henke

Straitjackets, blindfolds, restraints—Samantha Ballanger used any means necessary to rescue deluded people from dangerous cults. So when she retrieved a man from a kooky commune at the request of his wealthy aunt, it was a routine grab—until Sam realized she'd slapped her straitjacket on a Miami investigative reporter working a big story on the Russian mob. Oops! Now some powerful people wanted Sam and this man dead....

#62 FLAWLESS by Michele Hauf

The It Girls

An elite jeweler had been shot, diamonds embedded with secret military codes were up for grabs...and the übersecret Gotham Rose spies were on the case. Jet-set gemologist Rebecca Whitmore blazed a trail through London, Paris, New York and Berlin with her partner, British MI-6 agent Aston Drake, to track down the stones and snag the shooter. Could she stop the codes from falling into the wrong hands...before it was too late?

#63 STRONG MEDICINE by Olivia Gates

The Global Crisis Alliance had been field surgeon Calista St. James's *life*, until she'd been blamed for a botched humanitarian mission and dismissed as a loose cannon. Now, years later, GCA wanted her back for a delicate rescue operation in rebel-controlled Russian territory. Could Calista work with the man who'd fired her to free a group of hostages, or was this a prescription for disaster?

#64 ULTRA VIOLET by Ellen Henderson

Forget lost weekends—Violet Marsh couldn't account for five whole days! But when security firm Gideon Enterprises warned her that during that time she might have been subjected to genetic experiments without her knowledge, Violet dismissed it as nonsense...until she discovered her enhanced strength and sprinter's speed in a fight with a strange assailant. Who would do this to her? Violet wanted some answers—fast.

SBCNM0905